The Trials of an Half Orphan

Taniform Wanki

Langaa Research & Publishing CIG
Mankon, Bamenda

Publisher:
Langaa RPCIG
Langaa Research & Publishing Common Initiative Group
P.O. Box 902 Mankon
Bamenda
North West Region
Cameroon
Langaagrp@gmail.com
www.langaa-rpcig.net

Distributed in and outside N. America by African Books Collective
orders@africanbookscollective.com
www.africanbookcollective.com

ISBN: 9956-727-40-7

DISCLAIMER
All views expressed in this publication are those of the author and do not necessarily reflect the views of Langaa RPCIG.

1

In my primary school days I had friends who came from both rich and poor homes. Those from rich homes never fully devoted themselves to anything especially when it came to their studies and that often made me wonder why. The reason perhaps resided in the fact that they were accustomed to being well catered for and saw life from that perspective alone. Children from rich homes associated only amongst themselves and were always among those who performed poorly in class. What was even more intriguing about them was that they used gifts to buy friendship from the underprivileged that were more intelligent. My friend Kiel Emmanuel was one of those. I called him my friend not because we were friends in the true sense of the word. It was a friendship based on interest. He came to school in a car and was always neat unlike those of us from poor homes that had to go through bushes on muddy footpaths to get to school. During break, he went to the dinning shed and bought all the nice things little children from poor homes could only dream of. He often took me along to the dinning shed where he bought the nice things I could only dream of with no hope of ever laying my hands on. He gave me some but always made sure he reminded me of the fact that I had to compensate him during exams. Of course when payback time came, I always fidgeted to draw the invigilator's attention and he or she would waste no time in displacing me. When that happened, he would not know what to write and would remain examining the question paper. In order not to submit a blank answer sheet he would scribble a few words perhaps just to pacify some voices within him that might have been demanding answers. Sometimes he would walk out of the examination hall saying that some of the questions were wrongly set and would give his own proposal on how they were supposed to have been set. I would console him by blaming the invigilator for displacing me. He however always got promoted on trial bases.

There were moments I wished I were born into a wealthy home. My mother did a lot of farm work while my father was specialized in the tapping of palm wine. He carried most of it to the local market but not much money came in from sales. Farm produce were also sold if there were any surpluses and the money generated was used to pay my school fees and those of my younger brothers and sisters. Food was never a problem but the quality left much to be desired. The most important thing was filling the stomach. I felt terrible seeing my mother working herself to death to sustain her family. Her suffering spurred me to work hard at school knowing that it was the only path I had to take to avoid ending up in the same condition.

As if that were not enough, tragedy stroke when I got to primary five. My mother died and the date was February 22nd. I was still eleven and did not understand what death really meant or the mystery behind death as a whole. I saw many people walk into our family compound crying. A good number of them were shouting at the top of their voices with some asking why my mother had to disgrace them. My father too kept crying and asking who was going to assist him in raising the children. I felt really amused seeing my own father whom I considered the toughest man on the surface of the earth crying like a baby. However, his shedding of tears and the weeping of the different mourners was all drama to me. My mother's lifeless body was brought on a stretcher from a vehicle with an open back. She was laid on a little bed in the sitting room. Many people sat all-round the body either conversing or crying. A wooden box was soon brought in and my mother's body was put into it. It spent the rest of the day and the whole night in it. The next morning, a large hole was dug behind the house. A priest came in and a requiem mass was said. After that, the mouth of the wooden box was closed and some six men carried it behind the house where the large hole was dug. After a few words of prayer, the wooden box that contained my mother's body was lowered into the large hole and filled with soil. That was what I saw through the eyes of an eleven year old boy. I did not understand much about it then because of the environment I found myself in. Santa village was not very open to the outside world and I had never travelled out of it. Everything I knew was limited to what was found in it.

Things were never the same again after the departure of my mother. My father spent most of his time out of the house and whenever he returned, it was trouble. Any piece of paper that was on the floor or crumbs of bread on the table or any other thing that was not in its right place, became a pretext to have us beaten mercilessly. He had many concubines and we had to pay the price for anyone of them that annoyed him. Our house was strategically located and we could determine his mood from his movement far off. Whenever he was annoyed, he walked very fast. Whenever my siblings and I saw that from a distance, we either ran into the surrounding farm or into the bedroom and stayed there until it was bed time. With that kind of hostile environment, school became not just a place to learn but also a hideout from the wrath of my father. Whenever we were dismissed at the end of a school day, the thought of returning home was too frightening. The worse moments for us were the weekends and the holidays. No day went by without me or any of my two brothers, Joshua and Benjamin or two sisters, Quincy and Jane, crying. There were moments we had the impression that our father derived a lot of pleasure in inflicting pain on us. In the midst of all that, there was nowhere to go as such we just had to endure it. All of these brought back painful memories of our mother's passing on and the void it created.

As could be expected my father's actions had consequences. My performance in school dropped drastically and my elder brother ran away from home. My father did not bother to go and look for him. He just kept warning, threatening and saying that Joe, my elder brother was a thief and we were going to end up like him if we dared

3

to copy his example. My father's elder sister, Aunt Magdalene, visited us once and saw how her younger brother beat up my younger sister, Quincy for throwing part of her food on the floor, and decided to take her along.. I was still in primary five and was preparing to sit for the end of the year exam which was to take me to primary six then. I managed an average pass and moved to primary six which was the second to the last class to my completing primary school. But living under my father's roof meant that the sun was to remain permanently set and it was to rise only when I made up my mind to leave.

During the first week of school in primary six, Aunty Grace, one of my father's concubines moved into our family house with all her belongings. That was just seven months after my mother died. She was a nice woman and did all she could to protect us from my father each time he felt the urge to beat any of us. There were moments she got beaten up by my father for trying to stop him from taking out his anger on one of us. I can remember one particular incident on the 12th of September . That day, I returned from school and found no one at home. My younger brothers and sister as well as Aunty Grace had gone to the farm and I knew the farm in question. It was about some eight and half kilometres away from home and I decided to go and meet them there. Unfortunately for me, my father was with them at the time I got there and that marked the beginning of trouble for me. He left everything he was doing and started moving towards me shouting.

"Where are you coming from and where do you think you are going to?" he asked.

Gripped by fear, I was scared of saying something which might have made an already bad situation worse. It was Aunty Grace who tried to provide an answer in my place.

"He has returned from school and has decided to come and help with some of the things we might have to carry back home," she said.

Indeed, that was the reason why I followed them to the farm but my father was not going to take that as a good reason. The desire to have me beaten was already aroused and he had to satisfy it. He reaped off a branch from one of the fruit trees that was in the farm and had me well beaten. It did not end there. He kept kicking and slapping me on the way back home. To avoid him, I decided to put some distance between us by walking faster. But he continued each time he caught up with me. In the midst of all that he kept asking what I would have done if I was attacked by a wild animal on my way to the farm. Some passers-by who were also heading back to their homes from their farms saw what he was doing and pleaded with him to at least get home before punishing me for whatever crime I might have committed. But he asked them to mind their own business. When we got home that day, I entered the house to put down the load I carried. My father entered after me and locked the door behind him with the key. That prevented Aunty Grace or any other person from coming in to disturb him. He then grabbed a thin iron rod of about half a meter long and used it on me. He beat me all over my body with it. He hit me several times on the head with it. My head was swollen and by the time he let go of me, I looked like someone who had been stung by wild African honey bees. A severe headache started soon after. It has remained a problem ever since. Whenever I found myself in a place with temperature slightly higher than normal or did a lot of mental work, a terrible headache ensued. I could no longer read for more than 30 minutes without a break. Later on I began to wonder what he would have done if I had stayed home after school on that day. It was obvious that I would not have still gotten off the hook. He would have looked for another reason to have me beaten. Whatever the case, that act left an indelible scar that would remain with me for the rest of my life.

My father's brutality and heartless cruelty had severe negative impacts on me. One of them was that I became scared of any man that was old enough to be a father to me. Whenever I was in the presence of someone older, I remained silent and talked only when I was given permission to do so. Many other people I met outside our home had difficulties understanding my quiet attitude. Those I felt comfortable with were my classmates or kids of my age.

My father could be compared only to a chameleon whose colour could not be predicted. Only a week after seriously beating me up for taking a road infested with imaginary wild animals to meet them at a farm, he was the very one who asked me to come to that same farm and help in carrying some farm produce back home after school. I wondered where he kept the threat of being attacked by wild animals given that only hours had added to my age and not years. In resignation, I concluded that my father would always remain a stranger to me.

I successfully went through primary six and had to begin primary seven the following academic year. Over the holiday which ran from June to September, so much water went under the bridge. Aunty Grace had to put up with my father's violent behaviour but infidelity soon added to it. It was not that dating many women was something new but to Aunty Grace, it was a recent development. My father just couldn't keep his hands off women especially widows. I never understood how they could tolerate a man who was not only brutal but had a volcanic temper. Some of the women he dated were even married. I could remember once when I was still in primary five shortly before my mother died. I was returning from the farm with him and a man who had laid ambush along the footpath we took fired a shot aiming at him but missed. The gun the man used was locally made and took only one bullet at a time. It seemed the bullet he wasted was the only one he had. My father and I ran after dropping everything we carried. He ran faster than me and I could not believe my eyes. "*If everyone could see death, no one would have been dying,*" I told myself. The noise of the gun shot attracted the attention of some villagers who lived not far from the footpath who came out to see what was going on. My father on his part at some point after running for some time decided to walk back to see why there was a gun shot and I followed him. I'm sure he probably thought that it was one reckless hunter who didn't care to check if there were people around before firing his careless gun. When we got to the spot where the shot was fired, I discovered that the 10 litres jug of palm wine I dropped had all spilled out. The man who fired the shot was surrounded by some villagers. As soon as he saw my father coming, he surged forward and told my father to stay away from his wife. My father being a man who did not know when to stop talking responded.

"If you handled your wife well, she wouldn't have accepted me. If you cannot target something and hit it, tell me how you will successfully manage a woman. You do not have a child because you keep hitting the wrong target. Instead of telling me to stay away from your wife, you are supposed to encourage me to help you get out of childlessness," he said.

After leaving the scene, my father warned me never to breathe a word of what happened that day to anybody. I considered it naïve on his part because the people who were attracted by the gunshot got the story from the cuckolded man and were definitely going to spread the information. The small size of Santa village greatly favoured the spread of information especially those of scandalous nature. So if people did not learn of the incident from me, they were going to learn of it from the witnesses who were present at the scene. It was all a matter of time. Whatever the case, I heaved a sigh of relief as the palm wine container I dropped after the gunshot did not get broken..

However, Aunty Grace could not put up with my father's infidelity and decided to leave. Things got really bad for me and my younger ones after her departure. My father became much more violent. With no one left to prevent him from beating any of us to his satisfaction, it seemed he wanted to make the most of it. Any wrong pronunciation of any word or a delay in providing an answer to a mental sum was enough to make any of us cry. Even if any of us had the answer to any question he asked, fear was enough to make us give the wrong one. It seemed he was more interested in the mistakes any of us could make than the right answers to the questions posed. When one mistake was made, it gave him the opportunity to use the cane. I could no longer put up with the beatings and planned with my younger ones to do something really terrible to him. I thought of setting up a booby trap in our living room that would completely knock him off his feet giving my younger ones and I room to inflict maximum pain on him using any weapon we could possibly lay hands on. But my younger ones did not buy my idea and were too scared to try. With them unwilling to assist me do something; I considered that I have had enough. I was bent on not receiving any beatings and left the house with my books and some few clothes I could boast of. It was a Thursday morning and at that time, I was preparing to sit for the First School Leaving Certificate exam. That exam was capital because no one could be admitted into any secondary school without providing proof that he or she had succeeded in the exam.

2

When I left the house, I went to Pinyin, a neighbouring village which was found some 21 km from Santa. With no money of my own, I was forced to trek to get there. I decided not to go to school that day. On my way, just about six kilometres within the borders of Pinyin village, I found a house which showed no signs of life. From every indication it was abandoned or the occupants were probably far from the village. There was grass all over the compound, right to the door steps leading into what looked like a sitting room. On one end of the yard were two graves well-built and covered with tiles. I did not understand why such a beautiful house had been abandoned. I went round to the back of the house and touched the back door which led into the kitchen and it opened. I went in and moved round the whole house. It was void of furniture and other house utensils. I went into one of the rooms and set up my 'bed' using the little clothes I had. I was certain that no one was ever going to find me there.

Nevertheless, I did not know if it was fate or design but some things worked in my favour. The location of the school midway between Santa and Pinyin made things easier for me. I went to school regularly though I always got there very exhausted to begin classes at 07:30. I used the running stream which was behind the house for bathing and a source of drinking water. As for food, I often left school and went to our farm which was not too far from where the school was and harvested some. I sometimes got into the school farm as well as into the farms of total strangers to pick up what they had thrown there to rot away and manage just to survive. I harvested only food that I could roast like maize, cocoyam and plantains since I had no pots. Life was difficult but the fact that I was far from the nagging and anger of my father made me forget my plight. It was a matter of making a choice between two very bad alternatives. My plight made me think most of the time about my late mother and wished she was still alive. I equally thought of my younger ones who were still living with my father. I pitied their situation though the new one I found myself in was not any better. I was never too far from the corridors of malnutrition. Most of what I ate was dry and mostly roasted. With the complete absence of fruits on my food menu, stooling sometimes was not easy. I was conscious of the risk I was subjecting myself to but it was better than being beaten all the time by my despotic father.

Two weeks to the month of November, I fell sick. I was lucky that the seriousness of my illness manifested itself not when I was sleeping in the lonely and deserted house but at school. I was suffering from advanced malaria. I started feeling a lot of cold and pains on all my joints while in class. I felt weak and could not write. I soon passed out. That was what one of my friends narrated to me when I regained consciousness at the Santa District Health Centre. My father was alerted and told where I was. He came to the District Health Centre at 10:00 on that fateful Thursday. I expected him to start barking like a dog but he didn't. I could not tell if he behaved himself because he was in a hospital and there were many people around. All the same, he was very calm and stared at me most of the time. When it was 10:30, he asked all my friends who were around me to leave with the reason that he wanted to talk to his son. My three friends obeyed and walked out of the room. He began by asking me why I had to run away from home. I told him that I was not his son but a slave and asked him if he ever stopped for a while and tried to put himself in the position of those he inflicted pain on. He got impatient and shouted at the top of his voice.

"Who do you think you are talking to like that? It is only that you are sick….. If not, I would have given you the beatings of your life here," he said.

The loud threatening voice drew the attention of some nurses who came in to call him to order. He promised to behave and they

10

left the room again. That gave me more courage and I took off from where he ended.

"I have promised myself that no man alive would ever lay his hands on me again. I left the house because I got tired of you and the ill-treatment you meted out on my younger ones and I. I don't know why you bothered to come here when you were informed that I was sick. You are very mistaken if you think that I would leave this place and come with you. If you were the one that was on this sick bed and I was alerted, I would have prayed that you go and rot in the hottest part of hell. That way, you would not frustrate or inflict pain on anybody ever again. You will die a childless man because as soon as I start making money, I would come and get all my younger ones. You are a danger to them," I said boiling with anger.

"If someone would have told me that you would one day have the courage to talk to me the way you've just done, I would say it's a lie. I think that malaria has done something to your brain. If that was not the case, I don't know where that courage is coming from. How can you wish death for me your own father? If I beat you, it is not because I hate you. It is because I want to correct you," he said.

"I was told in school that when someone has only a hammer in his toolbox, he might tend to think and see every solution to any problem as a nail. You saw only the cane as the solution to all problems. You have made all your children to hate you. I have told you that you would end up alone and I will do everything possible to see that it becomes a reality. Someone like you does not deserve to live among human beings," I said.

He was really taken aback by my harsh words and I could read the surprise on his face through his eyes which he opened much wider.

"So, do you really hate me to that extent? Our people say that we are not supposed to spare the rod and spoil the child. I knew I was doing the right thing by using the cane to correct you and your brothers and sisters," he said.

11

"I am not against the fact that parents should use the cane on their children. I am reproaching you for over doing it. Too much of a negative act has disastrous consequences. You are a threat to me and my brothers and sisters. It was better you never engendered us if you were to do so and treat us like wild animals," I said.

We remained silent for about twenty minutes. I did not know what was running through his mind. He sat in a very pensive mood and I was sure that if we were at home, I would have received the punishment of the century. I used the 20 minutes to revisit all what I said to him. It was then that I was able to measure the full weight of my words. I thought that I was too severe on him and softened my mind a little. I think if he had made any request at that moment, I would have given in. But he didn't. The picture of him inflicting pain on me and my brothers and sisters ran through my mind. I hardened up again and it was then that he decided to break the silence.

"I would like you to come home and help me look after your brothers and sister," he said softly.

I could not believe what I just heard. The words were like those of a cruel killer in a horror movie trying to feign kindness in order to lure his victims. I knew the kind of people who could change and the man who was in that hospital room at that moment with me was not one of them. If I accepted and moved back home, he would have given me some time to settle down and then look for the slightest incident to punish me for running away from home. There was no need asking him to promise never to beat any of us ever again. He needed me back home and was going to agree to everything but he was not that type that kept to his promises. He was my father and I knew him just too well.

"Why did you come here? Was it just to come and ask me to come back home so that you would continue your beatings from where you left off? Well, you wasted your time because I will never spend a night in your house again. If I ever come there, it would be to see my younger ones and not you. To me, you now belong to history. If you wouldn't mind, I want you to leave now," I said.

His eyes widened as I asked him to leave. It seemed he was living a fairy tale. It was unheard of that a son or child would ask the father to leave. If he told anyone about it, I was definitely going to be the condemned one. In a conservative village like Santa, it was an abomination and tradition frowned at it. However, my father left the room as I said with disappointment written all over him. For the three days that I spent in the District Hospital, he did not come again to see me. I think my words really hurt him and I wondered if he was going to take it out on my younger ones. Uncertainty clouded my mind and I had to have the doubts cleared. I planned on rushing to our family home as soon as I was out of the district hospital to see how my younger ones were faring.

I was discharged on a Friday and I left straight for the new place I considered home. Since it was a weekend, I decided to remain indoors and planned on going to see my younger ones only on Sunday. I became more careful and to avoid contracting malaria I put on all my clothes before sleeping. But I was still vulnerable to pneumonia as the nights especially around 02:30 were usually very cold and I did not have warm clothes.

Sunday soon came and I left for our family home at 15:00. I knew my father's time table well and knew that he could not be at home at that time. I was very careful when approaching the house. I might have been very versed with his time table but there were still unforeseen, which I had to guard against. I saw my junior ones playing on the yard and that was an indication that my father was not at home. If they were not outside, that would have been an indication that he was in or he was not far away.

As soon as they saw me, they all ran to me asking why I had to abandon them. I felt terrible with that question and did not know what to tell them. They asked me if I had come to stay and were very disappointed when I told them that I was there only to see how they were doing. I then asked them how our father was treating them and they said that he was still taking out his anger on them. They told me that our father really got them well beaten on Wednesday when he came home fuming with anger and saw them playing. He asked them if there was nothing better they could do with their time. I realized that I was right not to have trusted him when he visited me in the hospital asking me to come back home. I did not want to stay there for too long because I did not want our father to see me even from a distance. If that were to happen, he would beat them. They all were weeping when I turned to leave. I was heartbroken but there was nothing I could do. I was unable to feed myself properly and could not take any of them along. I just told them that they had to bear the torments again for some time before I could come for them. With tears streaming down my face I just closed my eyes and left.

On my way back to my self-made home, I met so many American peace corp. volunteers. Many of them were in Santa and other surrounding villages. They gave assistance in the fields of agriculture, education and health. Many of them taught in the primary and secondary schools around Santa. One of them taught English in the catholic primary school I attended. He taught in my class and his name was Mr Finley Banks. He knew me by name as well as many of my classmates since we were not many in primary Seven. He was among the many peace corp. volunteers I saw that day. They were all heading to the direction of my home but lived much further from where I lived. I was a bit careful when taking the branch that led to the abandoned house and hoped that my teacher did not see me At least with the house isolated and the frontage very bushy, I did not at any one moment think that someone would ever come there to look for me or anything. Filled with that conviction I opened the back door, went in and roasted a few coco yams which I ate for supper. I drank a good quantity of water after eating and revised my lessons after that. All that took me up till 18:15 when I decided to go to bed. There was no electricity and I could not read in the dark. I had no money to buy candles and each time darkness fell on the village and its environs, I was forced to go to bed.

3

At about 19:30, I heard a knock on the main door. I had never opened it since I occupied the house because I did not have the key. I thought of remaining silent to give the stranger the impression that no one lived there. The knock on the door persisted and the person knocking said that he was going to knock down the door if I didn't open up. I could recognize the voice as that of Mr Finley. I did not know how serious he was about knocking down the door if I didn't open it but I saw his presence there as an opportunity to make a new friend to whom I could open up my heart. I responded to assure him that there was indeed someone there and asked him to go round and enter through the back door. I opened the back door and he entered the house. He had a torch in his hand and used it to examine the environment I lived in. He saw the mat I laid on and a few roasted cocoyams I kept at one end of the room to eat as breakfast the next morning before going to school.

"Are those the graves of your parents in front of the house?" he asked.

I just bent my head staring at the floor and did not say anything. He took my silence as a confirmation to the question he asked.

"I'm so sorry to learn that you are an orphan. I'm not an orphan but I know many people and children who have lost their parents in war-torn countries like the Democratic Republic of Congo, Iraq, Afghanistan, Pakistan as well as some countries where HIV-AIDS is ravaging the population like in Southern Africa. I know how difficult it is," he said pointing the torch at my roasted cocoyam. "Don't you have any extended family members who would have taken you in after the death of your parents?"

I still did not say anything.

"You don't have to say anything. I understand the trauma. I will do anything I can to help you. But first, you are not going to sleep here anymore. You could get sick. I would like that you come with me to my house…that's if you don't find any inconveniences," he said.

Wordlessly, I picked up my few property and we both left the abandoned house. Some 40 minutes later, we were at his house. It was not his personal house but that of an indigene who decided to give him to live in since he was doing some charity work which benefited the whole community. He opened the door and turned on the light. We were in his sitting room and it was well equipped with a large cupboard with all sorts of breakable plates in it, a set of very expensive chairs, a large wool carpet on the floor and a large TV set and deck. The house was covered in ceramic tiles. That was more than any wealth I have ever seen in my life and I was scared even to step on the carpet. My teacher could see it and urged me to make myself comfortable. After seating on the smooth comfortable chair for a short while, he took me to the guest room and told me that from that day on, I was going to be living there. He showed me the bathroom as well. I had a shower and joined him in the sitting room where we both watched TV.

While we were in the sitting room, he asked me how long I had been living in the abandoned house. I told him that I had been there for three and a half months. He asked me if I had ever been ill while I was there and I said yes précising the illness. He told me that he was going to take me to the Santa District Health Centre for a thorough check-up. I did not speak unless I was certain that I had the permission to do so. Thanks to my father, I had learnt to be quiet even though it was not so from the very beginning. The relationship I had with my father was so much built on fear and it soon had to extend to others. Mr Finley was no exception and all his attempts at getting me part with the grip of fear failed.

I thought of telling him that I ran away from home as well as the reasons that motivated me to do it. But the fear of being taken back to our home where my ruthless father was, terrified me. The possibility of him learning of it sooner or later was so great and if that were to happen, he was certainly going to either loose trust in me or hate me. There I was caught between a hard place and the deep blue sea. I did not know how to get out. I decided to leave everything in the hands of fate. From that moment, I knew something was happening and it was that my destiny was taking a different direction.

Mr Finley and I left for school the next day and he took me to the Santa District Health Centre for a check-up as he promised the previous day. It was discovered that I had malaria 1+. I was prescribed some drugs and encouraged to take them as prescribed by the physician. Mr Finley assured the physician that he was going to personally make sure that I took the drugs and at the right time. I must confess that Mr Finley was God sent. My health and physic greatly improved. My performance at school improved as well. Mr Finley drew up a personal time table for me. I had time to go and play with my friends, read and watch TV. Reading was mostly within week days and visiting of friends and watching TV was limited to the weekends. However, I followed my personal time table strictly and that had a very huge impact on my performance in the First School Leaving Certificate exams. I passed in List A when the results were published.

With my first certificate already in my pocket, I wondered what I was going to do after that. I really wanted to go to secondary school and the school fee was much higher than that paid at the primary school level. Mr Finley who was particularly happy with my performance asked me if I wanted to go to secondary school and I eagerly said yes. He told me that he was going to take care of my school fees right up to the university level if I was capable of making it there. I was extremely happy and thanked him immensely. But one thing remained which kept torturing me and I dreaded it very much.

It was how Mr Finley was going to react the day the truth about my life was going to get to him. I was scared he might hate me and withdrew his promise of helping me with my education. Whatever the case, only fate knew what was in store ahead.

Three months still separated me from my first day in the secondary school and with the promise of Mr Finley to see me through, I was confident the day shall come to pass. Something happened during those three months that cast a dark shadow over my future and I thought my dreams in life were going to evaporate forever. Mr Finley started dating one of his female colleagues who happened to have been my class five teacher. We were fond of calling her Aunty Grace. She was very beautiful but very strict and that explained why though in her late twenties she was still single. She knew me very well and was present at the funeral of my mother when she died. She was also aware of my father's brutal behaviour. Mr Finley brought her to the house several times and she got to know that I was living with him. She narrated my story to him and he was very furious at me. That Thursday evening that he learnt of it, he came home fuming with anger. He asked me why I let him believe I was an orphan and did not tell him I ran away from home.

"I have never at any one time told you that I am an orphan. And talking about orphans, I am not different from one, am I? He or she who told you that I ran away from home certainly gave you explanations on why I had to do so, right?" I asked.

The anger in him fizzled away with my question. I was careful not to let him know that I knew who must have narrated my story to him. He tried to make me understand that it was illegal for him to be housing me without informing my father or any of my family members. I told him it was not a very good idea to do so. It was true that in other skies, his act would be considered as kidnapping but I did not want him to see it that way. I told him that if he tried to look for any of my family members especially my father, I was going to run away. Suspicion crept into our relationship for a while but the good thing after the dust settled was that he did not try to look for any of my family members. He felt that it was better for me to stay with him than run away again into uncertainty. Besides, he was not that type that was violent and did not like men who found pleasure in inflicting pain on others. That said, things got much better between us after that.

My next huddle was Aunty Grace. She started coming to the house too often. Each time she came, she brought along one or two of her property and did not take them back with her when leaving. Within a short period of time, she had settled in the house. She became the mother and Mr Finley was the father. Unfortunately, I was not the son to complete the family structure. I became more of a house boy doing sometimes most of the house work even though there was a housemaid. Her name was Jessica and she was very hard working. Aunty Grace did not like the idea of having a female housemaid in the house. "Female housemaids are not to be trusted because they turn out to be husband snatchers," she always said. I didn't know why she started referring to Mr Finley as her husband. May be he had proposed to her or had given her the impression that he was going to marry her. Well, that was just a guess which was still clouded by doubts in my mind and only time was going to expose the reality. What I hated particularly about her was her authoritative attitude. She did nothing and was only giving instructions and orders. Whenever she was in the kitchen cooking and needed something which was just a meter or two from her, she would not go for it but would call for either Jessica or myself to come and get the thing for her. I was always mad whenever she called me to come and get something and give her when she could just reach it by stretching her hand. With time, she got really pissed up with my behaviour and kept insisting that I do most of the house chores. She saw a rival in Jessica who was overtly beautiful and attractive and wanted Mr Finley to send her away. If I was obedient and did all what she wanted, she would have used it as a pretext to pile pressure on Mr Finley to make

21

Jessica redundant. I was not prepared to play her game. Jessica was from a poor home and I understood that perfectly well because I too came from a poor home. Mr Finley hired her not because he really needed her services but because he wanted to help her. Because I did not want to play Aunty Grace's game, she became very cruel to me. She changed the social atmosphere in the house. Each time food was served on the table for four persons, she made sure that Jessica and I ate in plastic plates while Mr Finley and herself ate in breakable plates. I saw it as humiliating and decided to be eating in my bedroom or in the kitchen. That was the life I was used to before Mr Finley came into my life. Jessica too decided to avoid the dining table and preferred her bedroom. Mr Finley was a man who did not act in a hurry. He always took his time and observed situations. That was what I admired most about him. So, on the evening of the last Friday of November, when I was in year two in secondary school, the table was set as usual. There were two breakable plates and two plastic plates. While Aunty Grace and Mr Finley were at table, Jessica and I walked in and dished our food and started moving towards the kitchen. It was then that Mr Finley decided to stop us.

"Come back here children," he said. "I have been doing some observations for some time now and have noticed that plates placed on the table no longer reflect the unity I have always wanted. There are two breakable plates and two plastic plates. This is not what used to be. Is there any explanation to this?"

"In our African tradition, children are not supposed to be eating among adults. Adults have their own places while children have theirs," Aunty Grace said.

"Even at table?" Mr Finley Asked.

Aunty Grace did not say anything. She was busy enjoying her meal.

"I have realized that the kids no longer eat at table as before. They eat in their bedrooms or in the kitchen. Is that part of the

22

African tradition too? In what part of Africa is that custom practiced?" Mr Finley asked.

"This tradition is practiced all over Africa," replied Aunty Grace.

"I have many friends around this continent and I've been to their homes. They eat with their children on the dining table and the plates are all identical. Does that mean that they are no longer Africans?" he asked.

"Many people are turning away from our tradition. They go to school, acquire knowledge which they use to question our tradition. They have decided to cut themselves from their roots. I am not going to be like them. If we begin to mix with our children, how would they respect us?" Aunty Grace asked.

"I think those that are questioning the so called tradition have the right to do so. I think parents that eat with their children at table want to avoid developing a cat and mouse relationship with them. That has nothing to do with mixing up or loosing respect. Whether it is an African tradition or not, I don't want to see it practiced under my roof. That kind of tradition is creating division and I don't want to see it again," Mr Finley said in a very severe tone.

With that last sentence, he went to the cupboard and got some two breakable plates which were identical to those already on the table. After placing them in front of us he got the food flask and served Jessica and I himself. That act was a slap on the face of Aunty Grace and I knew Jessica and I were going to get it really hot from her. She left the table for the room as soon as Mr Finley said that he did not want to see signs of division in the name of tradition in the house. That alone was already an indication that tough times lay ahead for us the kids.

Mr Finley left us and went to their bedroom probably to talk things out with her. But as soon as he got to the room, a heated quarrel ensued. Jessica and I could hear them from the sitting room where we were. After a short while, there was dead silence. We soon saw Aunty Grace emerge from the room with some of her personal belongings in a small bag. It was obvious she was leaving us for a while or for a very long time. Somewhere within me, I was happy that peace was going to return to the house with her departure. But, I felt bad because of the impact her departure was going to have on Mr Finley. "Even planned separations are painful," people always say. Though he was angry with her for behaving badly and unwilling to make amends, I did not think he wanted her to go but she made up her mind to leave and there was nothing he could do to stop her.

Out of all that drama, I considered myself really lucky because it was happening at a time when I had left the primary school. If that was not the case, I'm convinced that Aunty Grace would have made life difficult for me there. For some days after the departure of Aunty Grace, Mr Finley looked really sad. He spent most of his time in his bedroom after work. I asked him once if he was going to kiss and make up with Aunty Grace since her absence was having a lot of impact on him. He told me that if there was someone to make a move towards reconciliation, it was not him. He added that he did not ask Aunty Grace to leave and just wanted her to realize that people must move with the changing times. He asked me not to worry as I tried to blame myself and Jessica for causing trouble between him and Aunty Grace.

"You have only helped to make me realize the kind of person she really is," he said.

I knew how he was feeling and told him how terrible I felt. However, on the first weekend after the departure of Aunty Grace which was a Sunday, I went for 06:00 mass and returned at 08:00. Mr Finley was in the sitting room watching a televised church service. I entered when the preacher just began his homily. He started with a short story.

"There were two friends who wanted to go to heaven," he began. "One of them was fat and tall while the other was a bit short and of medium size. The fat and tall one was called Samson while his friend was called Johnson. On the day which was arranged for them to begin their journey to heaven, each of them was given a cross to carry. Samson accepted his own cross and carried it without complaining. Johnson also carried his but kept complaining that it was too heavy and each time he did that, it was shortened. They soon got to a place where there was a bottomless pit and they had to place their crosses over the pit to cross to the other side. Samson was the one to go first. He placed his cross and crossed to the other side with ease. As soon as he was on the other side, his cross over the pit disappeared. It was the turn of his friend to place his own cross over the pit. He did but it could not reach the other side because it was already too short. He could not go across to the other side and so could not enter heaven. Many of us are like Johnson. We always like to find the easy way out of difficult situations. When we have problems with our wives, we go complaining about them to our friends or we opt for divorce. When we do that, we are not different from Johnson. We see our wives as heavy crosses and want them shortened.... We are faced with an exam and have it in our heads that it is difficult....We resort to cheating as an easy way out.... We are not different from Johnson who wants his cross shortened. We are not supposed to see obstacles or difficulties as punishment. We should see the cross or difficulty as an opportunity for us to share in the passion of our lord and saviour. So, when faced with difficulties, we should pray to our maker to give us the strength and perseverance to bear it. Our maker is very just and would not give anyone a cross which he or she cannot carry. If we are unwilling to put in a little effort, we would end up like Johnson at the mouth of the pit."

Mr Finley listened to the homily with a lot of attention. He nodded most of the time in the course of the homily. I imagined that perhaps he was telling himself that Aunty Grace might have been his cross and by not taking the first move to reconciliation, he was finding the easy way out. I was just guessing and nothing was certain yet.

4

On Wednesday the following week, Mr Finley informed me that he had applied to be moved to another school. I did not ask him the reason why he had to take such a move but thought that he might have done it to avoid confronting Aunty Grace. However, he left the house late again that afternoon and returned only at 21:00. That was the first time he returned home so late since I Moved into his house I went and opened the door when he knocked and did not ask him what kept him out for so long. He did not say anything to me either. We all went to bed after wishing each other good night.

Keeping late hours continued for the next few days and I knew that someone was keeping him out. It must have been only a woman. And the woman started coming to the house. Surprisingly, it was Aunty Grace and she moved back to the house eleven days after she left it. She was friendlier when Mr Finley was at home and a bit harsh when he was away. She abandoned the habit of calling me or Jessica to come and get something which was just a few meters from her. Mr Finley stopped coming home late in the night. I wondered why he did not go in for a new catch. Probably, he must have said to himself that it was better to stick with the devil he knew than with the angel he was still to discover. However, our new found harmony was to last only for three months.

On Saturday the 16th of May, Aunty Grace asked me what I was really doing in the house of Mr Finley as I did next to nothing as house work. I was not happy with her question as I was the one in charge of keeping clean Mr Finley's shoes as well as her own shoes. I also made sure that no grass grew around the house and took care of the flowers or garden. I did not see why she said that I was not doing anything. By so doing she reminded me of my father. With the anger in me, I asked her why she came back. That was definitely not the right question to have asked at that moment. But it just slipped out of my mouth and I had to accept the outcome. Aunty Grace had some real harsh words for me.

"You are a miserable fool who has been rescued from the gutters at the hands of hunger and now that you have been fed and washed clean, you have the guts to ask me stupid questions," she said.

I did not say another word after that. I just walked into my room and carried everything I had as belongings. I walked into the living room where she was and she asked me where I was going.

"I'm going back to the gutters where I came from. I had enjoyed this luxury to the extent that I've forgotten that I came from the gutters. Thank you for reminding me," I said with a lot of cynicism.

She tried to stop me not by pleading or trying to cajole as a mother would do when she sensed that a situation was getting out of hand but she was issuing orders. I could not stand it coupled with the fact that she just trampled on my pride. I told her that we were all strangers in the house of Mr Finley and she had no right to be treating me like a pauper. I left the house as soon as I told her what I had on my mind.

I went back to the old abandoned house Mr Finley found me in less than 4 km away towards my former primary school. There was much grass around the house since there was no one there to clean it. I went into the house through the back door as usual and set up my former room. The only difference was that I wasn't going to sleep on my clothes but I had a mattress which could be inflated and deflated. I took it out of my box and inflated it and waited for the night to come. While waiting, I tried to imagine what the situation would be like when Mr Finley returned and could not find me at home. I was certain that Jessica was going to tell him all what transpired. I knew the kind of man he was and he was not the type who would tolerate the kind of words Aunty Grace uttered. I knew he was going to take action and it was not going to be long from then.

At 20:25, I heard a knock on the back door. I stayed still and behaved as if there was no one there. There was another knock but I did not budge. The knocking became insistent and was accompanied by a voice. It was the voice of Mr Finley.

"I know you are in there and I will knock down the door if you do not open up," he warned.

I told him to go away and leave me alone. He insisted that I open the door so that we could talk. I still was unwilling to open it and told him that maybe Aunty Grace was right to say that I belonged to the gutters. After much pressure from him, I decided to open the door.

"You are the first who came into my life and not Grace. If there is someone I should part ways with, it should be Grace and not you. I will not allow her to come between you and me. She already has something doing to earn a living. She can move on with her life, with or without me. I took you in because I wanted to see you stand on your feet. If I allow you go now without knowing where you are heading to, I would have failed in my intentions and God would not be happy with me. Your place is in our home and not here. Please come home with me," he said.

"Aunty Grace said some really nasty things to me and I wouldn't want to go back to that house where I would have to confront her. I would prefer to stay here and avoid her hurting words," I said.

"I know the kind of things she said to you. Jessica told me and Grace confirmed it to me but added that she said them out of anger. But she cannot and will never come between you and me. For that, I can assure you. In fact, she will never bother you again," he said.

"What do you mean?" I asked.

"What I'm saying is, Grace and I have decided to go our separate ways. She obviously cannot be my cross and I think she is too heavy for one man to carry. She is just too difficult and thinks mostly of herself. I just could not continue with the relationship after learning the kind of things she is capable of saying to someone vulnerable instead of being a loving mother," he said.

I did not know what to tell him but I was definitely not sorry for Aunty Grace. She was too hard and was that type that would step on others if she were in a position of power. She was not yet the wife of Mr Finley and was already showing her colours. I just knew that if she was made legitimate wife in the house, she would try to control everything. I thought it was better for me to take my distance before things really start crumbling on my head.

Mr Finley helped me to put my scattered items together and helped me to carry some of them. We got back to the house at 20:00. Jessica ran up to Mr Finley and informed him of the departure of Aunty Grace. Mr Finley responded by saying that he was aware of it. That was the only thing he said and went to my room to keep some of my things which he held. After depositing the things he went straight to his own room. However, Jessica was very happy with the departure of Aunty Grace and I could see it on her face. That meant that there wasn't going to be any shouting and hurtful insults around the house. Peace finally came back to the house again and it was going to remain for the next eighteen months. I went through my book work with a lot of encouragement from Mr Finley while Jessica did her house chores. Mr Finley became the mother and the father as he went to the market and did most of the cooking. Life was perfect.

In my last year in the secondary school, precisely on May 07th, I was getting ready to sit for my G.C.E Ordinary Level examinations when Mr Finley's five year stay in Cameroon came to an end. The exam was scheduled to begin on June 10th and run for three weeks. I felt really terrible hearing Mr Finley tell me that he had to move over to Italy. I saw the bright future I had dreamed of vanish before my very eyes and wondered how I was going to face the uncertain future. I had always dreaded the day he would come to tell me that he had to leave but knew all the same that it was going to come someday. Mr Finley could see the sadness written all over me as he told me the sad news. But he tried to dispel my doubts and reassured me that he was still going to support me in all my educational endeavours. He further reminded me of the promise he once made to me that he was going to take care of my tuition to any level I wanted to go on the educational ladder. That reminder made me a little bit sceptical not because I doubted him. He kept all his promises he made to me for the whole time I lived with him and I had no reason to doubt him even for a second. But it happened at that moment perhaps because he was going away and maybe the kind of life where he was going to was very different from the one in Cameroon. I had seen and heard of wives who ended up frustrated after their husbands went abroad for greener pastures leaving them behind with catalogues of promises. Besides, there were friends who went far away promising to do this or that but none of them ever materialized. With such experiences from other people I knew, I doubted Mr Finley a little. I was just a few weeks away from my exams and was not supposed to let the separation affect me to breaking point. That was not the only stumbling block at that moment as I equally wondered where I was going to put up after his departure. I did not know if the landlord was going to be nice to me as he was to Mr Finley to the extent of giving him his house free of charge. There were some people who were nice to foreigners but not too hospitable to their neighbours and countrymen. I feared, prayed and hoped that the landlord would not turn out to be that type. All the same, my instincts told me that I just had to trust Mr Finley and try to dispel all the worries in my mind.

Jessica on her part felt really terrible too. She was a wise girl and managed what she was paid carefully. She gave part of her salary to her father to keep for her. Mr Finley gave her some money which she added to her savings and planned on opening a tailoring workshop for herself. She intended making herself useful before anything else because she was not the kind of girl that would tolerate nonsense from any man.

"A woman has her dignity only when she bears the name of a man. That is how society has made it and that is why women who

31

broke up with their husbands do not drop their ex-husbands' names. Men nowadays have decided not to marry women who cannot contribute to the family's financial income. I want to make myself useful and by so doing, get a good husband who would respect me," she kept telling me each time we talked about marital issues.

But I kept warning her of the opposite outcome. All around, there were men who had turned themselves into vampires with the intention of making money out of women who were financially viable. Other sincere men tend to be scared of successful women. But Jessica believed that a woman who lived in comfort could attract any man she wanted. Though she was not prepared to take shit from any man, it did not mean that she was hard. She knew her rights and knew when to be humble for the sake of peace. That was the reason why she once got really angry with me when I compared her to Aunty Grace. According to her, Aunty Grace was hard but foolish and forgot that she was always going to remain a woman no matter what, despite her level of education. However, the eminent departure of Mr Finley was bound to separate Jessica and I. She was very hard working, beautiful and intelligent but she was much older than me. I was not interested in having secondary thoughts perhaps because I was too shy or because Johnson, her boyfriend was there already. All I could think of was book work and improving my condition and that of my younger ones. She finally packed out two days before Mr Finley travelled.

5

On May 15th, Mr Finley left for Douala where he had to board a flight for Italy. I woke up that day and left the house earlier than the other days. I did not want to watch Mr Finely pack his things and leave. The pain would have been too much for me to bear. I tried crying all the tears out of my body on the eve of that day he had to go and resolved that I have had enough. He consoled me as much as he could and told me that he was going to call me every week via the landlord Mr Steven's phone,. He equally promised to send money for my upkeep and school fees and added that if I needed anything, all I had to do was just tell the landlord. On that day, I returned at 17:00. I could feel his absence in the house but his large portrait on one corner of the house filled some vacuum in my heart. I sat staring at the portrait for a long time. I had to learn how to live with the idea that he was no longer going to be there to encourage and support me at least physically. Nevertheless, one thing became very preoccupying to me and it was if the landlord was going to allow me continue living in his house free of charge. I could not find an answer and only time could tell. I went to bed that day at 19:06 without reading. I did not have the zeal to do so. My spirit was too heavy to concentrate on book work. I felt like Mr Finley left with not only part of me but also my future.

At 04:50 the next morning, I was awoken by a persistent knock on the door. I could recognize the voice as that of Achilles Otto, the fourth child of Mr Steven. He had his father's mobile phone in his hand and handed it to me as soon as I opened the door.

"It is Mr Finley. He wants to talk to you," he said.

I took the phone and was very happy to hear the voice of the one I considered father again. He told me that he arrived safely and was calling from his hotel room in Italy. He asked me how I was feeling and I told him how terrible I felt with his absence all over the house.

I narrated my previous day to him. He remained silent for a moment after listening to me and then urged me not to allow his absence affect me as I was going to face an important exam in the weeks ahead. He went further to say that he was going to call me every morning if that was going to help maintain my psychological stability. I told him that it was not necessary and promised to do all to stay focused. He then wished me a nice day and promised to call again the following week. We ended on that happy note and his voice continued re-echoing in my head long after he hung up.

I went to school that morning feeling lighter and prepared psychologically to face the lessons of the day. The nice and encouraging words of Mr Finley even from afar were having an effect. He kept his promise to call and everything went back to normal.

That notwithstanding, my landlord came and announced to me that I was going to move into his uncompleted and abandoned building just a few meters from the one I was living in. That was no problem to me but what was shocking was that the announcement came when I was barely three days to the commencement of the official examination. With no electricity in it, I wondered if he was going to allow me study in his house at night with his son. I asked the landlord if he could allow me stay in the house at least for the time I had to sit for my exam. He was adamant.

"Someone has to occupy that house in the shortest possible time. I don't want that he comes here only to realize that it is occupied. Besides, I did not build this house for charity. I built it to fetch me some money and someone is on the way to give me the money," he said.

"There is a guest room outside the house. Can you negotiate with the new tenant to let me occupy it just for the time I have to sit for my examination?" I asked.

"Sorry son, the new tenant has mostly young girls as children. A young man like you could constitute a real danger. In addition, who would pay the electricity bill for the time you would be there? You don't expect me or my new tenant to foot the bill for you, do you?" he responded.

I could not understand why he could give the house to someone like Mr Finley free of charge and not me. I asked myself if he had no thirst for money when he gave it to Mr Finley. '*Human beings are indeed difficult to predict*,' I said within me. I had no choice than to move to his abandoned house which had perforated walls. The only room that was manageable really had large holes on the walls. Anybody passing by the house could see almost everything that was inside. I went and reaped off some plantain leaves as well as some plastic papers I could find along the road and used them to block some of the holes on the walls. I spread a large plastic paper on the floor which was not cemented. After doing that, I opened my portable bed which Mr Finely gave me and inflated it. It occupied most of the room leaving just a little space for my other items. I placed the two pots Mr Finley left me with and some plates as well in one corner of the room. After setting everything up, I stood back and compared it with the one Mr Finley found me in. The differences were clear. The room at the abandoned house was better, with good walls and cemented floors. But I could not pack and go there because I wanted to be close to living people and not graves. Though there was a roof in my new room, there was no ceiling to shield me from the very cold nights and mosquitoes. I had no choice but to make it as comfortable as I could. "A beggar has no choice" is what I always heard people say. Since I was living the situation I knew exactly what they meant.

For the three days that separated me from my first examination subject, I went to my landlord's house and read using the security light outside. It was usually on from 18:30 to 21:00. Sometimes it was tuned off before 20:00 and I was forced to go back to my room and touch my way to bed. When it happened like that I often felt that my landlord was being wicked because he knew I was outside his house and also knew that I was preparing for the first very important exam of my life. His son Otto was still in his 4th year in secondary school and was not under pressure like me. If we were maybe in the same class, my landlord would have allowed the light on perhaps for much longer. However, on the eve of the exam, there was power failure in the evening and I was forced to do my last minute studies under the moonlight. I could not see anything as the moonlight was not really bright. I pleaded with Otto who went to their kitchen after his mother just left it and got some wood with one edge still glowing. I kept swinging it from left to right to maintain it in its glowing state and that was what I used to prepare for my exam.

On the day of the exam, I woke up very early and prepared for school. I did not have anything to eat. My landlord's wife was going to the farm that morning and passed by my room. She wished me luck in my exam and asked if I had something to eat. I told her I had nothing and she went back to her house and brought some beans in a plate and a loaf of bread. Beans was something definitely not to be eaten in the morning. It reacted more or less the same way as a sleeping pill. I thought for a while as she handed the meal to me whether to eat it or not. Sitting in an examination hall on an empty stomach was not a good idea and eating that beans was going to push me to sleep. There I was again in the middle of a situation with a very tough choice to make. At the end, I decided to eat very little of the beans and more of the bread. I drank a litre of water to limit the effect of the beans on my system. Thank God the effect was minimal.

I got to school at 07:20 and waited for the exam to begin at 08.00. I did not open my books following the advice our chemistry teacher gave us that it was not advisable to read less than 30 minutes before an exam. He did not give us any reason why but I decided to follow his advice.

At exactly 07:50 the invigilators started checking the candidates into the examination room. Only one student was allowed per desk and there was no room for cheating. There were three invigilators in the room to handle sixty five candidates. I liked it that way as I was fully concentrated only on my script without any distraction from a mate. At 11:00, the first subject ended and we had to move out and prepare for the second paper which was scheduled to begin at exactly 14:00. Only a maximum of two subjects were programmed each day and the intention was to give the candidates an opportunity to prepare and write stress free. But candidates who did not prepare well wrote with a lot of stress. I got comments from them soon after the first subject was over. Some speculated and read only specific topics. Unfortunately, there were no questions on the topics they read. Our teachers always warned us against speculations. They always asked us to read everything. Generally speaking, students who got involved in speculations did not fully invest in their book work. Our teachers kept reminding us that formal education and pleasure did not go together. Some of the students especially the girls, referred to some of us who took book work too seriously as bookworms. That did not bother us as we knew what we were looking for. At least book work was the area where we, the dedicated ones had an advantage over those who dedicated more time to pleasure. However, those who often called us bookworms went to the dinning shed and bought all the nice things money could possibly buy. I did not have money and only had to watch them enjoy themselves. My mouth watered as I watched them eating. I only prayed that the time for the commencement of the next subject could come soonest so that we get back to the examination room.

At 13:50, the invigilators started checking the candidates in for the second subject of the day which was Geography. When we were all set, a bell was rung for the subject to commence. It lasted for two and a half hours. I felt really exhausted at the end of it and was itchy to get home. I walked with those who lived in the direction of my 'home'. William and Wilson were among those but they lived much further from where I lived. On the way, our discussion was mostly centred on the first two subjects of the day and the frustration of some lazy school mates. When we got closer to where I lived, I slowed down and asked them to go ahead without me. When they asked why I was slowing down, I advanced a slight headache as the reason. I thought they were going to take my excuse and leave me as I had wished. I was wrong. William said that it was not proper for them to leave me in difficulties without doing something. I appreciated his caring attitude but insisted that they go ahead without me. I did not want them to start asking questions about where I lived. I was ashamed of the abandoned house with perforated wall in which I lived and did not want anyone to know that I lived there or let alone come to visit me there. I decided to hatch another plan and it was to tell them that I had a running stomach and had to get to the nearby bush to pass out the mess. I started behaving as if I was really in pain and dashed into a nearby bush. The way I went about my drama caused Wilson to laugh though he tried hard not to. Once in the bush, I stayed there intentionally for much longer than usual. They kept calling me and I kept asking them to go without me. William thought of a devilish thing to say to get me out of the bush.

"If a snake meets you in that bush, what would you say?" he asked.

That was something I had not thought of. The image of a big snake with its fangs piecing through my flesh and emptying its venom into my system became too terrifying. I knew it was just my imagination but anything that was in the form of a rope that touched my leg or any other part of my body made me skip with fright. The initial idea of playing delay tactics in the bush vanished and getting out became more pressing. I dashed out of the bush as fast as I could and joined my two classmates on the road. They sympathized with me and told me that things would get better once I got home. I still maintained the look of someone in serious pain on my face. They believed that I was really in pain and Wilson proposed that they carried me in turns on their backs. Letting them do that was going to cause them to want to know where I lived thereby making complete nonsense of my whole drama. I told them that it was my stomach that had some problems and not my legs and insisted on walking on my own adopting the pace of a snail. I told them that it was no use waiting for me as I was very comfortable moving at that snail pace. I thought of going to where William lived to do some reading since I did not have electricity and told him that I might be at his house that evening. Convinced that I was telling the truth that I could make it home on my own despite my stomach troubles, they hastened ahead much to my delight. Once they were about 300 meters away from me, I increased my steps and dashed to the branch which led to where I lived before one of them could get worried and decide to come back.

At 17:15, I was in front my landlord's house. His wife handed a little bowl of porridge yam to me. I thanked her immensely and she went on to ask how the first papers went. My response was very positive and she smiled. She encouraged me to work hard and added that God was going to see me through.

Mrs Angelica, my landlord's wife was a very nice woman. She was the exact opposite of her husband. Those words of encouragement would never have come from him. It seemed he had problems with people who were successful. He was that type who measured success only by his own standards. He tended to criticize anyone who was richer, more powerful or more successful than he was. However, he was not my problem and I knew what I wanted. I was not prepared to let anything stand on the way to my success, not even my landlord. Nevertheless, the kind words of Mrs Angelica reminded me of my mother. I cried a little when I got to my room and asked why death had to take her away. That crying soon carried me off to sleep and I woke up one hour later.

6

A t 18:17, I decided to finish the remaining beans I left in the morning with part of the porridge yam I was just given. I kept some of the yam to eat as breakfast the next morning before going to school. After eating, I left for the home of my friend, William. It was less than eight hundred meters away and I got there in no time since I was jogging. His room was outside the main house and he was about to shut his door when I arrived. Since he could not shut me outside, he asked me to come in. He was about to eat and probably did not want any intruders. He told me that Wilson was going to visit him that evening but it was definitely not for them to discuss bookwork. My friend did not come from a wealthy family. His room had a large family size bed but the floor was not cemented. The mud earth walls were not plastered and he used large transparent plastic papers to cover them from the floor to the ceiling. However, he shut the door after I entered and placed the food on his reading table for us to eat. Since he was a devoted Christian, he urged me to join him in thanking the Lord before sharing the meal. I got ready and he led the prayer in which he thanked the almighty God for providing the food and urged Him to bless the hands that prepared it as well as replenish the source of the food. He also asked God to bless those that were hungry and make it possible for them to share with us in spirit. He still had quite a lot to ask from God when there was a knock on the door. As soon as that happened, he ended the prayer prematurely and grabbed the bowl of rice and stew and sent it far under the bed. I was shocked by his actions looking back at the request he made in his prayer before the unexpected knock. He went and opened the door and the person who was outside was his kid sister, Juliana, who wanted to borrow an eraser. He took it and gave it to her and she left. I asked him why he sent the food under the bed and he said that he thought that it was Wilson who had arrived.

"You pleaded with God to enable those who could not share with us physically to do so spiritually because you knew that the spiritual sharing would take nothing from your food, right?" I asked.

"Do you know that you have a very big mouth? This food is not even enough for me and have you thought of what Wilson's appearance could do to the quantity? I was praying to God and not to you and so, stop speaking in the place of God," he said.

I ate just a little since I had already eaten in my room. I was there to honour my rendezvous though I made it clear to him from the start that it was conditional. I did not know what taking my books to go and read at his room would have looked like. I thought of asking him if it could be possible for us to be studying together in the afternoons and evenings but his reaction after the knock on the door prevented me from doing so. I was scared of what he might say concerning electricity bills. Most families in the village were poor and money was very hard to come by. I simply sensed that the high cost of a kilowatt of electricity was obviously going to come up and I did not want to hear it. I left him and went back to my room to prepare for the subjects of the next day.

At 19:00, I got back to my room and took my books and headed for my landlord's doorstep where I intended to read under the security bulb. I got there and sat down only for 15 minutes and the lights were turned off. The moonlight was up but it was not bright enough for me to read. I decided to head to the former house I lived in to plead with the new occupant, Mr Joshua, to allow me read. When I got there and knocked on the door, it was opened and he came out and closed the door behind him. He asked me what I wanted and I explained my situation. He asked me to get into the house and read for two hours only for that day. I thanked him for it and went in. I took advantage of the short time that was given to me to read thoroughly the first subject, Biology, which I had to face the next morning. At 22:15, I left Mr Joshua's house and walked back to the room I occupied. There was no time to prepare for the afternoon subject as there was no light and I planned on preparing for it soon after I was done with the morning subject. With that in mind, I went to bed.

The next morning at about 05:35 I was brutally awakened by a sting on my left leg. I jumped out of bed only to discover that I had some unusual guests. They were ants and they occupied almost the whole floor. I ran out of the room for a while before coming back. The ants were attracted by the porridge yam I kept the previous day. I carried the food outside and placed it there for a while. I wanted the ants that were inside the food to get out so that I could have something to eat before going to school. It was the only food I had. Throwing it away because ants had entered into it would not have been a good idea given that I had nothing else to eat. I got to school at 07:25 and things went on just as the previous days

At 17:30, I was back in the room with perforated walls I called home. I had just one subject the next day and it was scheduled to be in the morning period. I ate some bread Wilson gave me during break and rested for about two hours.

I went to read as usual under Mr Steven's security bulb. As soon as I sat down to read, he came out and started scolding at me. He asked me why I was sitting outside his house. I told him that I just wanted to read for the short time that the lights were turned on. He said my presence in front of his house at that hour of the evening was giving him a bad name. I responded that since he had once asked me who would be paying for my consumption of electricity, I could not dare knock on his door to let me in to read. That drew the attention of his wife and she came out to confront him.

"Just leave that child alone. Do you want to make him believe that you are not aware that he is always out there trying to read? You deliberately turn off the light sometimes when you know that he is out here. I have told you several times that your wickedness would bring ill luck onto me and my children. If you are maltreating another person's child because you feel that he is not your son, God might decide to punish you by withdrawing His blessings from this family. You are a father and are supposed to be a father to any child that comes your way," she said.

Her husband was not happy with that sermon especially as it was said in front of me.

"Shut up woman! If I needed moral lessons, I would have gone to church and not come to you. Who has asked you anything? This is my house and I have the right to decide what happens around here," he retorted.

Mrs Angelica was not that kind of woman who would stay quiet when wrong things were happening around her.

"I know what is troubling you inside. You are jealous of that boy. You are jealous of him because he is hard working and your own born children are not as hard working as he is. That is Otto there...he hates bookwork. Don't you think that Otto can see the seriousness in this boy and develop interest in bookwork? That is a child who has nothing and is fighting to be somebody. Otto is there and you give him everything. Yet, he is up to no good. You have spoilt all my children by providing them with everything they ask for. Now they are unable to do anything for themselves. Since you exiled that boy to that abandoned house, have you passed there even once to see how he is doing? Can you do the same thing to Otto? Life has a way of teaching people like you a lesson. That boy you are treating like an orphan will be the one to hold your hand someday," she said and went inside the house.

I started feeling the guilt of stirring up trouble between my landlord and his wife. I wanted to make amends by apologizing for the inconveniences caused. He did not say anything but just stood there devouring me with his angry looks without blinking. I was certain that the words of his wife were choking him and if he had his way, he would have taken it out on me that evening. My spirit was already dampened and there was no way I was going to concentrate again. The only thing left was to go back to my room and sleep. As I tuned to leave, Mrs Angelica called me back. As I turned to face her, I met her extended hand with a bowl of food in it. I took it and went to my room where I ate some and went to bed.

On the fourth examination day, I went in for the lone subject I had for that day. It was chemistry and I must say that my ideas did not flow as I would have wanted them to. I was psychologically disturbed and did not prepare well for it. However, when the subject was over after two and a half hours, I did not go back home. I stayed back in school to prepare for the next day's subject. I invited some friends and we formed a study group. I was very good at retaining things and did retain most of what we discussed. I did not bother much about reading at home. I did not want to be getting comments that were going to upset me especially if they were coming from my landlord. That strategy of reading in school before going home worked for the remaining four subjects.

I went through the examination successfully and looked forward to the release of the results which was supposed to be sometime in August. That notwithstanding, August was still a good number of weeks away and I was wondering what to do with the lengthy free time that was ahead of me. I thought of proposing to my landlord to employ me so I could do some work, in and around the house and even farm work in exchange for some money which I could use to buy some of my school needs in high school. But each time the thought came to my mind, there was some strange reluctance that held me back. I thought of the promise made by Mr Finley before his departure to Italy. I could not base my hopes entirely on what he said without thinking of a plan B. At last, I decided on going to Bamenda to look for a job. The distance that separated me from Bamenda was 45 km and I had no money to pay as transport fare. I did not want the lack of money to stop me from doing what I intended to do. I decided to trek to Bamenda.

June 24th, was the day after I wrote my last subject. I woke up very early and packed all my things in one box. Once that was done, I went to the house of my landlord and got his number. I had earlier informed Mr Finley of what I intended to do two days earlier when he called. I did not feel comfortable talking to him about financial problems as I considered that he had done a lot for me on that front already. *"If he was still calling me, it meant that he knew of my needs. There was therefore no need of reminding him of the promises he made,"* I told myself.

At exactly 07:25, I started my long trip to Bamenda on foot. I had never been there before and had no idea of how it looked like. The sun was bright but since it was the rainy season, such bright sunshine could give way to rain in a twinkle of an eye. I could not trust the weather and hated to think that rain might begin pouring down when I had not gotten to my destination. As I moved along, I was marvelled by the green small hills and trees in distant horizons. They acted as distractions from the exhaustion I started feeling when I had covered just 15 of the 45 km that separated me from my destination. There were moments I thought that it was insanity to have embarked on such a long journey. But turning back was not an option as there was nothing back in Santa for me to do to earn money. Besides there was no food and I could not continue depending on the charity of my landlord's wife. Bearing that in mind, I summoned all the energy I could and forged on.

Almost half way between Santa and Bamenda, I heard someone hooting on the other side of the road. I threw my eyes in the direction of the car that was hooting and saw that it was the father of my school mate, Kiel Emmanuel. He asked me where I was going to and I told him that I was going to Bamenda. "That is where I am going. Come on and hop in," he said. I did that excitedly and we continued the journey together. He was alone in the Toyota Corolla and was happy to have someone he could talk to. The first question he asked me was why I went ahead and left my friend behind.

"I always invited my friend to come over for us to study but he was never interested. If he is not interested in bookwork, no amount of pressure or effort on my part would help. Any success would be possible only if he shows the interest," I said.

"There you are right, my son," he said. "Kiel Emmanuel is my worst nightmare. I have done my possible best as a father to make him comfortable in life. I thought that by providing most of his needs, he would concentrate on his studies. But I have come to realize that it is all a waste of time. He seems to be praying that I die so that he can own all what I've worked for all my life. If at least he had learnt to produce and to manage things, that would not bother me. He knows how to do only one thing and it is to spend. Any son who can only spend and consume without being able to produce and manage is useless. If only he was like you, I would have been the happiest man alive."

His eyes watered as he spoke and there was also a lot of emotion in his voice. I thought of giving him soothing words but was afraid I might offend him instead. I had to say something all the same.

"I learnt in school that for us to appreciate the importance of an umbrella, the rain must beat us sometimes. You put the umbrella over my friend's head with good intentions. You did not want him to fail and justify it by saying that it was because he lacked this or that. But he has abused it. All is not entirely your fault. You were doing what you believed was best for him. Any good father would think only good of his children," I said.

"I wish my son could be as wise as you are. He is still in year two in secondary school whereas he is older than you. People who do not have children accuse heaven of being unkind to them. Those who have children regret the day they gave birth to them. Why is life that way? I always go back to the day your friend was born. There was a lot of joy. I felt like a man among men. But look at me now…I am a laughing stock looking at what my son has become. I don't know what to do with him anymore," he said.

I was becoming uncomfortable with the conversation and wanted to divert to something else. I was very nervous listening to someone pour out regrets. I searched through my mind and came up with a proposal I thought would give him some relief.

"With your permission sir, I would like to make a proposal. I want to suggest that when you get back home, call your son and have a chat with him. Ask him what he loves and wants to be in future. Bookwork is not good for everybody and you might be frustrated by the actions of your son. But maybe he does not have interest because he is in the wrong field," I said.

He promised he was going to take my advice. I was happy that someone like him made me feel I was important. He was there wishing I was his own born son while I was wishing he was my biological father. Promising to take my advice meant everything to me. That is why I had never forgotten that day.

Our conversation soon shifted to our destination which was Bamenda. He asked what I was going to do there and I said that I wanted to go and look for a job. I said it before thinking. What I said made him regret more having my friend as a son. But the deed was done and there was no way to reverse it. However, in his next question, he sought to know what kind of job I was going to look for. I told him that I was going to look for anything from a bartender, car washer, to a sales boy. He asked if I had someone in mind I wanted to go and work for. I told him that I knew nobody and was going to start a search the next day. He smiled and told me that finding a job was not an easy thing and those that were available could be gotten only through connections. That was one thing I did not like to hear. Obtaining a job through connections threw meritocracy to the dust bin and I wondered what all the certificates I was fighting to get would fetch for me under such an atmosphere. He pulled out his cell phone from his pocket and made a call. He called the person he was talking to Joel and asked him if he still needed a sales boy. I think the response he gave was affirmative as my friend's father promised to bring him an honest and hardworking boy in the next ten minutes.

When he hung up the phone, he told me that if a job was my reason for traveling Bamenda, I just got one and he was taking me to my jobsite. I asked him whom I was going to be working for and he replied that it was his friend Mr Joel. He then asked me if I had a place I was going to stay. Though I had my aunt in town, I was afraid that she was going to alert my father of my where about if I made her to know that I was in town. I just told him that I had nobody in town and had nowhere to stay. He told me that he was going to negotiate with his friend to take me to his house. I thanked him immensely and promised not to give him any cause to regret his gesture.

We were soon in town and drove straight to the Bamenda Main Market gate. He told me that his friend had a shop in the market and I was going to be selling there. He took me to the shop of his friend. His friend got up and welcomed us and then the two friends left me and went into an inner room. It was Mr Joel's office and there, they chatted and laughed loudly. They emerged 45 minutes later and Mr Joel looked at me and smiled.

"My friend here has said so many good things about you and I am tempted to trust you with my soul if what he has told me is anything to go by. Finding an honest sales boy has been a real nightmare for me. I have had so many who come looking so saintly at first but before long, they steal and make away with my money. I never thought that I could come and be spending time here when there are young men out there who could be helped. How can I help people who are unwilling to help themselves? Honesty is not too much to ask for, is it? I have even employed women as I got frustrated with the males but they proved to be worse," he said.

"I am not going to tell you that I will be honest but I am not that type of person who takes pleasure in hurting people or making enemies," I said.

"I don't know but I feel I'm not making a mistake this time. Just try to make yourself comfortable while I see off my friend. I will be back in a few minutes," Mr Joel said and left with his friend.

He returned a few minutes later and asked me to tell him more about myself. I did and told him that I wanted to work because I needed money to take care of my education. He asked me if I had a girlfriend. I felt embarrassed as I could not understand why he had to ask me that kind of a question or what having a girlfriend had to do with the job I badly needed. I told him that I had one goal at that moment and it was earning money to further my education. I later on understood why he had to ask me that kind of a question. He believed that the sales boys before me were motivated to steal his money by girlfriends. But I think that was not a good measuring rod to determine who would rob him or not. All the same, I told him the truth and he was pleased with what he heard. We then moved to the amount he had to pay me for the short time I was going to be there. I did not come up with any amount but told him to treat me like a son. He looked at me with amazement but did not say anything. No documents were signed. If at the end he decided to cook up lies about me stealing his money or goods, there'll be nothing I would do. I was certain of one thing though, and it was that heaven never forgot the vulnerable.

Mr Joel went ahead to write prices on little pieces of papers and pasted them against the items in the shop. That was intended to facilitate my mastery of the different prices. The shop was quite large with different items in it. There was a provision store section which was the largest, a section of kitchen utensils and a third one which was made up of building and construction materials. I did not see anybody else there apart from himself doing the selling and that intrigued me to ask him if he employed just one worker or more than that at a time. He said he employed just one at a time. I told him that it was a mistake doing that as it was dangerous for just one person to take care of sales, issue receipts and take down records. From my observation, he in fact made it easier for his employees to rob him or if at all they did rob him. According to him, employing more than one worker was going to be too costly as he had to spend much to pay them at the end of each month when he was not sure of making much profit. I told him that the shop was too large for one person to manage. Some customers could not be honest and with just one person doing almost everything, the chances of theft were too high. I made him to see that even an honest worker could suffer losses in a large shop as his without help. He saw a lot of sense in what I said and promised to bring in his daughter to assist me.

7

We left the shop on that first day of work at 17:00. Mr Joel led me out of the market and we went to his Toyota Hilux and drove home. It was just 30 minutes' drive from the Bamenda Main Market. The name of the neighbourhood we drove into was called Finch Street. A gate was opened as soon as the gate man heard the sound of the vehicle. I was marvelled by the kind of house my boss lived in. It was a small duplex which was well equipped. There was also a boys' quarter. I was taken first to one of the rooms in the boys' quarter where I put down the little personal items I took along. The room contained a bed, bathroom, toilet and a little kitchen at one end plus a TV set. After showing me to my room, Mr Joel took me to the main house where he introduced me to his wife and four children. They were Adam, Justine, Rose and Josephine. His wife's name was Genevieve. In front of the family, Mr Joel told Rose that she was going to assist me in the shop starting the next day. I left them soon after the announcement and went to my room where I had a shower and returned for supper. After eating, I went back to my room and watched a few news items on BBC and went to bed.

We went to work the next morning at 07:30. Rose was charged with recording all what was sold and keeping her eyes on customers especially male young customers. They were particularly very dangerous. Some of them organized and came in, in groups. While some created a distraction by demanding and seeking prices of items, their friends were busy stealing and hiding under the large jackets they wore. A good number of the male thieves and a few female thieves were caught thanks to the surveillance cameras put at very strategic points in the shop. An unfortunate one who got caught was called Samson. He had to suffer for the crimes of those before him. He came in on my fifth day of work with three other friends. He got a packet of chewing gums and went to the counter and was distracting Rose. As he was doing that, one of his friends was with me asking the prices of items whereas the prices were pasted on them. The remaining two were busy stealing and hiding under the huge jackets they wore. Unfortunately for them a customer who happened to have been a police officer was coming in and saw what they were doing and decided to raise an alarm. Two of them managed to escape while Samson and one other were arrested. Samson was lucky that his father was a wealthy man who had to go and bail him out of police custody and equally paid the sum of three million francs to my Boss. I don't know what happened to his friend. Mr Joel decided to employ a guard after that incident who was always at the entrance collecting bags and other things customers came with and returning them to the owners when they were about to leave. He made sure that what was taken out had a ticket showing that the item had been paid for. Theft reduced and profits increased.

Just a month after I started working at Mr Joel's shop, Rose did something which was beyond imagination. We sold a 50 kg bag of rice and she proposed that we issue no receipt, keep it off the records and share the money equally among ourselves. I could not believe that Rose would decide to team up with me, a stranger, to rob her own father. I asked her to register it and threatened to move to her desk to do it myself if she was unwilling. She was very angry with me and decided not to talk to me for the whole of that day.

Late in the evening of that same day, Rose was out on the yard taking some air. I had some words for her and thought it was the right time to tell her. I walked up to where she was but she was very aggressive.

"What are you doing here and what do you want?" she asked.

"You have asked two questions and I don't know which one to begin with," I said.

"Don't try to play smart with me. I proposed something which would have benefited both of us and you stupidly turned it down.

Anybody else in your shoe would have played the game without a second thought. People like you shall never progress," she told me.

I remained pensive for a while wondering the kind of world I found myself in. I thought that it was important that I settled the issue with her without raising dust. She was an adult and I considered myself as a big and civilized boy. There was therefore no reason why we could not speak like two grownups. So, I tried to let her see the gravity of indulging in such an act.

"Rose, I come from a very poor home. I know my position and people from poor homes like me stand no chance when they find themselves on the wrong side of the law. I want to stay out of trouble. You should be thankful to God that you have a father who has confidence in you to the extent that he has decided to entrust his business into your hands. I thought you would have been the one to reprimand me if I came up with that kind of indecent proposal but you are instead the one trying to lead me into it. That act you attempted is the same as going and organizing a gang to come and rob your father's house," I said.

Her eyes widened as I mentioned the word gang. She opened her mouth to say something but the words refused to come out. She remained silent and was looking elsewhere.

"Let's say I agreed and we stole the money as you requested, who would you have been robbing? Would you have been robbing yourself or your father? You would have thought that you are robbing him but indirectly, you are robbing yourself because everything thing he is doing is for your sake. He is there toiling for you and I think you should help him make a better future for you. I wish I had a father like yours. He is a good man and does not deserve any of what you proposed we do today. I believe that we are two adults and should behave like adults. We are going to end this conversation here. What happened will remain between the two of us and next time when you want to do something to someone, first of all put yourself in that persons shoe," I said.

Though I talked and hoped that everything was over, I was still afraid of what Rose could do. I did not quite know her well. But the fact that she had the courage to ask me to be her accomplice in robbing her father made me fear for the worse. I did not know what lies she could cook up to feed her father with so that he would hate me. The thought tortured me all night and I did not know what to do. My fears were finally laid to rest the next morning when she was the first to knock on my door to say 'good morning.' All went well for the remaining time I served there.

However, one week after that incident, precisely on August 27th which was a Friday, something unusual happened in the house of my boss. He left the house that day with his wife to attend the burial ceremony of a friend who passed away in a ghastly car accident. Rose and I went to the shop as usual. My boss passed by the market when we closed the shop and picked us up and together, we returned home. When we got to the gate, my boss hooted for a long time but the gate was not opened. It would appear the gateman left much earlier that day. My boss concluded after the hooting that perhaps there was nobody at home. He pleaded with me to go and open the gate and I did. He drove in and parked in the garage. I did not go straight to my room before coming to the main house as usual. I decided to accompany my boss into the main house to keep some of the foodstuff he bought on his way back from the burial of his friend. While we were outside the main door, we could tell that the television in the sitting room was on. That was an indication that there was someone in the house. My boss knocked hard on the door and a voice from within asked who it was. It was the voice of Justine. Once my boss spoke, we could hear hasty footsteps inside the house. The sound made by the TV went off all of a sudden. Everything was dead silent. When she opened the door, my boss asked her what she was doing that she could not come and open the gate. She responded that she did not hear the hooting sound of the vehicle. My boss then moved to the where the TV set was placed. He discovered that it had been disconnected from the socket. He looked at the deck and saw that it was not only on, but there was a disk still playing inside. Justine probably forgot to disconnect it as well. My boss took the TV cable and plugged it and it was then that we discovered what Justine was watching. It was a pornographic movie.

"No doubt you could not get the hooting of the car! You were so concentrated on this thing and I'm sure that if a thief broke into this house, you would not have heard," Mr Joel said.

He just smiled uneasily after saying that and said to me when everyone had left the sitting room that if his daughter could be watching that kind of a movie alone, it meant that she was already mature. But then, I wondered if she was there watching the film alone as my boss thought. The answer to my preoccupation did not delay in coming. My boss's stomach started rumbling as we stood close to the TV set in the sitting room. He might have consumed something which did not agree with his system at the burial ceremony of his late friend. He ran into the corridor which led to the closest toilet. When he tried to open it, the door wouldn't open. It was locked from inside. His wife did not come out of the car with us. She remained in the car to listen to the program 'Women and Development' on Radio Hot Cocoa. My boss did not take his own key to their room that day. He called Justine and asked her to hurry to the car and get the key to his room from her mother. She ran out but delayed in coming. When she finally came, my boss had already passed out the mess in his trousers. I could not stand there to see it. So I left for my room. His wife was alerted of the mess and she rushed into the house to clean it up. I waited in my room until I was convinced that the mess in the main house had been taken care of. Just when I left my room and was about to enter into the main house, I was pushed down by a young man of about 24 who was struggling to find his way out of the compound. He succeeded to run right out of the gate but was caught by neighbours who heard the alarm raised by my Boss's wife. The neighbours gave the young man some serious trashing before pulling him back into the yard of my boss. The neighbours thought that the young man was a thief and it was when they threatened to kill him that Justine came out and confessed that she knew the young man. It then dawn on my boss that Justine might not have been watching the porn film alone and that the young man must have been behind the locked toilet door. He then asked the neighbours that were pounding on the young man to leave him alone which was done. He asked that the young man be taken to his car so that he could take him to the hospital for his wounds to be taken care of. When that was done, my boss drove out again.

Since I got into town, I had just three places I went to…the shop, church and back home. I did not know why people adopted some attitudes towards certain behaviours. I did not understand why people caught someone whom they considered a thief and preferred to kill him than calling the police to hand the criminal over to them. Were there no other crimes that were worse than stealing to warrant the death penalty? I decided to ask Rose why considering the case of the young man who was just taken to the hospital.

"People in this town have lost faith in the police. The police are too corrupt. You can catch a thief now and hand to them and tomorrow you will see that same thief out in the street. Once the criminals are in the hands of the police, they are asked to share their stolen booty into two parts in exchange for their freedom. That is why people prefer to kill the thieves once they are caught and not hand them to the police," she said.

"That is terrible to hear. How can someone have the courage to hit another to the extent of killing him without any remorse? In Santa, that is very unheard of. What about the innocent? They must be paying a heavy price. Just look at that boy who has been taken to the hospital. He was just mistaken for a thief and the crowd was prepared to kill him. Is this how life in town is?" I asked.

"You have not seen anything yet. What just happened out here is even minute. You can feel sorry for the thieves because they have not visited you yet. The day they would come and rape your daughter or wife or tear open the stomach of your pregnant wife, you would learn not to feel sorry for them," Rose said.

Goose pimples covered my whole body when she said that. I felt like I was living a nightmare after what I heard fall from Rose's lips. *'Well, that is town life and I still have enough time to get used to it'* I told myself and left. I did not want to be in the main house when my boss returned. I knew there were going to be tensions. Society frowned at a child who took a partner and made love in the house of his or her parents. My boss was definitely going to be fuming with anger when he returned because what Justine did was a blow to his pride. I didn't want to be there. It was his family problem and he had to sort it out himself.

My boss did return at 20:30. There was a lot of yelling in the house. He blamed more his wife for not doing her job properly as a mother. I wondered why he blamed her for the mistakes of Justine. Perhaps he just needed someone to apportion blame on. I did not see how his wife would have been policing a girl like Justine who was already 17 and above. One thing was certain though and it was that Justine needed to be schooled on sexuality and the dangers that stared her in the face on that path. It was not supposed to be the job of her mother alone but that of both parents.

Nevertheless, just a week to the reopening of the new academic year which was going to be my first year in the high school, my boss asked that I give him the list of my textbooks as well as measurements for my uniform. I did and he took care of those ones. I asked him to come so that we take stock as well as do an audit of what had come in as profit. He did and all the records were ok. He called his friend who brought me to him to say how grateful he was. I too was happy because I made my boss happy. Rose on her part thanked me immensely for making her realize how lucky she was. She appreciated her father more and the efforts he was putting in for her sake and the sake of her brother and sisters. I appreciated her for reflecting over what I said on the evening of the day she wanted us to rob her father. It was thanks to that reflection that she had a change of heart and could better appreciate having a hard working and caring father. However, on the eve of the day I had to travel back to Santa which was a Saturday, my boss's wife took me to the market and bought me some new clothes and shoes. I had almost everything I needed to begin the new academic year in style. I considered all that as the fruit of loyalty and honesty.

The next day which was Sunday, my boss gave me the sum of 60.000 francs and told me that I had a bright future ahead of me if I maintained the good behaviour. He equally gave me his old mobile phone he was no longer using and some pairs of shoe. With the money, I planned to take care of my school fees and feeding for some time. He asked me to come to Bamenda any time I had the chance to give a helping hand in the shop. I promised I would and he accompanied me to the taxi park. We got there at 08:12 and there was a taxi that needed just one passenger to be full. I occupied the only seat remaining and the vehicle hit the road at 08:20.

8

The road was tarred and any right thinking person who saw the car which was still in a good state would have imagined that the journey was going to be a comfortable one. Far from it. The vehicle was a Toyota Corolla which was designed to carry a maximum of four persons. But we were eight of us in it and comfort became a very rare luxury. Anybody who dared to complain received heart breaking comments shockingly not from the drivers but from fellow passengers in the car. "If you want to be comfortable, buy a car," they would often say. The amazing thing about it was that we went through some checkpoints manned by policemen and others manned by road safety teams sent to the field by the ministry of transport. They were not there to see to the safety of passengers and road users but to squeeze a few francs from drivers. Once the drivers paid the amount those who manned the checkpoints asked for, they were free to carry passengers even in the booth of the cars and no one would bother them. The passengers in the car were all quiet probably praying that the 45 km journey come to an end as soon as possible.

30 minutes after leaving Bamenda, we finally got to Santa. I could not walk properly as part of my body was almost paralyzed due to the fact that I was squeezed in the vehicle. The driver offered a joking apology.

"If we do not carry more than the required number of passengers, we would not realize anything at the end of the day. It is our country and we have to live with the situation," he said.

"So, for the sake of realizing something at the end of the day, you are prepared to sacrifice human life for money?" I asked.

The driver did not respond but looked at me with a stern expression on his face. I could read in that expression that he was not happy with my comments. He moved to the booth of the vehicle to offload the luggage of the passengers. The little box I had was taken out of the booth but the little traveller's bag I put all the shoes my boss gave me was nowhere to be found. I actually waited and saw it tied in the booth of the vehicle before I boarded it. I told the driver that one of my luggages was missing and the only thing he said was that maybe it had fallen off along the way. I asked him what he was going to do to get it back and he said that if he found it on his way back to Bamenda, he would bring it on his next trip. I waited at the motor park for him to load and take off. He finally left two hours after we got to Santa. He didn't show up even at 17:00 when I left. My shoes were gone and the only pair that I had left was the one I had on. I still hoped to return some other day and the driver would hand the bag to me.

I got back to my room with its perforated walls at 17:20. I got there faster because I had money to pay for a commercial motor bike. I went and got more papers and leaves to block more holes that appeared on the wall. I had to also replace some of the old ones that had been there for some time. After doing all that, I took the six loaves of bread and a five litre tin of palm oil I bought for my landlord and took to his house. Lucky enough for me, he was in. I intended meeting him in person to find out if Mr Finley had called in my absence and what messages he left for me if there were any. He was very happy with what I brought and told me that Mr Finley had been in touch. I asked him what Mr Finley said but his response was that their discussion had nothing to do with me. He also added that Mr Finley promised to call within that week I returned as he was informed of the eminent reopen of the next academic year that week. I found that very hard to believe and sensed that he was not telling me the truth. I did not ask him any further questions and left for my room. I prepared my uniform and the only pair of shoe I had left. At 19:15, I heard a knock on the wooden door of my room. It was the wife of my landlord and she had a dish of rice and stew in her hand for me. She thanked me for the things I brought for her and told me that God was going to bless me abundantly. She held my two hands and sprayed spittle in my palms. That was considered a blessing and a prayer to God to fructify the works of my hands. By doing that, she was playing the role of the mother I no longer had. She proved to me by her actions that one's mother was not necessarily the one who must have given birth to him or her. I thanked her for supporting me materially and morally. I went to bed at 21:00 with a lot of optimism for the next day.

The next morning which was Monday 7th September, I woke up early and got ready for school. I got there at 07:30 and was part of the assembly on the school yard. The principal of the school welcomed those of us who were new to the second cycle but promised to personally come and talk to us in our classes later in the day. We dispersed into our various classes at 07:50 and waited for the different teachers to come present their scheme of work as well as their time tables. There were no lessons for us on that first day but we had some orientation on what awaited us ahead in high school. The principal of the school during the orientation urged us to be very hardworking as the school was expecting a lot from us in terms of good results. Those of us who were present promised to uphold the good reputation of the school. I was making my promise from the heart but could not tell if my mates were sincere. The authorities were satisfied with the pledge that not withstanding

I left school at 13:30 but did not go straight home. I went to see my younger ones. I bought some small items I knew they loved and took along. When I got closer to our family home, I was careful to make sure that my father was not at home. I heard my younger ones playing on the yard and walked in with confidence. I gave them what I bought for them and supervised them eat up everything. I made sure no trace of what I offered them could be seen. If my father were to come home and discover that they had eaten something strange, he was going to kill them with beatings. My kid brother, Joshua, told me that our father had warned them never to associate with me because I was a very bad child and a thief. He also told me that our father had poisoned the minds of the neighbours against me and that they had to run and alert the neighbours each time I came to the house in his absence. The neighbours in turn would raise an alarm for me to be caught and beaten. Those were the firm instructions of my father to my younger ones. I knew that he was a hard and cruel man but I would never have imagined that he would one day try to turn my own blood brothers and sisters against me. I could not understand how a man would decide to erect a wall of separation between his own children. After listening to what my kid brother told me, I concluded that my father was not only cruel but he was a heartless monster. I hugged them and wished I could stay longer with them but I had to go away with a very heavy heart. I was completely devastated after learning the kind of 'thing' I had become in the eyes of my father. The word 'Thief' kept echoing in my head as I headed back to that place I called home.

I got in front of my landlord's house at 15:40. I had the intention of going straight to my room to have a rest. My landlord's wife stopped me outside and pleaded with me to assist her son in his studies. She complained that her husband always asked her to leave his son alone each time she tried to force him to devote some time to his studies. She equally complained of him using the cases of some young boys who had gone to the university and could not find jobs upon completion of their studies and were back in the village tilling the soil to back up his protectionist attitude. I felt like asking her why she was telling me what her husband was doing. But on second thought decided against it. Her words felt like those of a drowning woman who was prepared to cling to anything even to a serpent to stay afloat.

"He has turned all my children to useless things. He believes that in order to please a child, one should not force him to do what he does not want to do even if it is for his own good. He feels that everything a child wants should be granted. He believes that doing everything for a child is the only way to make a child happy. My children cannot do anything on their own because they have developed the habit of getting things done for them by others. When they shall be brandished as useless in future, I shall be the one to carry all the blame. My husband would forget that he was the architect of their failure in life. Please my son, help me. He will be writing the Ordinary level this year and he is already preparing to fail," she said with tears streaming down her eyes.

For a moment or two, my wounded spirit stopped bleeding and the pain of learning my father considered me a thief suddenly vanished. I promised I was going to assist her son. She wiped the tears off her cheeks and asked me not to go away as she moved into the house. She returned a few minutes later with a bowl of white yam in one hand and cabbage sauce in the other. She handed both to me and asked me to get quickly to my room and have a rest. I wondered why she mentioned the word 'quickly' but I just obeyed and went to my room as she instructed.

I got to my room and ate part of what was given to me by my landlady and tried to open some textbooks I had. I could not concentrate as the events of that day revisited me and battered my spirit with the strength of a wild wind. I abandoned the books and went to bed very early. I had imagined that my thoughts were going to allow sleep carry me off as I longed to forget the events of that first day in the high school. But that was not the case. I pondered over what my younger ones said and cried for a while. It was in the middle of the sobbing that I fell asleep. But hardly had I gone deep in sleep when I began dreaming. In it, I went to the night club after school and was returning very late in the night with a group of friends. We were making a lot of noise and my father could make out my voice. "Martin," he called out. I did not answer and asked my friends to try to cover me. My father then decided to call my second name instead of the first he always called me with. "Smith," he called out again. I still did not respond and decided to hide in a nearby bush. I asked my friends to move away without disclosing my hideout to him. They did but my father found me and held me by the arm. He started kicking and punching me. I was crying and looking for ways to break loose from his grip. I soon had my chance when he thought he found a cane and was trying to pick it up to use on me. I freed myself from his grip and started running away in the dark night towards a very big river. He began chasing me with no intention of letting me go without using the cane he just picked up on me. I soon got to the river bank and jumped with the intention of drowning and freeing myself from his cruelty once and for all. But someone caught me in the air and we both landed back on the bank of the river. I tried to see the face of the one who saved me but I couldn't. The person soon spoke and I could recognize the voice as that of my late mother.

"Why do you want to kill yourself? Have you thought of your siblings before doing that?" she asked sobbing. I started crying and asked her why she had to go and allow me in the hands of my cruel father. The only thing she said was that she was part of nature and had answered the call of nature when she was called. Just then, I heard a whip land across my back. I cried out in pain and turned round to see who had beaten me. It was my father and he stood with his back to the big river below. Without a second thought, I pushed him and he was in the air on his way down the big river. I regretted my action immediately after I initiated it and was shouting as I watched him falling into the river. That shout carried me out of my sleep and equally attracted my landlord and wife who came knocking on my door at 02:35 to find out what was wrong with me. I rose, opened the door and told them that it was a nightmare. My landlord turned and went back but his wife got into my room and prayed with me. I thanked her for being such a nice and caring mother. She wished me goodnight and left for her house. I had a sound sleep for the remaining hours before dawn.

I got up at 06:20 and got ready for school. Classes started fully on that day and it was going to be the routine for the next four months. That was the length of time the first of the three terms in the school year lasted. I got up each morning, got ready for school, went to school, returned in the afternoon, had a bath, went to bed and the routine lasted through the four months. I went to church on Sundays as well. Mr Finley called me as often as he could just as he promised before leaving Cameroon. I never took on the issue of money with him because I knew that he was well aware of my situation. Our conversations were mostly centred on my book work and how I was doing. My answers were always positive and perhaps that was why he never asked me about my financial situation. I still had part of the money I earned while working for Mr Joel and so had no problem of feeding. My landlord's wife always supported me as far as feeding was concerned. Generally speaking the first term went hitch free for me.

Nonetheless, towards mid-December, I was worried about how the end of the year was going to look like. I was thinking particularly about Christmas and the feast of St. Sylvester. I wondered how my younger ones were going to spend it and if it was safe for me to take something to them. Given that they were not starving and the money was not much to buy something for them, I decided to stay put and prayed that the feast days come and go fast. I spent the eve of Christmas night in church and took part in the midnight mass. It ended at about 02:30 and I went back home. I did not go to church for the 08:00 mass as I was already in the midnight mass. I spent the day sleeping and left my room only at 15:00. I stopped first in the house of my landlord to wish them a very merry Christmas. Of course, my landlady invited me in and gave me a plate of rice and chicken stew. After eating, I went for a long walk. But feeling alone and seeing just trees and sceneries which I was already too familiar with, it became boring and I decided to head back to my room. I slept for the rest of the day and the greater part of the night.

I got up the day after Christmas and was wondering what I was going to do with the whole week that still laid ahead of me before the feast of St. Sylvester. There were no jobs to be done in Santa and I could not spend my whole time brooding on books. I had to be involved in something positive or I was going to land into some trouble. I searched through my brains for what I could possibly do. I even thought of accompanying the wife of my landlord to the farms to help her till the fields. That was not a bad idea but I needed a job from which I could generate some income. I then thought of what Mr Joel told me about coming in to give a helping hand when I had the chance. I decided to travel to Bamenda to go and see if I could make something after assisting for that one week.

I got up on the morning of December 26th and informed my land lady of where I was going and my intention for doing it. She appreciated me very much but regretted the fact that her children could not take initiatives like me. To console her, I asked her never to ever relent in praying to the Almighty for them. She wished me a safe journey and stood in front of her house watching me as the distance between us widened with every step I took. I could feel her gaze trailing me as I moved away. I could not help feeling for her because she kept living in a state of uncertainty wondering what her kids were going to become in future. I was some sort of consolation as she found happiness in assisting me with food and giving me advice as if I were her own born son.

9

I got to Bamenda 35 minutes after leaving Santa. I alighted at the Commercial Avenue and walked to the shop of Mr Joel inside the Bamenda Main Market. He was in his office in the shop and walked out as soon as I greeted Rose and he heard my voice.

"Welcome my son. Have you come to assist me for this week?" he asked.

"Yes," I said.

"It is a good thing you did. I thought that customers would reduce after the preparations for the feast of nativity but I was wrong. People had their projects especially in building and construction. People still stream in here to get building materials and we badly need a hand to help in transporting them from this place to the main road outside this market. Welcome again. You can begin work right away," he said.

I got down to work right away. I was involved more in the transportation of items bought by customers to waiting vehicles or hired taxis outside the market gate, than selling. The work was more exhausting as I had to do a lot of transportation many times in one day. We returned home each day at 17:00 and I occupied the same room in the boys' quarters I left some months earlier. I was well fed and pleased to give a helping hand at a time it was most needed. Mr Joel's wife was nice as usual and offered me some clothes and a pair of shoes at the end of that nativity week.

On the eve of the feast of St. Sylvester, my boss handed 30.000 francs to me as compensation for the one week I spent with him. That was a lot of money to have earned in just one week. There were people who did much harder work but needed 60 days to make that amount. I was very lucky to have met a man like Mr Joel who was human in the way he did things. I travelled back to Santa and was part of the late night mass to render thanks to the Almighty for watching over me throughout the year and to witness the transition to a new year. Of course I was always optimistic that the next year would be better than the previous one though for me, the battle against hunger remained a permanent one. The New Year was not going to change that. The promise of Mr Finley for sponsorship and financial support not coming to fruition made the future more uncertain. But as people always say, "where there is life there is hope", I still had to keep the faith despite the uncertainties ahead. I spent the New Year day just as the day of nativity. I slept all day and the only persons I went out to wish happy New Year to were my landlord and his family. With some money in my pocket, the second term was definitely going to be a less tough one. I looked forward to going back to school as the dust of the feast days started to slowly but steadily settle.

Three days after the feast of St. Sylvester marked the beginning of the second term in the school academic calendar. I received a knock on my door when I was about to leave for school on that first day of the start of second term. It was my landlord and he handed me his cell phone and said that Mr Finley was on the line. I wondered why he did not send his son as usual. However, as soon as I placed the receiver on my ear and said hello, Mr Finley greeted me very warmly and then asked if my landlord had giving me the school fees and the pocket allowance he always sent for me every other month. I could not believe my ears as the words 'fees and pocket allowance' fell from my lips unconsciously. Mr Finley could read the surprise in my unconscious words and asked the question again. I told him that I had never received a dime from my landlord as money coming from him. He was very shocked himself that he ran out of words. He promised to call me later and hung up. My landlord who had been watching me certainly sensed that there was something wrong. I think he saw the surprise on my face as I turned and looked at him when Mr Finley mentioned my fees and pocket allowance. He started walking towards me when he saw that my conversation had ended.

"What did you people talk about?" he asked.

I did not answer immediately but stood there in front of him staring straight into his eyes without blinking. So many things were running through my head. I could not qualify the kind of person I was seeing in front of me right there. I could not find words to describe his actions. He got uncomfortable with my looks that he decided to ask why I was staring at him.

"Should I begin with the second question you've just asked or I should go back to the first?" I asked. He did not respond. I did not want to disrespect him or to be rude by not answering his question. I told him what Mr Finley asked me.

"What did you tell him in response to his question," he asked with eyes wide open.

"I told him the truth. Is there something else you expected me to tell him other than the truth?" I asked.

"I thought you were big like that there was something in that your head. I expected you to use it to know that telling him the truth as you call it, would jeopardize my relationship with him. How would I ever have the courage to face him? If he ever had plans for any of my sons, I think they have all evaporated now. It is your entire fault," he said.

"You have children, don't you? Don't you punish them when they tell lies?" I asked.

"I punish them for telling lies for lies' sake. When they tell lies, I try to find out why they had to lie. If it was to safe a situation, I do not punish them. There is a lot at stake in this situation and you have messed up everything. You have spoiled my relationship with Mr Finley and any prospects he had for me and my children is now gone," he said.

"You keep talking only about yourself. What about me? Is it because I am not your born son that you feel I do not have any interests?" I asked.

He did not give any response to my last question. He left me and went back to his house fuming with anger. Since I was already in my school uniform and was about to leave before Mr Finley called, I locked my room and started off to school. The actions of my landlord troubled me a lot. I could not believe that he could be so mean. I remembered what his wife once said to him in my presence about her children receiving punishment for the crimes of their father. I began to feel that what she said was true given that none of his children was doing anything worth the name. His first son Josephs who was about 37 years old was a night watchman in town and categorically refused to get married. His second son Augustine just left the house some six years earlier after disagreeing with his father over the sharing of property. His third child who was a female got pregnant while she was in her third year in secondary school. She left school as a result to take care of the baby but picked up another pregnancy before the child was eight months old. She had long left the house and I leant from Achilles Otto that she moved to Douala where she was involved in some petty trading to support herself and her children. Achilles Otto was born after her and he was in his fifth year in secondary school. Some of his mates were already in the university. He was asked to repeat a good number of classes because he did not have the required scores to earn promotion to the next classes. His mother kept complaining of her husband spoiling him just as his elders. If he could punish me by not giving me the money which was sent through him, then heaven had every reason to frown with him but his children were the ones paying the price for his transgressions. I let the thoughts to rest for a while once I got to school as I did not want them to disturb me during lessons.

That notwithstanding, Mr Finley called again later in the evening that same day at 20:00. My landlord did not send his son but came himself. When he knocked my door and I opened, he walked into my room and handed the phone to me. I thought that he was going to go out so that I could discuss with Mr Finley freely but he remained rooted in my room. I asked him to excuse me but he refused to go out. I was the one who went out and shut the door behind me. I went some distance away before letting Mr Finley know that I was on the line.

"I had a very bad day today son," he began. "When I got to that village and that man offered me his house for free, I thought that he was a good man. I had been sending your pocket allowance every month and had been asking myself why you never offered a word of thank you each time I called you. I thought you had turned into an ingrate and by asking if you've been seeing all the money I sent, I wanted to verify my thoughts. Now, I know the truth and it has really spoilt my day.

"One act of kindness should not make you conclude that someone is a good or nice person. Human beings are like the chameleon that is always changing its colour. One act of kindness might be a trick to better attract the prey to the trap," I said.

"I think there you are right son. I have been so blinded by the one act of kindness from Mr Steven and he has dealt with me and you," he said.

I then told him of what happened immediately soon after he left Cameroon. I told him of the room in the abandoned house I occupied then, with its perforated walls. He was shocked and asked me to go and look for another room elsewhere and he would send me some money to pay for it. I told him that it was not necessary as I was just a year and a few months away from my GCE Advanced Level certificate. His concern was my comfort and I understood that. He then asked if I had something like a pen and paper to take down his phone number and I said yes. I did not have a pen and paper out there but I had my mobile phone in my left pocket. I took it out and typed the number as he dictated it. He equally gave me the phone number of one of his friends, Keith Richardson who worked at the American Embassy in Yaoundé. He promised to send me some money through him so that I could get a mobile phone. It was then that I told him of the one which was offered to me by Mr Joel. He asked me to give him the number which I did. He promised to call me from then on, on my mobile and then hung up.

I went back to my room and saw my landlord sitting on my bed. He had his eyes fixed on me as I walked in.

"Why have you done this to me? I talked to Mr Finley about my second son and he promised to help me take him over to America. Why have you frustrated me and my son," he asked.

"I have not frustrated anybody. You have frustrated yourself and your son. How did you expect me to tell Mr Finley that you've been giving me money when you've never done so? Have you ever given me money that it came from Mr Finley? Have you ever made me to believe that he had ever sent money to you to give me before withholding it back?" I asked.

"My wife has been giving you food. Where do you think the money was coming from to buy the food? You used to come and use my security light to read for your exams. Do you know how much a kilowatt of electricity cost? Where do you think the money was coming from for me to pay for that electricity which you were using? Besides, you had lived in that house which I removed you from for the length of time Mr Finley was here. If I decide to calculate the rent for all that length of time, would you be able to pay?" he asked.

"If the rent was your problem, you should have at least told me that Mr Finley was sending money for me but you were going to take it as the rent for the length of time I lived in that house. You took the money and decided on what to be done with it alone leaving me out. You forgot to remember that I was the reason why he sent the money to you. Have you ever asked yourself why he did not send the money directly to me and had to send it to you instead? Well, it is because I am too young to be given a national identity card and the money would not be given to me without it. He sent the money to you because he knew that that you had children and would never had imagined for a second that you could behave funny. He had confidence in you and you just betrayed it. If he had promised to

74

help you with your second son, you would have used it as a motivation to obtain what you wanted by being honest. You are a father and if I was in your place, I wouldn't have done something like that. Do you want to make me believe that a child you call your own must come only from your womb? Mr Finley is a white man. But I am as black as you are. Yet, he calls me his son and treats me as his own born son. To you, he is insane, right? You are an old man and should have known better that nothing done under the sun can be hidden for ever. So, instead of sitting there and blaming me, you should go back to your house and search through your mind and figure out how you are going to right your wrongs," I said.

He bent his head and stared at the floor for some time before lifting up his head again. I did not take my eyes off him and he did not dare to look at my face. He stared elsewhere before speaking.

"I admit that it was wrong for me to have taken a decision on something which concerned you, alone. I expected that you were going to use your head and save me this embarrassment. That is the hope of my son gone and one source of my income lost. So, from now hence, you are going to be paying rent for this room. 2000 francs will be the amount you would pay," he said and left.

I had no problem with paying the 2000 francs he said I would pay but it was his selfish attitude which made my stomach rumble. But that did not bother me much as I already knew the truth as well as knew that money was no longer going to come through him. With that soothing thought in mind, I went to bed.

I went about my studies normally and saw my landlord less often after that incident. I sometimes felt that I indeed helped in frustrating the dreams of my landlord's second son. I did not feel guilty but remained constantly filled with the satisfaction that a mask had fallen. I felt really happy and smiled each time I thought about the incident. I just couldn't explain it. However, everything went well until towards the end of that second term when Jeremy decided to humiliate me in class.

Jeremy was a classmate who was not very intelligent and did not take book work seriously. He was huge and bulky and physically strong too. He was aware of his physical strength and became a bully in school. He always sat at the back of the class and often made senseless comments when some teachers he did not like were in class. When he was ordered to get out of the class each time he disturbed, he would refuse saying that he did not pay his school fees to come and be staying outside. The principal was always solicited to come and restore order in the classroom. The only good thing about him was that he knew his limits and had never tried to lay his hands on any teacher. He knew that dismissal was the penalty for such an act and resorted to verbal attacks and outright stubbornness. Each time he wrote a test and failed, the teachers came to class and read out his script and the class often jeered at him. He decided to turn his anger and frustration towards those of us who were intelligent. He saw us as those responsible for the humiliations some teachers subjected him to as we scored high marks. He did not miss any chance to make any of us, the bright students uncomfortable. March 16th was the day I fell in Jeremy's trap. We were writing our second term exam and the subject that day was chemistry. The only pen I had on me that day suddenly stopped flowing. I was not allowed to go out in the middle of an exam. So, I indicated to the invigilator and got up to plead with the class if anybody had a spare. It was Jeremy who spoke from the back of the class.

"Has poverty hung on the neck of your father that he can't afford to buy even a common pen for you?" he asked.

His question provoked a lot of laughter in the class. I was not amused at all. I felt really humiliated that day. I knew that he was like that and that was supposed to prepare me psychologically for his insults but it did not. I was totally destabilized and was unable to write much even when I was given the pen I asked for. I managed only an average mark in that subject because of Jeremy's action. It had an effect on the term classification. I left the second position which I occupied in the first term to the fourth. I hated Jeremy for it but was bent on bouncing back during the third term.

During the third term exam, Jennifer slipped from the first to the 5th position after receiving a verbal insult from Jeremy. According to her story, Jeremy wanted to go out with her and she asked him to have the Advanced level certificate first. Instead of being an encouragement, it infuriated him and he decided to call her a professional sex worker during exams. Jennifer took it really hard and it dealt a blow on her to the extent that she missed two subjects. Society frowned at sex workers and those who were stigmatized with that name were considered outcasts. Some students and classmates took up the rhetoric and that was what further compounded the situation. Jennifer carried the matter to the authorities and Jeremy was suspended from school for three days. Antoinette slipped to the 4th position because she fell sick and did not write all the examination subjects. I must say that the down fall of the two girls benefited me as I moved back to the second position though I was targeting the first spot.

I went to the second and last year in high school the next year with over three quarters of my other classmates. Out of 96 of us who were in the previous class, 85 of us moved to the next class. 'The goats were separated from the sheep' as the teachers always said.

Jeremy was among those who were asked to repeat. It was a relief to those who suffered humiliation in his hands. He was not ready for it and planned to go and seek for admission in another school. We did not have bullies in our new class. Those who were in that last class knew where they were heading to and the excitement of getting into a university was a motivating factor to work hard. I paid the rents for the room I occupied as my landlord wished. I did not go to his house and his son was the only connection between us. He always sent Otto to come and collect his money from me. I assisted him in his studies in fulfilment of the promise I made to my landlady. He did not accept my assistance easily. He was older than I was and found it humiliating to be receiving lessons from me. I had to ask his mother to plead with him to accept my assistance. Mr Finley cut communication with my landlord and he was very unhappy about it. I went to the house of the tenant who occupied the house I left and made an agreement with him to assist in the paying of electricity bills. It was Mr Finley who gave me the go ahead. He accepted the deal and I went there every evening and carried out my studies both for classroom exams and the official GCE advanced level exams. The difficulties of reading under moonlight and security bulbs when I was preparing for my GCE Ordinary level exams became a mere souvenir when I was writing the GCG Advanced level. The house of my landlord was very close to my room but I could not go to him with the deal of assisting with the payment of electricity bills. If I did, I would have been paying his electricity bills plus mine. He was a man who would take advantage of every situation to make profit. I wondered why he made his life that way.

Moreover, I did not pack out of my room soon after writing my last GCE Advanced Level paper. I stayed put for a while since I had no place I could move to. I discussed with Mr Finley about my desire to go to the university and he asked me to travel to Yaoundé and get information on registration, fees, lodging and feeding. I had to get the information and call his friend, Keith, who worked at the

American Embassy. You might be wondering why I had to leave Bamenda City which was closer to Santa and travel to Yaoundé which was some 315 kilometres away, for university studies. Well, the thing was that there was no state run university in Bamenda. That does not mean that there was no university in Bamenda. There was a mission university and it was beyond the reach of poor people just like most mission secondary schools. So, most students who graduated from high school had to cover the 315 kilometres for further studies. That was costly but it was better than getting into the mission university. So, I left Santa on August 20th at 20:00 to go to Bamenda town where I had to board a bus for Yaoundé. I got to Santa Motor Park at 20:20 and found a taxi which was heading to Bamenda empty. I got in and was the only passenger. I was to remain the only passenger till we got to Bamenda up station hill. When we got there, I felt like easing myself and pleaded with the driver to stop. He did not hesitate but did not remain on the steering wheel after I stepped out. He came out to ease himself as well after shutting his door. We went a few meters from the vehicle before doing so. When we were through, we returned to the car and got back in without looking in the back seat. It did not occur to any of us to look behind because we knew that only the two of us were there. It was when the car was on the move that we realized that we had company. Our guest was a young girl of about 23 and she was as naked as the day she was born. The driver halted abruptly and we both dashed out of the car and tried to run away. But after a second thought we both summoned some courage and returned to the car. The driver decided to pick up a big stick just in case the lady tried to act funny. He opened the back door of the car where the lady sat but ran back a few steps soon after, while at the same time prepared to use his stick. The lady in the car asked us not to be afraid and assured us that she was harmless. We got closer but carefully and she narrated her ordeal to us.

"I am from that hotel there," she said pointing at Green Hill Hotel which was some 500 meters away. "I was in a room there with a man since 15:00. We had some drinks and ate some chicken after which he asked me to accompany him to the room. We went to the room just some 45 minutes ago. We had fun and just lay in bed resting. I tuned my back as soon as we were through and was facing the opposite side as I began to feel useless and wondering when this kind of life I'm living would end. I did not know what was going on behind me. I don't know if it was fate or design but something asked me to turn and look at the man I was in the room with. I turned only to realize that the man's head had transformed into that of a python and the rest of his body was transforming too. I am lucky that he did not lock the door of that hotel room. I jumped down from the bed and ran out shouting at the top of my voice. People in the other rooms came out and the workers in the hotel ran in the direction of the room I ran out from. As I'm talking to you, I don't know what is happening there right now. So please, if you can drive me to Kennedy Street where I live, I would forever be indebted to you."

We could not be insensitive to her predicament. The driver got back on the steering wheel and we all drove to Kennedy Street which was 3 km from Vatican Travel Agency where I intended to alight. The driver had initially planned to take me to that travel agency and after doing that, stop work for the day. Going to Kennedy Street increased not only the distance but the time as well. There was not much traffic congestion in town that evening and we took no time in getting to Kennedy Street. Once we arrived there, she thanked the driver immensely and alighted. She disappeared into the neighbourhood and we went on our way.

I knew the taxi driver like most of his colleagues was going to comment on what he saw and heard. He started just when the girl alighted.

"These young girls who sell themselves for money are those who want to get things the easy way and making love to pythons is the ultimate price to pay. She is lucky that her python man did not lock the door. If not, she would have ended up in his stomach. When are they going to learn that these things that move around in expensive suits are not human beings? Strange stories like the one she narrated are told on radio and television every day. Yet it has not rung a bell in the heads of these young girls. It seems their brains have been opened and the word 'No' erased. They find it really hard to say 'No' to any man that approaches them especially if he is wearing a suit and driving in a car. It is really a pity," he lamented.

"It is unfortunate young girls fall prey to these vultures called rich men. But how are they supposed to know what man is a real and which is a python just by looking at them?" I asked.

"Must these young girls go out with men? Must they lean on men to survive? Yet they would be clamouring for equal rights with men. Why can't they begin by fighting for self-reliance before clamouring for equal rights with men?" he asked.

"The world is a male dominated one and I don't think that it is going to change any time soon. You cannot really blame them for looking for men to take care of them. Besides, there is poverty everywhere and occupying the few job openings is not easy. One must have a connection somewhere who knows another connection for one to obtain a job. With no prospects on the horizon, can you really blame them for leaning on men?" I asked.

"We still have vast uncultivated lands which need man power. How many of these young girls would accept to go and till the soil? They see farming as a mean job. They see themselves as modern girls and would want only white collar jobs and as a result fall in the claws of these unscrupulous employers who would exploit them sexually and physically. It will not be surprising to me if we discover later that the young lady we dropped off a while ago went out with her python man in the hope that he might help her secure a job. What people fail to know is that everything else can fail someone but not the soil. If the worse comes to the worse, you would at least recover what you invested in it. If this taxi business fails, I will go back to my village and till the soil," he said.

I agreed with him. However, I was not very used to town life and was not versed with human beings transforming into animals. It was terrifying to me. I had lived in Santa for most of my life and was versed with stories of people practicing witch craft. I had never seen anyone practicing it but everything I knew about it was just mere stories. For instance, if someone was building his house and it collapsed before it was completed, it was associated with witchcraft. The owner either accused a neighbour or someone he had some problems with for breaking down his house or he went to a witch doctor to find out who made his house to crumble. Bad site or poor erection of the walls or poor construction of the foundation was never to blame in such situations. Only somebody must have been responsible who must have been an enemy. In the same vein, if an owl landed on someone's house at night, someone was responsible. Witchcraft was associated with any happening that could not be explained scientifically. I had never really believed in it partly because of my formal education and the religious doctrines I received in church. Ardent traditionalists called those of us who criticized the belief in witchcraft as agents of the imperialists who had been brainwashed. What was annoying about the witchcraft belief was that people almost never asked 'what', but 'whom'. The victim was always out to apportion blame and not look for possible causes. Once someone was pronounced guilty of practicing witchcraft, he or she had to face punishment ranging from the payment of financial damages to his or her victim to banishment from the village. Of course the innocent were those who paid the highest price. But the issue of people transforming into animals was a new phenomenon I was getting acquainted with.

The driver dropped me off at the gate of Vatican Travel Agency at 21:00 and I went in and booked for my trip. The bus was scheduled to take off at 22:00. It was already too late to go visiting or calling Mr Joel. So, I just sat in the waiting room reserved for passengers watching TV.

At exactly 22:05, the bus hit the road with 70 passengers on board. There were some passengers who were conversing and others who just sat quietly thinking perhaps of their different problems. There was music playing in the bus. Since my immediate neighbour in the bus was a total stranger, I did not know how to go about starting a conversation with him. I was not good at making friends easily because I was that shy type who still had a lot to learn about life away from my village setting. He did not talk to me either. That was an aspect of people who lived in towns or cities as Rose told me. They just loved minding their own business. With nothing for me to do I just sat nodding my head to the Makossa rhythm that was booming in the bus. I tried to sleep after a while but the thought of people transforming into animals came back to me. Covering my eyes became a serious problem more especially as the coat which was worn by my neighbour was almost identical to the colour of python skin. Could that have been just mere coincidence? I decided to become the self-appointed night watchman keeping watch to make sure that no one dared transform into anything. The idea of transformations was more in my imagination and that fear kept me awake all night. There were a good number of people who tried to have some sleep but the bus jumping into potholes prevented them from doing so. Some of them insulted the bus driver for directing the bus into the potholes. Their reason for blaming him was that they believed he did it on purpose because he did not want to be awake alone. The driver would apologize but that did not stop him from getting into another pothole.

When we got to Yaoundé at 06:30 the next morning, there were some people who had swollen eyes because they were unable to sleep or barely slept all night. I was very tired and needed to sleep but the beauty of the city took all that away. There were beautiful flowers along the streets, well tarred roads and pavements, well decorated buildings and some towering sky scrapers. I was marvelled by what my eyes saw and considered Yaoundé the most beautiful city in the world. My native Bamenda was nowhere close to the beauty of the capital city. I understood then why most of my classmates dreamed of going to the university in Yaoundé. But I could not allow the beauty of the city derail me from what I went there to do. There was enough time to get back to Bamenda and then return to Yaoundé to admire the splendour of the town in its entirety. So, I stopped a taxi and announced my destination to the driver. I was taken to the school and fortunately for me, I met Lillian, a school mate who was a year ahead of me in the high school. She asked what I came to do in Yaoundé and I gave her the details. She took me all round the university campus which covered hectares of land before taking me finally to the university secretariat. There I was handed a prospectus for freshmen. 'Freshmen' too was a new term I had to get familiar with. I asked Lillian what it meant and she told me.

After getting the information I needed, I went with Lillian to her room at the student residential area which was not far from the university premises. There, I got information about the amount different rooms cost. The 4.5 x 6 meters room with a water system toilet at one corner Lillian occupied cost 15000 francs per month and she told me that she had to pay for ten months before she was allowed to pack in.

"That is the rule and landlords are never prepared to compromise. If you do not have the ten months, you go elsewhere. If you pay this year and the next year you do not have the full ten months to pay, you would be evicted. The landlords have the phone numbers of their tenants and before the academic year begins, they would call all of them to find out if they have all the year's money. If you say that you don't have all the money, someone else would occupy your room by the time you come back to school. What we have here are called shylock landlords," she said with a sigh.

I knew that her father was just a poor farmer and could not afford the 15000 francs per month she paid for her room. Besides, I did not know any of her relatives who were wealthy or abroad who could be assisting her. I asked her how she managed to pay for her room. It seemed my question landed like a bombshell and she laughed nervously before attempting an answer.

"My father cannot afford to pay for my room because my younger ones also need to go to school. I am not going to remain a little girl all my life. I have to use my head and squeeze a few francs from here and there. With the extras, I add to what my father gives me. There are rooms with external pit latrines which cost less but you have to understand that prestige is an important element in the life of a student here. I hope you do understand," she said.

I agreed that I understood what she was saying. But in reality, I did not understand what she meant by using her head to squeeze a few francs from here and there. What I could make of what she said was that she was perhaps doing a part time job or jobs to make some money. I wanted to ask her why she did not go back to Santa to assist her parents raise money for her fees and rents for the following academic year. But I swallowed my question because I felt that I was getting too much into her private life. I decided to shift our conversation on how to secure a good room which was not too expensive. She proposed that if I had a friend who was coming to Yaoundé too, we could arrange and take up a single room so that cost would be minimized. I saw that her idea was good given that I was not that type that kept a girl friend or girlfriends. But the problem was going to be with the friend who might be that type who loved women. I did not like inconveniences and dismissed the idea of putting up with a friend. I asked her to help me secure one and she promised to do so. I gave her my phone number to use in reaching me when she found it.

I decided to call Keith, Mr Finley's friend and informed him of my findings. He told me that he was going to inform his friend but insisted on seeing me that day. I directed him to the student residential area and he said that he knew where that was. He told me he was going to use one the embassy vehicles. That was going to be easy for me to spot him once he was in the area. I had never seen him before and that was an opportunity for me to meet him. I informed Lillian of his arrival and also told her who he was. We both left her room to be along the road in the neighbourhood where we could spot him.

He was there in 45 minutes and I introduced Lillian to him. I told him of what I had decided with Lillian as far as securing a room was concerned and he went ahead to get her number. Lillian was going to call him once she found a decent room and he would take care of the bills. We then moved to Lillian's room for him to know where she lived. After doing that he took us out to a drinking spot in town where we had a few drinks and also ate roasted fish. As we sat eating and drinking, he did not take his eyes off Lillian. He looked at her deep in the eyes that sometimes she was forced to bend her head. Lillian was a pretty girl and I would have had no problem seeing them dating. After all, they were two adults and had the right to do whatever they pleased with their lives. We separated after all the eating but before leaving, Mr Keith promised to call me and to Lillian, he promised to see her later.

I planned to travel to Santa that same day but the thing was that I was going to get to my destination late in the night. If that were to happen, I would have had to sleep in the bus to wait for dawn. Lillian knew of that and urged me to spend the night and travel the next morning instead. Well, that was a bit disturbing to me as her room had just one bed. I asked her if we were going to sleep on the one bed I saw in her room or she had other plans. She told me we were going to sleep on her bed. I told her that I was going to go and book for my trip and travel later in the evening. But she insisted on me spending the night.

"If you are afraid of sleeping with me on the same bed, I will go and sleep with a friend while you occupy the room for the night," she said.

That was better than having all the discomfort of the night. I had never slept with a girl and the fear of not performing as I should when the occasion presented itself scared me.

My relationship with Lillian was not clearly defined. I looked at her as a senior and as a sister but I did not know how she looked at me then. Way back while we were still in secondary school, she always tried to defend me from those who tried to bully or humiliate me. She even received some beatings in the course of trying to defend me sometimes. She fought hard to know where I was living but I was determined not to let anybody know, not even her. She was in love with me but I always pretended not to notice her enticing moves. It was unheard of for a girl in a senior class to have something to do with a boy in a junior class. A thing like that was always considered as an abomination. It was normal for boys in senior classes to look for girl friends in junior classes. Girls on their part had to look ahead of them and not look backward. School rules and regulations forbade intimate relationships between students. But the rules on unhealthy relationships were violated too often. I was shy, naïve and lacked the courage to open up to any girl even if she took the first step towards me. Poverty was another hindering factor coupled with the school rule. If I'd opened up to her, the news would have been out sooner or later and I dreaded being involved in public scandals.

I could remember while I was in her room that she put on a very transparent blouse and a very short skirt. She tried at some moments to push up the skirt higher so that I could see her pant. Though we were over 300 kilometres from the eyes and cheap gossips of Santa, I kept asking heaven what it was about to let fall on my head. What scared me most was not even getting involved in the sexual act but picking up a sexually transmitted disease and also not being up to the task. Back in school, my female friends always sat and discussed what they did with their boyfriends in private. They mocked and laughed at their boy friends' incompetence as they couldn't satisfy them in bed. The news soon spread in school and the boys in question became laughing stocks. The boys in question became known as 'women in trousers'. I was scared of being a laughing stock too if I failed to perform as a man. That was why I preferred having Lillian, a distance away from her room than being in the same room with her.

We went back to the student residential area at about 19:30. We did not go back straight to Lillian's room. She took me and we went round the neighbourhood visiting her friends. The visiting lasted till 20:50 when we decided to head back to her room. I knew she was going to pick up something like her night wear and leave but she still had some time to be in her room. That was increasing the risk of falling into temptation for me and I did not like it. I asked her when she was leaving and where she intended to go and spend the night. She ignored the first part of my question but told me that she was going to sleep with Anastasia who was some tree doors away on the same block. I was relieved that she was going to go but she had an embarrassing question for me.

"Have you ever made love to a woman," she asked.

I had my eyes on her when she asked the question but let them fall to the ground as I bent my head. She saw my mood change and understood everything. By the standards of most of my male friends, any man who attained the university level and had not known a woman was a eunuch. I did not know what she was thinking of me. I opened my mouth to speak but the words got stocked in my throat.

"It is not a disaster. That shows that you are still clean and pure. Guys like you are very rare. Don't worry… I am going to help you," she said.

"How?" I asked finding my voice again.

"You don't want me to sleep here with you and I have to respect that. Maybe some other time when you'll be ready," she said and left with her night wear and a tooth brush.

I could not sleep all night. I thought that by pushing her to go out and sleep at her friend's I was going to have a peaceful night sleep but she put 'thorns' in my head before leaving. Those thorns tortured me all night that at one point I began to feel that it was better to have allowed her stay and let what had to happen, happen.

Lillian knocked on the door the next morning at 06:30 and asked me how I spent the night. I sighed and she asked why. I sighed again.

"You will get old quick when you turn your stomach into a warehouse where you store your problems and do not want to share them with anybody," she said.

"I did not cover my eyes the whole night," I said.

"Is it because of what I said? I knew it was going to torture you," she said.

"You knew? If you knew it was going to disturb me, why did you say it then?" I asked.

"If it tortured you, it means that your body is ready and can react to….never mind"

She did not complete the sentence even after some insistence from me. All she said was that I had to eat something and then move to the travel agency and book for my trip if I did not want to get to Santa at night. I got out of bed, brushed my teeth and had some tea with a loaf of bread before going. She accompanied me to Vatican Travel Agency. She went and paid for my bus ticket and we both waited for the time the bus would hit the road. The time came at 08:00 and I said goodbye to Lillian and she asked me to remain pure in heart and body. I still watched her through the window of the bus as the distance increased between us. She too stood and watched the bus as it disappeared out of sight. With my eyes hurting inside as if filled with sand, I tried to find some sleep as I could not sleep the previous night. I did have some sleep in the course of the journey though the potholes on the road could not allow me have enough of it. I knew I would have enough time to sleep and catch up once I got to my destination. I finally got to Santa at 14:50. There was nothing more comforting and sweet like sleep.

11

Close to two weeks after my return from Yaoundé, precisely on July 9th which was a Thursday, I got out of my room in the evening after sleeping all day to take a walk. I bumped into Pricilla who was on her way home from the farm. She had her five years old daughter, Emily, with her. Her son, Jackson, who was just five months old, was strapped on her back. I greeted her and she complained of tiredness after working all day. I soothed her by telling her that the earth never failed those who worked hard to make a decent living. She smiled and I asked her if she was going to work in the field again the next day and she said yes. I told her that I'd love to accompany her there since I stayed home all day suffering from boredom. She smiled and told me that she had no money to pay me after that. I asked her not to worry about money. We promised to meet at the same spot I met her the next day for us to move to her farm. I continued on my way and returned to my room at about 20:40 and lay on my bed.

As I lay in bed, I remembered Pricilla and our secondary school days. She came to Government High School Santa from Bamenda town and entered in the third year. I was in year two then and could realize that she always put on a large pullover whenever she was in school. I heard rumours then that she was impregnated by our Geography teacher, Mr George, who always left Santa and went to Bamenda town four times a week to see her. Pricilla's parents were highly religious and were afraid of their reputation. They did not want anything that could put it in jeopardy. So, they went to the police and reported the matter but insisted that the matter be treated discreetly. Our geography teacher was summoned and asked to sign some documents. Since Mr George behaved positively, Pricilla came to Santa and was living with him while at the same time going to school. By sending her off before her pregnancy became noticeable, her parents tactfully avoided having a tarnished reputation. Well, that was a story I got by listening to gossips. I found no need to go in for any verification because the evidences were there in front of me to see. Mr George was fortunate that he had his house already. However, by virtue of the fact that she was impregnated by one of our teachers, she was admitted into our institution and allowed to study until when she could have her baby. Any other girl who picked up a pregnancy was sent home to go and have the baby before returning to school. It seemed Mr George did truly love her though he was more than twice her age. He was 32 then while she was just 16.

Her husband being a public service worker meant that he was not free from transfers. Some of the transfers did come when the person concerned least expected. That was what happened to Mr George. He was forced to go on transfer, to Victoria Bay situated some 250 km from Santa, just two years after Pricilla started living with him. A good number of male teachers and some big boys in the school were determined to take advantage of her husband's absence. So, they clashed over her. I blamed them for doing something so mean as to trying to go out with a married woman. Pricilla was a very pretty girl and child birth did nothing to reduce her beauty. Whether she dated some of the male teachers and the big boys or not is a different story. She stopped school after obtaining her GCE Advanced Level Certificate. She was an intelligent girl and did love to go to the university. But her two children were more important and she had to give up her dream of going to the university.

She was involved in farm work because she did not want to buy everything from the market. Besides, she had nothing doing and farm work was the only activity that could keep her busy. Her husband provided her with all the money she needed but depending on him all the time for money was what she disliked.

I met her the next day at the spot we agreed to meet. She had her two children, Emily and Jackson with her. The farm we had to go to was some four kilometres away. The road to the farm was not bad and commercial motor bikes could go there.

We arrived at the farm at 07:20 and our intention for going so early was to do some serious work before the rain came in to disturb. I went in to survey the environment as soon as I climbed down the bike. The land covered so many acres and Pricilla told me that it belonged to her father-in-law. Since she was one of the lucky few who was in very good terms with her father-in-law, he asked her to farm as much as her strength could permit her.

She got to the farm that day with the intention of clearing and tilling a portion of the farm she allowed to lay fallow the previous year in order to plant beans and potatoes to harvest in the dry season. She had to do the clearing using a hoe but with me there with a cutlass, she limited herself to gathering the cleared grass in one heap which she had to later on cover with some soil and burn. Before we started work, she gathered and arranged some dresses in the baby's plastic bath and put him in it. After doing that she placed him under a pear tree which was not out of sight. So we could then keep an eye on the baby while we worked. She instructed her little daughter, Emily, to stay close to her kid brother under the tree. But she was very stubborn and preferred to be with us where we were doing the clearing and gathering of grass. Jackson was very sensitive and could sense when he was alone. He cried most of the time when he was awake and the refusal of his elder sister to stay closed to him made things worse. Pricilla decided she would allow him cry for some time before going to carry him. She allowed him to cry for a little while and when she went and breastfed him. He fell asleep in the process. He was to sleep for the next 45 minutes.

At 10:15, he woke up and started crying since he found no one around him. Pricilla pleaded with her daughter to go and play with him. She refused. He continued crying but the crying soon gave way to laughter as if he was playing with someone or something. Just then, I was feeling really thirsty and the drinkable water we brought was kept under the same tree Jackson was. I decided to go and quench my thirst as well as check on him. As I got 15 meters to where the baby was, something beyond imagination caught my attention. There was a black snake that had wrapped itself on the baby and was dangling its head in his face. When it dangled on the left and the baby tried to tough its head, it dodged and moved to the right and continued dangling. When the baby tried to touch its head again on the right, it dodged and moved to the left. The baby found it to be funny and that explained why there was that play laughter.

I was too marvelled to shout. I just stood there watching with my mouth wide open. I don't know if it was fate or the instinct of a mother that prompted Pricilla to look in my direction, but the way I stood was enough to tell her that something was going on where the baby was. She immediately dropped her tools and ran to where I stood. She saw the snake wrapped round the baby and shouted at the top of her voice. Immediately the snake got the noise, it sensed danger, left the baby unharmed and ran away. We saw it running away and the direction it took. Pricilla ran to where the baby was and took him out of the plastic bath. She wasted no time in striping him of all his clothes looking for a spot that the snake might have bitten. She found none and put his clothes back on. She decided not to put him again in the plastic bath and leave him under the tree but preferred to strap him on her back. She became very terrified even to go close to the grass. She suggested that we go back home but I reminded her that we had not done much for the day. But she said that she was not going to touch the grass again. I told her that she had to just sit and watch me work for at least two hours before we head home. She agreed and I worked for the next two and a half hours.

While on our way back home, our conversation was centred on the snake incident.

"Why did you not run to chase the snake away from the baby," she asked.

"I was afraid that I could do something stupid to frighten the snake and it would harm him. I was really marvelled to see it playing with the baby. He was not anyway in danger. I think that shout you raised would have made it panic and harm the baby when it was not its intention to do so," I said.

She was really taken aback by the words that fell from my mouth. She even stopped walking and starred at me for a while.

"We are talking about a snake which was wrapped round my baby. It was a black snake and I know that black snakes are poisonous. So, I don't understand what you mean by 'he was not in danger', she said.

"I had once visited my uncle in Wum and he had a dog and a three years old son in the house. The dog was a wild dog and no one would dare go a meter close to it when it was eating a bone. Even my uncle himself could not try. But his three years old son always went close to the dog when it was eating a bone and would even try to pull the bone out of the mouth of the dog and it would do nothing. I'm not sure that what happened in the farm there a while ago was any different. Even the wildest beast would not hurt a harmless and defenceless child. Were you not told that God watch over the very little ones? That was the hand of God at work," I said.

She admitted that the hand of God might have been at work but disagreed with the rest of my explanation.

"Some years ago in pinyin village, a woman put her son in a plastic bath just as I did with my baby, and placed him in the yard where she was peeling potatoes. Her phone rang in the house and she left the baby and went to answer the call. When she finished answering it, she came out only to realize that her baby had been partly eaten up by a pig. Is it that the pig didn't know that the baby was harmless and defenceless? What can you say about that?" she asked.

"The pig is a cursed animal and that is why Moslems don't eat it," I said.

"So are snakes. Isn't that why it crawls on its stomach," she asked.

I did not know what else to say. I just remained silent and she raised both hands as if to receive something from heaven and thanked God for saving her son. She equally thanked me immensely for assisting her that day in the farm. She invited me to come to her house the next day which was Saturday. She wanted me to come and share a meal with her. It was her way of thanking me for a job well done. I accepted and we parted on the path that led to my room. She had to advance about a kilometre before getting to her own house. I got to my room and had a bath. I felt really exhausted after doing that because I had not done hard work in quite a while. The only thing left to do was to go to bed and I did just that. I was to wake up only at 09:05 the next day which was Saturday.

I could not go to Pricilla's house that early. It was abnormal to visit someone in Santa village during the morning periods unless it was a matter of life and death. After inquiring, all I was told was that it was tradition and I was just supposed to take it as it was. I decided to spend that time by weeding around the abandoned house and fitting in more papers in more holes that appeared in the walls. I also revisited some of my high school note books and textbooks.

At 14:15, I left for Pricilla's house. Since it was just a kilometre away from where I lived, it took me no time to get there. Her house was simple and modern but it was not fenced as most modern houses in and around Pinyin village. However, as I approached her yard, I could see Emily and she sat backing the road into the yard. There was a dog that squatted in front of her. It saw me but did not bark because it was eating with Emily. I stood for a while and watched what was going on. The food the little girl was eating was rice and stew. When she took a spoon full of rice, she got the next spoon full and put in the mouth of the dog. I found that really fascinating and decided not to disturb. When the food in the plate got finished, it was time to eat the meat and the little girl decided to let the dog have the first bite. But the dog ate up everything and she got really furious.

"You fool, I will not give you anything again," she shouted landing a slap on the jaw of the dog.

It was then I decided to signal my presence.

"What is it baby?" I asked pretending as if I did not know what was going on.

"Is it not this foolish bully? I have given him meat to bite a little so that I can eat the rest but he has eaten all the meat," she replied.

"Don't worry. I will tell mummy and she will give you another meat, ok?" I said.

She said yes and I held her hand and led her into the sitting room. There, I sat on one of the beautifully made chairs and waited for Pricilla to come. While waiting, I decided to feed my eyes on the pictures on the wall and the beautiful artificial flowers that covered the whole sitting room. I promised myself that I would decorate my house likewise when I had one.

Pricilla soon came into the sitting room from the kitchen and asked why I did not send her daughter to come and call for her. I told her that I had no plans for the afternoon and was not in a hurry. I then went ahead to tell her what transpired between her daughter and the dog.

"That dog is the best thing that has ever happened to my daughter. I was furious from the start when I saw her eating in the same plate with the dog but with time, I had to give up. The best thing I do is to take the dog to the pet clinic every month for check-up and vaccination. That is the only way to prevent the dog from infecting my child," she explained laughing.

She went to the kitchen and brought a plate of rice and stew for me and another slice of meat for her daughter. She ate three-quarters of the slice and gave the remaining one to the dog. I really saw that she really loved the dog and her threat that she would not give anything to it again remained just a threat.

Pricilla asked what she could offer me to drink. I told her that she could give me a mug of water. She asked if I did not want beer and my response was that alcohol was not good for young people. What prompted me to say that was that there were so many university graduates in Santa and since there were no jobs for them, they drowned their frustrations in alcohol. People were issued licenses to open beer parlours as many as they could. They could be found every 50 meters in every neighbourhood. That was not all….churches were opened almost in every neighbourhood and sometimes only a family made up a congregation. Youths who could not drown themselves in alcohol found solace in the churches. I began to see alcohol as a tool in the hands of those in authority who wanted to remain in power for as long as they wanted. Brewery companies in the country gave a lot of prizes ranging from TV sets, T-shirts, caps and free bottles of drinks to those who consumed their products. Free bottles to be won were always in their thousands and millions and many youths delved into drinking in the hope of grabbing the alluring financial and free bottle prizes. That to me prevented them from thinking and putting into use all the knowledge acquired from school. I got really worried and wondered why a government could get really greedy and would want to drown its own people in alcohol. Back in the countries of those who opened the beer companies, there were regulations by government to prevent the sale of beer and other alcoholic drinks to youths below certain ages. I wondered why the same regulation could not be effected in my own country. Yet the same authorities kept singing in their speeches that the future of the country lay in the hands of youths and at the same time they turned around and destroyed the same youths with alcohol. I was not going to fall in that stupid trap and I always discouraged my friends from taking alcohol each time they invited me out to go and drink with them. Of course, they often called me a woman each time I turned down their offers. It did not bother me since I knew what I wanted to make out of my life.

Pricilla was marvelled at my attitude and that prompted her to further ask if I had a girlfriend. I said no and asked her why she was interested in me having one.

"To find a boy who does not smoke, drink and is hard working is very rare these days. It will not be good for you staying just like that. Some lucky woman is supposed to be enjoying those good qualities you possess," she said.

I just smiled but became uncomfortable with the conversation as it shifted to my private life. I hated talking about things that involved my intimacy. She proposed that she was going to introduce me to her sister. It sounded funny to me and I began to wonder what I was going to tell her sister if at all she ever did introduce her to me. I had always dreaded the day I was going to find myself in a room with someone of the opposite sex. I decided to change the topic by asking her if she missed her husband. She did not have time to provide an answer as the baby started crying in the room and she went to attend to him. She spent about 10 minutes in the room and when she returned, I told her that I had a rendezvous with someone at the Santa motor park. She reminded me of what I said earlier about having no plans for the afternoon. I told her that I forgot about the rendezvous and it just came back to my mind. I then thanked her for her hospitality and rose from the seat on which I sat. As I was making for the door, she asked when I was going to come and visit her again. I did not give her a clear cut answer. I just said that I was just a kilometre away and could see her at any time. I was afraid that she wanted to know when I would come so as to arrange for her sister to come over. That answer as well as the rendezvous lie was just an escape route.

12

I got back to my room that afternoon at 16:25 and was feeling bored. I thought of my younger ones and wondered how they were doing. I also thought of what they told me the last time I visited them and the sadness of that day came back to me again. I did not want that to spoil my already good day and I decided to step out to go and say hello to my landlord's wife. I got to her house when she was just stepping in from the farm.

"Have you eaten anything today?" she asked. I did not say yes or no but smiled. She went in and returned with a plate of porridge potatoes. While I sat on the steps leading into her house savouring what she gave me, she asked what I intended to do once the GCE Advanced Level examination results were out. I told her of what I went and did in Yaoundé and what Mr Finley planned to do for me. She still praised my hard work and determination to make it in life. I could feel the emotion in her voice as she spoke. It was the same as all other times I spoke to her about my future. There was pain in her heart and I could feel it. She took some of the things out of the pail she brought back from the farm and cleaned them up before taking them into the house. She went and threw the dirt behind an old abandoned car parked on one corner of her yard rusting as the hours, days, months and years went by. Perhaps that car was a reflection of the gloom that enveloped her each passing day as she was uncertain about the future of her kids. I considered that my presence there was adding to her frustration and decided to eat faster. I wanted to go as fast as possible and not remain there reminding her of what she could only imagine but having no hope of ever seeing what she imagined materialize. I thanked her after eating and said good night before going to my room. I could not think of anything else but working hard in school, picking up a job and returning to save my younger ones from my father when I left my landlady. That was what occupied my mind until I fell asleep.

The next day was Sunday and the first thing for me to do was to go to church. I left my room at 07:20 and I was at the church door at 07:55. Mass started at exactly 08:00. After the first, second and gospel readings, it was time for the homily. The priest started it with a short story.

"There was a very rich man who lived in a large mansion," he began. "He had a beautiful wife, children, cars, servants and guards. He worked hard so that riches would not one day run dry. So, one day, he came back home after working hard the whole day. He was tired and after super with his family, he went to bed. The tiredness pushed him to sleep in no time. Hardly had he slept for long that he started dreaming. In his dream, he met our lord and saviour Jesus Christ. He invited our saviour for lunch in his house the next day. Our saviour accepted the invitation and promised to at his home the next day at the agreed time. The rich man got up the next morning, called all his servants and ordered that the healthiest sheep be caught and slaughtered. He also ordered that a lot of food be cooked and asked his wife to personally do the supervision to ensure that the taste was impeccable. He equally ordered that some of his servants go to the city and get the best wine they could fine as well as beer of different sorts. His servants were really curious and marvelled at the type of preparation their master asked them to make. That of course was bound to raise some questions.

"Master, are we preparing for a party?" one of his servants asked.

"No, we are not preparing for a party. We are going to be honoured with the visit of the most important man the world has ever known and will ever know. His name is Emmanuel and he will be here at lunch time today. I don't want any mistake in the food and the surroundings must be thoroughly clean," he instructed.

Everything was done and set just as the rich man had imagined and instructed. He asked all the servants when they had finished

104

working to go clean up and put on their best clothes. The guards were asked to leave their posts and allow the gate wide open. They did and everybody and everything was set. They all sat waiting for lunch time when the August guest was to arrive. At exactly 12:05, there was a knock on the door. Everybody in the house turned their eyes in the direction of the door to really see whom the guest was that the master had to make a lot of preparations for. When the door was opened, what the expectant eyes saw was indeed a person but the person was an eye sour. If you must know, it was a beggar who had not taken a bath perhaps for weeks or months and was really stinking. The rich man was really disappointed and furious that he ordered his guards to pull the beggar out of his yard and to allow him only several meters away from his gate. That was done and the guards soon returned and the waiting continued. At 12:20, there was a knock again on the door and it was opened. This time, it was a leper. Some of the servants exploded with laughter and others asked if all the preparation they made was only to welcome outcasts. The rich man was very disappointed and asked that the leper be kicked out. Since the intruder was a leper and could not move faster, the guards carried him and when they were out of the gate, they dropped him like a log of wood. At 12:30, there was yet another knock on the door. When the door was opened, it was a mad man that stood outside. The mad man was also kicked out as the first two before him. After the dismissal of the mad man, the waiting continued but no one came again after that. The rich man who was very unhappy asked his servants to eat up everything they prepared. He went to bed very unhappy.

In the evening while he was asleep, our lord came to him again in his dream. The rich man asked Jesus why he did not come for lunch to his house as he promised. Our lord said "I came to you the first time and you sent me away. I went and came again the second time hoping that you would soften your heart but you didn't. You still sent me away. I summoned some courage and came again the third time and you still sent me away. Now, I will not come again to your house."

"But my lord, I would never have sent you away. I personally invited you to my house. How could I do that and turn you away again," the rich man asked.

"A beggar came and you sent him away. That was me you sent away the first time. A leper came a short while later and you sent him away. That was me you sent away the second time. I summoned courage for the third time and came as a madman. You still sent me away. Now, I cannot come again."

That story is to tell us that we are supposed to treat and welcome everybody that comes our way with all honour and respect without taking into consideration, social status, class, financial situation, sex, race or origin. We are supposed to see our lord and master in everyone that comes our way because He lives in every one of us. How many of us turn to look at those lepers and mentally impaired people when they come to our doors or close to us to beg? We either turn our faces and look at the opposite direction or turn up the glasses of our cars when we see them coming. Does that cancel the fact that they are there? Of course not. They shall always be there to remind us of our indifference. When we even want to offer them something, we give them what we consider as good for the dogs. When we treat them like that, how do we expect our lord to visit us or let alone dine with us when we had rejected him in such people? Let us pray that as we leave this church today, we would develop a new approach towards people no matter how they look and where they come from."

I went home that Sunday feeling really edified. The story of the priest remained stock in my mind as I walked all the way back home. I also hummed some of the gospel melodies that were sung in church as well. I went straight to my room after leaving the church. There was nothing there to do and I did not like it because thinking of the sad moments of my life was going to occupy my mind. I forced myself to sleep and fell asleep for another three hours.

At 15:00, I woke up. There was nothing for me to occupy myself with as usual so I decided to get a commercial motor bike and head to the Santa motor park where I could watch people enjoying themselves since it was a weekend as well as watch cars get in and out of the park. I left my room, walked to the road and stopped one commercial bike rider and told him where he had to take me. Just about two kilometres from where I got on the bike, I saw a group of other commercial motor bike riders coming from the opposite direction. They were about eight of them and each bike had three people on it. They were noisy and I sensed that there was something amiss. They bypassed us and barely six hundred meters from where we bypassed, the guy who was taking me to the motor park kept turning and looking back. I asked him why he kept doing that but he just smiled uneasily and did not say anything. I also turned back to see what he was looking at and saw the group of bike riders coming after us in top speed. Without announcing, my rider left his bike and dashed into a nearby bush leaving me on it. With the engine still running and having no idea on how to manoeuvre it, I just let it fall to the ground with me. The heated exhaust pipe lay on my right leg and was burning like hell. The bikes all halted where I fell and one of the guys came and helped lift the fallen machine off me as I cried in pain. While he gave me some assistance, his other friends staged a man hunt for the guy who ran into the bush abandoning his bike. He did not run into the bush to join them in the chase but stayed with me. I wore a jean pair of trousers and that prevented the exhaust pipe burn from being severe. The guy who helped me must have been in his mid-20s and he introduced himself to me as Samuel. I asked him why they were after the guy who ran into the bush.

"Some two fellows robbed my kid brother of his commercial motor bike at gun point some two days ago at 14:00. After making away with it, they dismantled it and sold the parts to this guy we are after now who is trying to be smart. The two thieves who robbed my brother are already in police custody and we want to take him there to join them," he said.

I was stunned as anyone else who might have heard that kind of shocking revelation. He went on to examine the engine on the motor bike he lifted off me and said that it was the engine of the bike seized from his kid brother. He added that he could recognize the engine from a number that was inscribed on it. I told him that if the guy they were chasing was aware that the parts he bought were stolen, then he was supposed to be punished.

"He is guilty. If he is not, then why did he run away when he saw us coming after him? It means that he was fully aware that the parts he bought were stolen and he went ahead to buy them all the same. He will have to go and face the music as the rest of his accomplices," Samuel said.

Just then the group of young men who delved into the bush for the long chase soon re-emerged with the criminal in their grip. Punches and slaps landed on him from every angle. The blood in me froze as I watched them inflict so much pain on him. Blood started oozing from the guys nose as the slaps and the punches continued to rain on him. I pleaded with Samuel to do something to stop his friends from inflicting further pains on the guy. He asked them not to beat him again as I requested. They all obeyed. Then Samuel spoke to the criminal to the hearing of everyone present.

"Simon, I can assure you that no one would lay a finger on you if you tell us where the remaining parts of that bike are. Already, I know that is the engine of my kid brother's motor bike which you have mounted on that your old bike," he said pointing at it.

It was then I knew the name of the guy who accepted to take me to Santa Motor Park. He was not willing to say where the other parts of the stolen bike were. The friends of Samuel threatened to beat him again. I pleaded with them not to do it and to allow me talk to Simon.

"These guys are here to get what belongs to them. They have been able to recognize the engine of their stolen bike with you. If you have the remaining parts, please just go and hand them in and get this issue done with. Those pieces of metal are not worth a drop of blood you've spilt here. They have said that you were not part of the robbery. You merely bought some parts which you needed though you knew they were not clean. Just by virtue of that fact, your situation is already better than that of those who robbed the bike from its owner. Please be wise and help yourself," I said.

Some of the guys there supported me in what I said and urged him to cooperate. My words indeed had some effect on him and he confessed that the remaining parts of the stolen bike were at his house. The wounded guys decided to accompany Simon to his house. I was convinced that since Simon decided to cooperate, no more pain was going to be inflicted on him. I decided to take a walk back to where I lived since I had not gone far before the incident took place.

While I was walking back, I kept thinking that if the guys who robbed someone of his bike were already in the hands of the police, it meant that they knew already much about the case and should have been the ones to come for the arrest of Simon. I could not understand why the police had to stay back and leave violent young boys to come and fetch a criminal. I did not know what to make of it but I did not think that after receiving all the beatings from the young men, Simon had to be punished a second time with imprisonment for the same crime. Those in authority always said that 'Cameroon is Cameroon. That meant that what was abnormal elsewhere was acceptable as the norm in Cameroon. Elsewhere it would have been unheard of, for civilians to go and carry out an arrest except the police was unaware but in Cameroon, the police could fold its arms and allow an angry crowd beat a suspected criminal to death. And most of the time, the innocent paid the heavy price. The only thing I could do was sigh as I walked back home.

When I got back to where I lived later that evening, I went to my landlady and showed her what I had on my leg. She went into her kitchen and brought an egg and applied the egg white on the spot burnt by the exhaust pipe. It hurt a little and she told me that the egg was going to help the wound heal without leaving a scar. I did not know how far that was true but there was nothing wrong with verifying. However, a little over 48 hours after the stolen bike incident, I left my room in the afternoon at about 14:20 and decided to head towards the Santa motor park on foot. My intention was not to get there but just to exercise my legs. Three kilometres from my room, I found a young man and recognized him as one of the guys who was among the young men who had Simon well beaten the Sunday they caught him. I greeted him and introduced myself. He recognized me and apologized for the embarrassment I was subjected to that day. I asked him what they found at the house of Simon when they got there that day.

"We got there and he went and showed us a spot behind his house which we dug. The different parts of the stolen bike were inside. But some parts like the wheels were in his bedroom under his bed. After assembling all the parts, we rebuilt the bike. We then used it to transport him to the police station where he is presently locked up though we discovered that he is a father of four children and his last child is just two weeks old," he said.

"That is really unfortunate," I said and we parted on that sad note. I moved just a few meters from where we parted and decided to make a U-turn. While I was walking back home I rang Mr Joel to find out if there was some work. He asked me to come over if I had nothing to do because there was always work to be done at the shop in the market. I promised that I was going to be with him in town the next day. So that evening, I packed everything of mine in my traveller's bag. I moved to the house of my landlord and informed him and his wife that I was moving out and was not certain that I was going to return soon. My landlady was sad to hear that I was leaving and asked me to come and visit them whenever I could. I promised to do so. Her husband too on his part was sad not because I was leaving but because I had caused trouble between him and Mr Finley and according to him, I did it because I wanted to benefit from Mr Finley's generosity alone.

"He is helping you to progress and if you are leaving, it means that he is making things better for you. What will happen to my son whom he promised to help? You have made him to shove my son aside and now he is concentrating on you. We shall all rip the fruits of what we sow," he said.

His words were really aching. I felt really hurt and his wife too, as she left us in the sitting room for the kitchen. I rose and left for my room without another word. I did not want to sit there receiving taunting words from my landlord. I felt that he was someone I had to avoid getting close to. At 20:24, I was in bed.

On Thursday morning, I woke up at 07:20 and said goodbye to my landlady. I told her that if I had to someday return to that place, it would be because of her. I then got on a commercial motor bike which took me to Santa Motor Park. I was in Bamenda town 35 minutes later. I went straight to the shop inside the Bamenda Main Market. He was in and welcomed me as soon as he saw me. He reminded me that he had earlier told me to come over at any time I had some spare time because there was always work. He then took my traveller's bag and went with it home while I remained in the shop attending to customers. He returned an hour or so later and we did the work till 17:30 when we all went home.

Everyone was excited to see me as I was equally excited to see them. We chatted about life in Santa and I told them of the kind of things that happened there. Abortions, dumping of babies in bushes and dust bins, sexually transmitted diseases, witchcraft, stealing of farm produce were some of the things we talked about. After supper at 19:45, I went out on the yard to have some fresh air. Rose came over to where I was and told me that she loved the simple and innocent way I reasoned and acted. I told her that a little elaboration was going to be of tremendous help because I did not understand what she meant or what she was driving at. She ignored what I said but instead sought to know in her next question if I had a girlfriend. I told her that I did not and was curious to know why that was of interest to her. So, I ask her why. She just smiled and said nothing. I wondered why the issue of me having a girl friend or not kept coming up. The surprising thing was that the issue was raised most of the time by ladies.

A long silence followed after my question to Rose. In a short while, I had the feeling that the one meter distance between us began to narrow. She came quite closer to me and spoke again.

"You are so young, handsome, innocent, caring and very hard working. No woman would observe you even for a week and would not feel something for you. I have for all the time that we've been working in the shop doing just that and I think that you are a very nice person," she said leaning on me and caressing my left hand.

A wave of heat ran all over my body as she did that and I withdrew myself from her. I asked her not to ever do such a thing again. She tried to apologize but I did not allow her get through with what she wanted to say. I just cut her short and told her that I was tired and went to my room at the boys' quarters. She was a beautiful girl, I must say. I was scared that her apologies might push me to move over to console her and who knew what might have happened? It was better to pre-empt things before they got out of hand because 'the body has its own reasons which reason itself might know nothing about.' Besides, Rose's father had already a positive impression about me and I did not want any careless youthful adventure to spoil it. Isn't that why he always wanted me to come each time I had any spare time? If he were to one day suspect that his daughter was 'insecure' and I was the predator, my links with him would cut automatically. I was not prepared to see that happen and I was bent on preserving the image he had of me at all cost.

13

I went to my room and locked the door behind me. I did not want to face the temptation of the minutes earlier when Rose leaned on me. I did not want to think about it and in order to completely take my mind off my mind, I decided to turn on the TV. The channel I tuned to was Hillside Television. It was a private TV channel in the City of Yaoundé. The program on the air at 21:00 was 'SOS, Break the Silence.' The program started with the presentation of some guests who happened to have been a woman and her 16 years old daughter. The woman introduced herself as Madam Susan and her daughter as Mariana. The presenter made the listeners understand that the guests were going to talk about something really terrible and sad but before he delved to their story, some images were first of all beamed to the audience.

The images that followed had to do with the arrest of a man who must have been in his mid-50s. The arrest was made some 48 hours earlier at his residence. The guests in the studio at that moment could be spotted in the images. After the images, focus went back to the presenter and the two guests in the studio.

"You must have realized in those images that there were no comments. The man who was arrested as you just saw there is called Mr Elias and the woman here is his wife and the girl by her side is their daughter. Mr Elias did something which people do not talk about easily when it occurs, though the victims may be suffering terribly. Our guests here have taken the courage to come here and talk about what led to the arrest of their husband and father. In other words, they have decided to break the silence. We will be right back after this short break," the presenter said.

That brief introduction was enough to chase any sleep from my eyes. I sat up on the lone chair in my room so that sleep would not carry me off

"My first question goes to Mariana. What led to the arrest of your father two days ago?" the presenter asked.

"For over four years now, my father has made it a habit to be giving me and my younger sister and two brothers, some tablets. He gave us the tablets every week and he always said that the drugs were to protect us against malaria parasites. We had no reason to doubt him since he is our father and we love and trust him. However, we realized that there was a special black pill he always included in the tablets he gave to my sister and I but not in those given to my two brothers. I too naively thought that it was because we girls had more delicate systems that the special black pills had to be added and so, had never bothered to ask. For over four years, he had fed us with those pills every week," she said.

She paused for a while and tears started streaming down her eyes. The presenter intervened to tell the audience that they had to bear with Mariana because what she was talking about was too painful. Her mother by her side took her into her arms and soon joined her in the crying.

"If you don't feel like going further, we could carry the program forward to another day when you must have been feeling much better," the presenter said.

"Oh No No, I will continue," Mariana said.

"Then, tell us what happened after you took those drugs for over four years," the presenter implored.

"It was two months ago that I decided to find out why he always gave my sister and I malaria tablets including a black pill. I took the malaria tablets and pretended to take the black pill with them. It was a Thursday in the evening at about 19:00 as usual. I say as usual because that was the time he always gave us the malaria tablets and about one and a half to two hours later, we would start feeling very weak and dizzy. So, that fateful Thursday, I did not take the pill and at about 22:00, someone sneaked into my room and came straight to my bed. I pretended to be asleep and the person took off my trouser.

It was then that I stopped pretending and wanted to shout. The person closed my mouth and threatened to kill me if I dared to. I could not recognize the person from the face since the light was turned off but I could recognize the voice as that of my father," she said with tears streaming down her eyes again.

She tried to continue but the tears and emotion in her voice could not let her. A brief moment of silence followed and the presenter decided to punctuate the program by bringing in the program's signature tune. The program continued after that.

"Did your father rape you that night?" the presenter asked.

"That night, no. But there was every indication that it was not the first time he was sneaking into my room. I discovered that the black pill was indeed a sleeping pill and it was intended to push me into a very deep sleep so that he would have his way. He threatened to kill me if I breathe a word to anybody and I became scared," Mariana Said.

"Did your father ever try to touch or rape you after you discovered his little trick?" the presenter asked.

"Yes he did, several times. He did not do it in the house. He often dragged me into a bush or to an abandoned house. Each time he dragged me to any of them and I tried to resist, he tied me up and then raped me. He monitored my movements. Each time I came home late, he would beat me and ask me to tell him where I was coming from or with whom I was. I would tell him that I have only female friends and he would warn me that the day he would catch me with a male friend, he would kill me," she said.

The images of the place Mariana's father often dragged her to before raping her were shown to the audience. The reporter then turned to Mariana's mother and asked her how her house looked like.

"My house is a simple one with a large sitting room and five bedrooms. My four children occupy one room each. I think that was what facilitated the abominable act of their father," she said.

115

"I would like to think that you occupy a single room with your husband. Did you ever notice any strange behaviour in your husband?" the reporter asked.

"I can remember that each time we went to bed, he left the room saying that he was going to the toilet or that there was too much heat in the house and he was going outside to have some fresh air. He always returned 30 minutes or one hour later to sleep. He did that two times every week. It was two days ago when the police came and arrested him that I understood why he always left the room and returned only a while later," she said sobbing.

"Madam, what did you do when you discovered what your husband had been doing to your daughters?" the reporter asked.

"I asked Mariana why she never told me that her father was abusing her. She told me of the death threats she received from him. I took my other daughter to the hospital to see if she had been abused too. The revelations at the hospital were so heart breaking. She is traumatized and behaves now as if she is not normal. The doctor who examined her told me that there are chances that she would never be able to bear children because the damage on her is very profound," she said and burst into tears.

A break was observed to permit Madam Susan regain her calm. When that was done, the next question was asked Mariana.

"Did your father continue to give you and your younger sister the malaria tablets with the black pill after you discovered him?" the presenter asked.

"Yes, he did and personally supervised us take it. I pretended to swallow mine and once he was convinced that I had swallowed it and turned his back, I went behind the house and spat it out. I left my room and moved to that of my sister and was sleeping with her. I made sure that the light was always on and I also stayed awake for as long as possible. Once he opened the door and saw me sleeping with my younger sister, he would shamelessly say that he just wanted to check on her to see if she was ok," Mariana said.

"One last question....how did the police get wind of the information?" the presenter asked.

"On the eve of the day of his arrest, he dragged me to that abandoned house you saw in the images and raped me. He gave me money to get a taxi and go straight to the house without stopping anywhere. I did not do that. I got a taxi and stopped at the police station. I could not take it anymore and decided to speak out irrespective of the consequences. The policeman I narrated my ordeal to promised to come and arrest him the next day and he kept his promise. It was after I got home from the police station that I opened up to my mother," Mariana said.

The time allocated for the program was fast running out and the presenter was forced to conclude the program. He concluded by saying that Mariana and her mother were very courageous to come out and talk about something which was supposed to be a family secret and which society still considered a taboo. He added that we were still over 150 years behind civilization and breaking the silence on the taboo subjects was one way of catching up with the rest of the world.

Goose pimples covered my whole body as that program ended. I could not believe what I just watched on TV. It happened in that Yaoundé I was going to move to in the weeks ahead. I began to understand that behind the beautiful city with well tarred roads, well decorated streets, and towering sky scrapers laid something horribly terrifying. I thought about the program for a long while and asked myself a lot of questions. *'What could really push a man to direct his sexual instincts towards his own children? If the man was no longer satisfied with his wife, why did he not go out and date single women instead of destroying his own children? What prevented him from going out? Was it the fear of expenditure?' I asked myself.* I soon realized that I was going to end up with more questions than answers if I went on thinking. I remembered what my literature teacher always said to us each time we treated a text which had to do with the sexual behaviours of some of the characters. "We are like goats and become helpless when we are gripped by the desire for sex," he always said. I concluded that Mr Elias' goat instincts caught him and he had the right to quell them down but the problem was that he decided to quell them on the wrong persons. That conclusion settled my thoughts and I went to sleep.

I woke up very early the next morning and took a shower in readiness to go to work at 07:30. Mr Joel had to take Rose and I to the shop that morning. While we were on our way, I narrated to them in detail what I watched on TV the previous night. They were not at all shocked by what I told them. They were instead marvelled at the idea of the black pills the man used to rape his children. Mr Joel commented that the issue of incest was no longer strange to them in town as they heard of cases on a daily basis. I asked if there were no punishments for such crimes and Rose said that the law prescribed ten years but money always had the upper hand. She made me to understand that once the rapist had the money to buy his freedom, nothing else could stand in the way. I sighed when she said that and felt irritated to learn that the state was powerless in the face of corruption and more victims were made each day. Perhaps that was the reason why the TV channel resorted to encouraging people to expose the perpetrators of such acts. Whatever the case, I thought that some of such horrendous acts happened in the home because people always believed that danger could only come from outside. But what was certain was that the acts of rape and incest came from people within the home. *'What is the human race degenerating into? Some people can no longer use their brains to make a distinction between those to direct their sexual instincts to and those they should not. Has man become so bestial in his sexual behaviour that he has over taken animals?'* I asked myself. The answers were certainly blowing in the wind.

We got to the market at 07:54 and opened the shop. I was worried about one thing and it was on what attitude to adopt towards Rose after the incident of the previous evening. For the most part of the morning period, I spoke to her only in the presence of her father.

When he stepped out or went to his office, the silence of death came between us. I did everything possible to stay away from her and she noticed it. It was in the afternoon at about 14:00 when her father stepped out of the market that she decided to confront me.

"Why are you avoiding me?" she asked. "Is it because of what happened last night? I'm sorry if I made you uncomfortable," she said.

"There is nothing wrong with having feelings for someone. It is something natural but where you direct such feelings may have some thorns. You know what your father thinks about me. How do you think he is going to feel if he learns that I'm having a love affair with his own daughter and doing funny things under his own roof? He has done a lot for me and I don't think flirting with his daughter is the right way to repay him for what he has done for me. No, that would be biting the very finger that feeds me and it is not proper," I said.

"That is the problem with you. You spend your time being careful not to hurt others that you forget you have to enjoy yourself. How many of those people you struggle not to hurt do struggle not to hurt you? Please stop thinking about others and forgetting about yourself," she said.

"We are not talking about just anybody here. We are talking about your father. Have you tried to put your leg in my shoe?" I asked.

"There you go again….always feeling only for others," she retorted. "You should…."

I did not allow her to complete that last sentence. I saw that we were going to keep arguing all day and so had to end it.

"What I'm doing has nothing to do with pleasing people. It has to do with what is morally acceptable as right. I am not going to give in to what you want simply because you think that I spend my time pleasing others. What you want will never happen and I don't want to talk about it anymore," I said bluntly.

I could read the disappointment on her face as I said that. I felt that I was a bit too harsh in the way I spoke to her and wanted to apologize. But after a second thought I gave up the idea because I felt that apologizing was going to create more room for her to invade me further. A brief silence followed and just then a customer walked in. When I was going to attend to him, Rose said to my hearing that 'we shall see.' I went and attended to the customer. When he was gone, I went to Rose and she recorded what was sold. I asked her what she meant by 'we shall see'. She responded that I was proving to be so tough and she was anxious to see how far I would go. I asked her if she was not planning to intoxicate her father's mind that I tried to abuse her. She replied that she was an adult and was already too old to be indulging in such childish acts simply because she wanted to get even. I felt some relief after she said that. Things seemingly went back to normal and we became friends again or so I thought.

At 16:00 Rose tuned to F.M 94 and it was news time on Radio Hot Cocoa. The presenter began with a human interest story. It had to do with a woman called Josephine who was already 43 years old and was dating a young boy of about 26. She knew that she had no future with him but had invested a lot, financially in him. She had a daughter of about 22 who was living in Bamenda and wanted to her to get married. Since Josephine had invested a lot in the young man and did not want her investment to go in vain, she invited her daughter to Yaoundé and told her that she had found her a husband. She happily travelled to Yaoundé and saw the husband and loved him but was unaware that the guy and her mother had been lovers. They dated for a while in Yaoundé and decided to come to Bamenda to begin their marriage arrangements. The younger sister of the young man was aware of the affair between her brother and Josephine. She opposed the planned marriage between her brother and the daughter of Josephine because she could not understand why a mother would date a man and then hand the same man to her daughter after a while. She was bent on doing everything to stop the marriage. She started by alerting Josephine's daughter of the love affair between her brother and her mother. That did nothing to deter the young girl who was bent on going on with their marriage plans. With that first plan having failed woefully before her very eyes, she hatched a second plan and it was to go to Radio Hot Cocoa and present her case. That was how the story became headline news.

Rose listened to that story with keen interest. She clapped her hands in disbelief when that first news item was done with.

"Abomination….wonders shall never end!" she exclaimed. "How can a mother use a man and then hand over the man to her daughter as a husband when she is done with him? Has the man become a handkerchief or what? I have heard many shocking things in my life but that one has surpassed them all. How would the girl's mother behave with the man when she comes to visit her daughter? How would the man behave when his wife is not around and he finds himself alone with his mother-in-law?" she wondered.

"I don't know why that is troubling you so much. The three characters in that story are all adults and I think that they know what they are doing. Sentiments are now involved and I was told that love is blind. Perhaps that is the reason why the woman's daughter gave a deaf ear to what the young man's sister told her. I think understanding is what is needed in the relationship between those two young people. I don't think whatever they do with their lives should be making headline news," I said.

Rose was stunned by what was coming out of my mouth. She could not believe that the Santa village boy could say something really surprising.

"From the way you sound, it seems that kind of thing is pretty normal to you. Tell me something, if you were that young man, would you accept to marry the daughter of your former lover?" Rose asked.

That question caught me by surprise and for a minute or two, I did not know what to say. I realized that saying things for the sake of sustaining a conversation was one thing and living the real thing was quite another. I felt like I was the boy in the story and so many roads were ahead of me and I did not know which one to take. But I had to say something to safe my face and knew that whatever I said at that moment was going to define or add to the image she carried about me from then on.

"Let's not get into conditionality. I am not the guy in the story and any answer I give you now may not tie with the situation if it was real. Let's leave it at the level of the guy and allow him live his life," I said.

"Martin Smith, you are very tactful there and I'm really impressed. You have carefully avoided putting yourself in the situation just like all the smart men I know. I think you should go to Yaoundé and register in the faculty of political science. It will really fit you," she said.

I smiled uneasily knowing fully well what she was thinking when she asked that taunting question. I did not say anything else after that because I did not want our conversation tilting towards male and female relationships. I was uncomfortable with them given that I knew what she wanted from me.

Rose and I behaved like adults and things went back to normal between us. At least that was what I thought because her behaviour seemed to suggest that she had killed the feelings she had for me. Cordiality soon took the place of avoidance and suspicion much to my delight. That was to last until the third week of the month of September precisely on Saturday 19th. That was three days to the day I had to travel to Yaoundé. On that fateful Saturday, Mr Joel, Rose and I went to the shop in the morning. We were all there until 14:00 when he left the shop telling us that he had an important business to go and take care of somewhere out of town. He did not precise where that was. Rose and I were left in the shop and towards the time we had to close, he called to inform us that he was not going to be back before 17:30. Customers were no longer coming and it was obvious that other shop owners in the market were preparing to go home. Rose went into her father's office and I heard something fall. A little scream followed. I was afraid that she had hurt herself and rushed in there to see if I could give some assistance. She stood close to the door when I entered the office and was indeed crying. She had broken a clay vase that was on her father's table. It was not expensive but looked really beautiful. I thought that Rose was sorry for breaking it and that was why she was crying. I picked up the pieces and was about to get out of the office when she threw herself on me. I did not see how I would have pushed her away seeing that she needed to be comforted. I held the broken pieces of the clay vase in my left hand and let my right arm go round her shoulder. Her right arm went above my right shoulder while the left arm went below my left arm. I could not determine if it was accidental or intentional but she pushed the broken pieces I had in my left hand and they dropped to the ground. She gripped me tight and her lips were pressed against mine. I was over powered by the situation. I felt like I was on board a train on top speed without breaks and could do nothing to stop it. I felt the same heat that swept through me over a month earlier when she leaned on me and tried to caress my hand. But that second time in her father's office, the heat was more intense. A crash was eminent. What I had been resisting, fighting and avoiding finally happened. Guilt started eating me up as soon as we finished consuming the act. So many thoughts started coming to mind at the same time. But there was some packing to do and the checking of records as well. That served as a temporary distraction from the mental torment I was going through. Verbal communication between Rose and I did not cease as we wanted to continue behaving as adults. After the packing and checking of records, we locked the shop and headed for the main gate which led out of the market.

Once we were outside the market gate, Rose expected that I would stop a taxi for us to take home. I did not do that and started walking instead. I thought that she was going to board one and go home without me but she decided to follow me on foot. She knew that I was mad at her and tried to use the opportunity to talk some sense into me.

"For how long are you going to keep behaving like a spoilt naughty child?" she asked. "You should have known that what just happened in my father's office a while ago was bound to happen. It was just a matter of time. It has happened and there is nothing you or anybody else can do about it now."

"There you are right. Nothing from now on would change the fact that something has happened between us. But one thing is clear and it is that I will never forgive you for pushing me into this mess. Do you know the guilt I feel inside me now? Do you think I can ever raise my head with confidence and look into your father's eyes? What will I tell God when I see Him on judgment day? Do you know what you have done to me?" I asked.

"I have told you several times that the problem with you is that you spend your time worrying about how other people would feel and forget that you too have feelings. What happened back there was just something natural and it happened because I wanted it to happen. A woman always obtains what she wants. That is what I wanted and there is nothing wrong in obtaining it. So please, grow up and stop behaving like a child," she said.

I saw her like the devil in person in front of me with no conscience thinking of only herself. I thought of telling her something really hurting that she would never want to see me again. But what was the use? Was that going to wipe away what happened or the pain I felt inside me? I began to run out of words and frustration was taking hold of me. I did not know if I should curse or hate Rose. She kept telling me that I had to focus on the pleasure of the act and the guilt would disappear with time. She even suggested that we find more time to be together. That was what got me really angry.

"I don't know why I've allowed you to be walking next to me and listening to all that shit you are saying. You want me to find time to be with you to make a bad situation worse. Do you have a conscience?" I asked.

"What do you mean by conscience? As far as I know, you are the one who have to control your conscience and not the other way round. Besides, a conscience should not stop someone from having fun. If you are really feeling guilty and want to appease your conscience, then marry me. That will lessen your burden," she said.

I got more furious with her comments and considered that I had heard enough from her that day. I stopped a taxi and we both entered and headed home. When we entered the gate, I went to the main house and greeted Mr Joel's wife and other people in the house as I was fond of doing. I moved straight to my room after that.

14

Things were not easy as I entered my room and lay on my bed. The full weight of my action at the shop started weighing down heavily on my conscience. The church teachings on crime and punishment especially as far as adultery and fornication were concerned were making matters really worse. The pictures of hell especially for fornicators and adulterers scared me out of my skin. The framed picture of Christ on the wall in my room only increased my guilt. I got up, took it down and covered it on the table. Doing that did nothing to lessen my burden as I could still see the picture in my mind's eye where it hung with the eyes of Christ looking down on me with fury. I did not know what to do.

I soon got a knock on the door. When I opened, Rose stood outside.

"I've been sent to call you to come for supper," she said.

I told her that I was on my way and she went back without saying another word. It seemed she knew what I was going through and did not want to do anything that would provoke me. I moved to the main table where everybody was already seated. I took my seat but was unable to dish anything for myself. I lost all appetite and was not interested in anything. Mr Joel got worried and asked me if I was sick. I told him that I was ok but he suspected some intestinal worms for being behind my probable loss of appetite. I told him that I took drugs against intestinal worms regularly. He then asked me to at least drink some of the red wine that was on the table. I poured the first glass and emptied it in a flash. I did the same thing with the second and third glasses. I poured the fourth glass full and started drinking slowly. It was already taking control of my wits and I took more to get drunk completely so that I could at least drown my trouble for a while.

I woke up the next morning which was Sunday morning at exactly 06:50 and did not feel like going to church. I knew that I was going to see the effigies of Christ everywhere in church and that was going to increase my guilt. Besides, my crime was one that was hammered on most of the time in homilies. I did not want a situation where I would start feeling that the priest probably prepared his homily having me in mind. I decided to stay in my room to think of what to do to alleviate my pain and guilt.

Later in the afternoon I received a call from Mr Finley. He informed me that he had sent money to his friend to take care of my fees, lodging and feeding. He added that all was already set in Yaoundé and it was better for me to travel there so that I could acquaint myself with the environment. His intention for suggesting that I move to Yaoundé was for me to acclimatize with the place as fast as possible so that it would not disturb my studies. It was a good suggestion and I promised to travel the next day. I told Mr Joel of my planned trip later in the evening and he had no objection to it. He encouraged me to be hard working as usual and added that his door was always open for me. His kind words increased the burden on my conscience and I hated myself for betraying such a nice man like him. However, he went to his room and returned with the sum of 40:000 francs which he handed to me.

"Feel free to call me if you need anything there in Yaoundé. People like you need all the trust and assistance you can get," he said.

Unknown to him was the extent to which those kind words were piecing my heart. I wondered how he would have reacted if he found out or ever got to learn that I fidgeted with his daughter. I prayed that the unholy day should never come. I thanked him immensely and told him that God was going to reward him tenfold for his generosity and kind heartedness. With money in my hands and my room already paid for in Yaoundé, I wanted to get far away. I wanted to get away from Bamenda because I felt that my pain was going to subside if I was far away from the crime scene.

The next morning which was Monday, Mr Joel took me to Vatican Travel Agency at 06:45. I had to book for the first bus because I did not want to get to my destination at night. Yaoundé was a place I was not used to yet and it was therefore imprudent to venture there at night. I said goodbye to Mr Joel and he left for central town where he had to take care of business. I sat at the resting space in the Agency premises watching TV while waiting for 08:00 when the bus would start off.

At 08:05, the huge bus left the Agency for Yaoundé with 70 passengers on board. The fear of hell and the fear of an accident lingered in my mind. That fear made me stay alert and any pothole that the bus jumped into made my heart leap. The end was ever close and I was alert to prevent it from getting to me. I became scared more of the unknown and the thought that God was angry with me tormented me. I imagined that if the world were to end at that moment in the bus, I was definitely going to end in the bottom of hell. What was I to do? At that moment, I did not know.

We finally got to Yaoundé at 14:30. I called Mr Keith when the bus got to Vatican Travel Agency Yaoundé branch premises and he came and took me to the room he helped secure for me. He did not spend much time with me at the room as he had a date with Lillian. I had to unpack my things in the boxes I carried and set up the room the way I wanted it to be. When I was done with the setting, I lay on my bed and my conscience started pricking me again. I had thought that going away from Bamenda was going to make things better for me but I was wrong. I learnt the hard way then that problems of the mind followed the individual everywhere. I could not function properly with a tormented spirit and so, I resolved that it was time to open up to someone. The only person who came to my mind was Lillian. Mr Keith told me that he had a date with her and so, I waited some three hours after he left before ringing his girlfriend. She told me she had finished with him at the time I called and was on her way back to the neighbourhood. I asked her to come quickly because I had something very important to discuss with her.

At 17:50, I heard a knock on my door and I knew that it was Lillian. I immediately asked her to come in.

"Welcome to Yaoundé and welcome to a new life," she said falling into my open arms.

She wasted no time in asking what was very important that I wanted to discuss with her. I narrated my ordeal and instead of feeling sorry or sympathizing with my situation, she laughed at me. That reaction was exactly the kind I wasn't prepared to get. I became scared that she was going to x-ray me to her friends. What was I going to do if that was indeed her intention? I pleaded with her to stop joking because I was going through a lot of psychological torture. She looked at my face and realized that I was really troubled and needed her advice instead.

"I felt exactly the same way I did that act for the first time. It happened after some resistance and I hated myself for falling into that sin. What did I not think or imagine? I considered it the worst sin I've ever committed. I felt my head was going to explode at some point and decided to confide in a friend. Do you know what he told me?" she asked.

"Not until you tell me," I replied.

"He told me that I should do it as many times as possible. That way, it would become normal and I would stop seeing it as a sin. I did it and it worked. I think you should follow my example and free yourself of those guilty thoughts," she said.

"What happened to your conscience when you kept doing it many times?" I asked.

"Doing it many times would push the conscience to accept it as normal. You have to impose on your conscience and not your conscience imposing on you. You are feeling really terrible because you've allowed your conscience to be the judge of your actions," she said.

"I disagree with you. You have literally asked me to kill my conscience and I don't want to be a man with a dead conscience. People without consciences have no souls and do not care about the feelings of other people. I don't want to be like them. Besides, that conscience which you say is controlling me has kept me out of many troubles I would have gotten into," I said.

"But it didn't stop you from fornicating. Look, you asked for my advice and I've given you what I think is appropriate. What happened was a manifestation of the heart's and body's desires. I don't see why you should consider something so natural as sinful and go tormenting yourself over it," she said.

Logically, what she said made some sense and was very soothing to the ear as well as the conscience temporarily. I would have taken part of it but indulging in another love making act was definitely out of the question. It was possible to pick up an STD in the process and I did not think that was reasonable enough. Being sceptical about taking Lillian's advice meant that my pain was going to remain intact. With no solution in the immediate horizon, I resolved to leave everything to time as I always heard people say that time healed all wounds. Nevertheless, I thanked Lillian for her advice and she left me at 20:25 to go to her room which was just a stone throw from mine. She said that she was going to 'flash' my phone when food was ready. She did 25 minutes later and I rushed over to her room and we had supper. I returned to my room after eating and crashed into bed. The long journey had its toll on me and I badly needed rest.

At 21:45, I went to ease myself and saw some whitish and creamy substance coming out of my genital. I did not feel any pain or any pricking and felt that perhaps it was something normal that happened to any man who just knew a woman. I did not imagine even for a second that what came out would have been the sign of an illness. I just finished easing myself and went back to bed.

Back in my bed, finding sleep was not easy. Images of an intense burning fire and me in it agonizing, kept running through my head.

Those were the pictures of hell that were painted in my mind while I was still in primary school and attended doctrine classes. I became scared to sleep. What I could manage was sleep in snatches. However, that was not the only nightmare I had to face. At 03:15 the next morning, I started getting some pricking in my genital. It was not yet too painful and I lay in bed on my stomach and it subsided after a while. I got out of bed and went to ease myself but passing out urine became painful. I did not understand what was going on. I thought of calling Lillian to tell her of what I was experiencing but was ashamed to do it. I kept it to myself and hoped that with time, it would go away. I was even naïve to think that what was pricking me in my genital could be washed out if I drank a lot of water. So, I got a litre of water and emptied it into my stomach. At 07:15 I went and passed out urine normally. With things seemingly back to normal, I thought that what was in my genital had been flushed out.

At 08:00, I got a call from Lillian to come for breakfast. I rushed to her room and had a cup of tea with some bread. We sat and chatted for a while about Santa and the kind of things that still happened there. I soon felt like easing myself again and decided to run to my room instead of using Lillian's toilet. I did not want that if some pains had to be involved, I should be groaning in her presence. So, I got out of her room and rushed back to mine where I went to the water system toilet to ease myself. Passing out urine became the hardest thing ever. I felt like the urine suddenly turned into razor blades or pieces of broken bottles which I had to pass out. When I finally did it, the pain subsided. I resolved not to take liquids of any sort and dreaded the moment I was going to pass out urine. With the pain temporally gone, I decided to go and discover new places in central town. Where I ended for the day was at the central post office. I did not get a taxi to go back to the student residential area but preferred trekking.

I managed to get in front of paradise hotel and there, the pain became unbearable. I was moving like a pregnant woman in severe labour pains. There was a lot of traffic congestion where I was. There was a lot of hooting too but one from behind me was really outstanding. I turned to see why the car was hooting with a lot of insistence. The person on the steering wheel waved at me and called me by name. I waited on the spot where I was until he could actually get to me. Moving a step became a whole lot of trouble as the pain in me showed no signs of diminishing. The person finally got to where I was and I saw that it was Henry Miles, my secondary school classmate. The government launched a campaign encouraging young boys and girls above the age of 17 to join the army while we were in the third year in secondary school. He was 18 and considered himself too old to be in the same class with some of us who were terribly young. He saw the army as the only way to get away from the 'humiliation' and decided to try his luck. He was finally selected and sent to the military training school. He did his training but went further. He did medicine though he was not yet through with his training the moment he met me. The pain in me was so intense that it could be read on my face. He was the only one in the Toyota Carina 2 he drove and I got in and sat on the passenger seat next to him. He was really happy to see me after a very long time. Unfortunately, I could not show the same enthusiasm because something else was terribly wrong with me. I apologized for being cold. He was a smart guy and could notice when things were not going right. He asked me what was wrong and I narrated my misadventure starting with the incident with Rose to the releasing of the whitish and creamy discharges. I supposed he knew exactly what it was as he did not ask any further questions about it. The only thing he told me was that all was going to be ok soon. The snail pace at which we were moving felt like eternity and it made me angry as that was an indication that my pain was going to last longer.

We soon got to Obili Round about and the traffic became fluid. I asked him if he was taking me to the hospital and he said no. He was taking me to his house in the Biyem Assi Neighbourhood. We soon got there and he took me to his guest room. There he left me and shut the door behind him as he went out. He returned almost immediately with two syringes. There was a liquid in each of them. He injected them in my waist, one on the left and the other on the right. Both legs paralyzed for some 45 minutes before getting back to normal again. I remained seated for the three hours that I was in his guest room. I could feel the pain going away as the liquid injected in me started taking effect. He gave me some tablets which I had to take for some days.

When he was certain that I was much better, he sat next to me and then burst into laughter. I was taken aback by such a reaction and asked him if he was alright. He stopped laughing and told me that what was amusing him was the look on my face at the time he found me.

"You looked like someone who was in the middle of something with a terrible stench. Have you ever heard of sexually transmitted diseases?" he asked.

"Yes," I replied. "I know of HIV-Aids, syphilis and gonorrhoea.

"Well, you are suffering from one of them and it is gonorrhoea. I think you are very lucky that it is not HIV which has no cure yet. You should take it as a second chance given to you by life. Many have not been so lucky. I would give you a full packet of condoms which you could carry on you everywhere you go," he said.

"You would give me condoms? I don't think I'm going to need them because I wouldn't want to have anything to do with women," I said.

"That is the problem. Did you plan to journey into the lady who donated that illness to you? It happened during a brief moment of weakness and you became really powerless. Those moments of weakness are very frequent especially when sexual feelings are involved. The body and emotions are very unpredictable and if you do not want to pick an illness worse than that one, you better be on your guard. You have tested it already and there is no way you can claim that you would stay away from women. They might be the ones coming to you and you must be prepared for anything. So, never say that you would never have anything to do with a woman. You know a woman and it has recorded at the back of your mind. Each time you will see a woman, you will imagine what it would be like having and feeling her especially if she is beautiful. That is what all this shit about love and friendship or relationship is all about. You have gotten to the stage and your body can respond to the stimulus. So, 'Never' has to disappear from your vocabulary because some of the things happen and you let them happen without being able to do anything. Listen, I learnt in one of our psychology lessons that life is in stages and any stage you miss or skip over, you would always go back to it," he said.

"Are you telling me that what I am going through is one of the stages?" I asked.

"Picking up an illness? No....your heart desired what happened and that is why it happened. Up in your mind, you want it but you are using reason to suppress it. You should really not be doing that. If you let it waste away and you get to the next stage, you would one day come back to it," he explained.

"All what you are saying about skipping a stage and coming back to it later does not make any sense to me. Are you saying that if I get married later which is a different stage after skipping this one you have just talked about, I would one day come back to it? What about adultery there?

"That is the religious side of it and it is behind the suppression of those feelings which your heart and body wish to be expressed. But psychology has its own reasons. Let me give you an example. You must have heard or known some men who have been married for about 20, 30, or 40 years and on some good day, the man packs out of his house and goes to spend some time with a younger girl perhaps in a student residential area like the one you live in. Good enough, you are here in Yaoundé and you would soon witness it. The man might spend about 2, 3 or 4 years with the fresh catch and on another good day, he would pack his things and move back into his matrimonial home. A man who behaves like that possibly suppressed one stage of his life and had to go back to it. Once that is done, they become psychologically satisfied and they can move back to their matrimonial homes complete and happy," he said.

I was mesmerized by all the explanations my friend gave on psychology. I believed in life after death and there was something I had to face after living this world. I would have used his explanations to sooth the pain in my conscience but it wouldn't have taken away the fact that I had to make amends with heaven. It was the beginning and the last place I could turn to and I could not hide under some justifications in psychology to avoid the reality. Though the explanations of my friend were sound and convincing, I told him that I had heard enough for that day. I really wanted us to change the topic and talk about different things. He asked me to go with him to his sitting room so that he could introduce me to his wife and four years old daughter. I was surprise to learn about that and he could read it on my face.

"Our people say that he who sleeps early wakes up early. When you have something doing, there is no need wasting time to get married. I have something doing and the best way I can spend the money I earn is on my family," he said.

I appreciated him for that and told him that I was going to follow his example. That prompted him to ask me how I was going to follow his example if I did not want to have anything to do with women. I smiled and he went ahead to tell me that his explanations were correct since I spoke of copying his example unconsciously. I just asked him to drop it and we left the guest room to go and see his family.

He had a pretty wife who was heavily pregnant and his daughter was pretty too. I dreamed and wished for a few seconds I had a family of my own. But there was something that was immediate and it was my university education. We had supper and I had to go back to my room. My friend gave me a packet of condoms as he promised and I took them. I had to accept the fact that I was human and could fall. He asked me to call him and come to the house always. That was because we were all far from our home town and there was need for us to take care as well as support one another.

I got back to my room at 21:00 and tried to find some sleep as I already ate at the house of my friend Henry. Psychologically, I was ok but my spirit was still restless. The images of a burning fire kept haunting me. With a few days left to the commencement of classes, a tormented spirit was not what I needed to start off. I had to do something about it. I decided that same night that I was going to go for morning mass the next day and meet a priest soon after.

15

On Thursday September 24th, I got out of bed at 05:15. The mass was to begin at 06:00 and I was thinking of what I was going to tell the priest. I wondered how it would be like when I entered the church and saw the pictures of Christ on the walls. The guilt I felt on the day of the mistake was definitely going to come back. I pictured the cross on the alter crashing to the ground as soon as I stepped into the church. That was frightening and I began to ask myself if it was a good idea going there in the first place. I had to convince myself that what I pictured in my mind was never going to happen. There was no pain more painful than a psychological one.

I got to the church gate at 05:50 and saw many Christians streaming into church. Most of them were hurrying and I wondered whether any of them had problems as burdensome as mine. I admired some of them who exchanged smiles and glances. They looked as though they were problems free and I wished I was like them. I entered the church and did not have the courage to take up my head and look at the crucifix that was on the alter. I also avoided looking at the walls to see the different pictures that hung showing Christ on the different stages that led to his crucifixion. I did not really participate in the mass as I kept imagining a voice calling me a hypocrite who deserved to be in hell. I thought I was going insane and wished for the mass to come to an end quickly.

The mass ended some 45 minutes after it started and the Christians began leaving the church. A few of them remained behind just like me. They had one or two things to discuss with the priest. I allowed everyone to finish with him before I went to him.

"What can I do for you my son?" he asked.

"Father, I don't know if I did the right thing coming here because I doubt if God is going to forgive me," I said.

"You must not say that. Every child who has gone astray and has rediscovered his or herself is always welcome in the house of God. I'm sure you know the story of the prodigal son in the holy book. God does not turn any child away who wants to come back home. What is it that you did which you think God cannot forgive you?" he asked.

I narrated everything that happened in the shop of Mr Joel with his daughter. I stopped at some stages because I was ashamed of uttering some words which I considered obscene. He assisted me by filling in some of the gaps. He asked me how I felt from the day it happened. I told him that at that moment we spoke, I was losing faith in life because I had it in my head that God had his back on me. I added that ever since it happened, my life had been a complete nightmare. I even told him of the crazy things I imagined before making up my mind to come and see him. When I was through, it was his turn to give me some advice.

"In the profession of faith, you make mention of your belief in forgiveness. Were you really saying it sincerely or you were merely reciting it because others were doing it? You committed a sin but you have realized and admitted that you committed a sin. That is what God our master wants. He is happy when his children realize their mistakes and make up their minds not to commit the sins again. He forgives you before you come to ask for one. God has forgiven you already. You are still feeling terrible because you have not been able to forgive yourself. Those who cannot forgive themselves cannot move forward. God has forgiven you and it is your turn to forgive yourself. It is only after forgiving yourself that you would find a peace of mind and spirit," he said.

I left the church premises that morning feeling light like a cotton seed that could be carried by the wind. I felt I could touch the sky as I walked back to my room. But I still had one preoccupation and it was Rose. I had to inform her that she was carrying a disease and needed treatment. How to proceed was my main problem and I was sure that she was not going to believe what I was going to tell her. But someway somehow, I had to do it. It was my moral duty to do so. So I got my mobile phone and rang her. It rang on end for the first time with no response. I rang again and she picked up the receiver.

"Have you realized that I am the woman of your dreams," she asked.

I accepted just for the sake of doing so and told her that our relationship could be a wonderful one if she went and did some clean up. Very excited, she told me she could pluck the moon for me so long as I was prepared to be her man. It was then I told her that I was receiving treatment for gonorrhoea. She remained silent for a while that I thought she had hung up. What I had previously imagined about her behaviour did not happen. She was very sober and receptive and promised to go to the hospital. I first of all thanked her for listening to me before telling her that going to the hospital was the wisest thing to do. Things went back to normal and I became whole again. I limited myself to school, bookwork, church and my room. I went out to have fun very rarely because I did not want to fail a course and be compelled to rewrite it again. Besides, I did not know how Mr Finley was going to take it if at all it ever happened. All the same, I had to do everything to avoid such a situation.

That notwithstanding, on the first weekend in the month of November, I went to pay a visit to my friend Henry Miles. It was a Sunday and he decided that we go out to town to Briketerie, a popular neighbourhood in Yaoundé. We got there at 15:00 and he drove to Hotel Kassam. It was a four Star hotel which looked very magnificent at least from the outside. I asked him why we were there and he said that he wanted to show me something. He pointed to some young boys and girls who were in front of the hotel. The youngest there must have been about 13 years old. I asked him what he thought they were doing there.

"Have you seen that little girl in a red gown?" he asked.

"Yes," I said.

"She is carrying a little tray on her head. You can see some oranges in it but let me tell you that she is selling more than those oranges. She is selling herself as well. I really admire her because she is the most honest person on the surface of this earth. She has chosen to be a tart and she is not hiding it. She is better than most of those your female university mates. They are disguising as students but in reality, they are professional wenches. How can you explain the fact that a girl comes from a very poor home and she is not working anywhere or doing anything here but is living in a room which cost 20, 30, 40 and sometimes 50.000 francs a month? They sleep with these big men and the sad thing is that some of the men are old enough to be their fathers. That explains why the rate of HIV infections among university students, especially girls is too high. Even some of the married women who come there for studies behave even worse. Cases if infidelity would be very frequent in that student residential area where you live. If you walk up to that little girl, she would ask you if you want oranges or if you want her. She is not ashamed of it and that is the greatest honesty I have ever seen. Most of those women you would find along the roadsides roasting fish or maize are not just selling that. They are selling themselves too. That is why you will always find them with assistants. When it is their bodies that the customer negotiates for, they hand over the roasting to those assistants. I will show you something on our way back. Men are not left out. You would see young men as those ones there going to sleep with very old women in order to get paid. This is Yaoundé and you will have to learn of the kind of things that go on here. I'm telling you all this because if you go flirting with any of your school mates, know that she might not have you alone and you can expect to pick up a sexually transmitted disease worse than the one you brought from Bamenda," he said.

I did not agree with the context in which he used the term 'honesty' in reference to the young girl and decided to make my point.

"Honesty is a virtue but I don't think that honesty should be what we should be attributing to that young girl. She is just about 13 and self-destruction is what I will use to describe her actions. The government has put in place a whole ministry of Social Affairs. Are they not supposed to take such young girls off the streets and protect those that are vulnerable from ending up there?" I asked.

"Ah the government. That is a bunch of confused, greedy and selfish group of persons. What would any of them benefit from taking that young girl off the street? Nothing. And so, there is no reason for them to do that. All they are interested in is benefiting from the advantages of being in government," he said with a sigh.

"If the government cannot take care of those vulnerable ones, the church is supposed to pressure it to do it or take up the responsibility entirely. At least when the men of God get together and take a stand, the government trembles. If the church can will such power, it should also exercise it by taking care of those young girls who are being exploited sexually, right?" I asked.

"Smith, you give me the impression that village you grew up in completely cut you from the rest of the world. Don't you listen to the radio? The church today is running neck to neck with the government as far as exploitation is concerned. The church is today a business enterprise. New ones in the name of Pentecostals keep cropping up every day and they are owned by individuals or family members. In other words they are family businesses. The leaders of such churches tax their followers and use the money to build luxurious houses for themselves and buy the latest and expensive cars you can think of. Do you know that some of them prescribe what their followers should bring for harvest thanks giving? The church is now in all spheres of social life. They have opened primary schools, secondary schools, high schools and universities. Of that whole lot, only their primary schools are at the reach of the underprivileged. Their secondary schools, high schools and universities are meant for the children of the rich. The fees have gone up to half a million. How many people who are not business men, bankers, high ranking civil servants can afford such an amount? Yet their teachers are the worst paid even though they work like slaves. They are paid menial salaries and the church imposes contributions and still curtail the very little it pays them. The poor things are condemned to be there because they have nowhere else to go. When it is time to construct such schools, the church imposes levies on its Christians and once they are opened, only the children of the rich can go there. I used to think that the norm in every society is to take from the rich or those who at least have enough to help the poor. But the church is changing that rule by taking from the poor and adding to what the rich already have. They are into medicine but I must admit that their drugs are at least affordable for now. Their prices are going up too and with time the poor would be side-lined from mission hospitals just as they have been side-lined from mission schools. They are not only into modern medicine. They are getting into traditional medicine too. You would imagine that after getting into schools and hospitals, the church would stop charging amounts from its Christians. They have come with the formation of what they now call small Christian communities. Every member of the church must belong to one. If you are not a member and something like death happens to you or your family member, the priest would refuse to come or do any other thing. They have instituted something they call Christian Contribution Cards. You have to contribute and the card marked every year. I have no problem with that but the churches use such contributions as a bargain before they do anything for you, your child or family member. Just take for example that you want to baptize your new born baby. You would have to go through the Small Christian community group to which you belong. They would ask you to bring your church contribution card and they would go

144

through their records to make sure that you have paid all contributions. If all have not been paid and until you pay, your child would not be baptized. That is why I say that the church has become a business enterprise. What has that poor new born baby done to be denied baptism? I get really angry sometimes when the church is mentioned. Is there any benefit in saving that child from sexual exploitation? Very recently the church has been the one exploiting young children like that one there. If you have been listening to the radio lately, you would have heard of the sexual abuse of young boys and girls in countries like the United States of America, Ireland, and Germany. The worse thing is that the church had engaged in a policy of cover-up for so long. I don't believe in the church anymore. They are supposed to be on the side of the disadvantaged and the vulnerable but they are not. It is instead perpetrating criminal acts against them. All the church is today interested in, is making money. So, please don't mention the church again," he warned.

"You seem to be forgetting that those who manage the church are human beings and not angels. If they have decided to allow pleasure from material things to over shadow their spiritual consciousness, then it is rather unfortunate. 'Do what I say and not what I do' is a common statement I hear in that student residential area. They use it in a variety of contexts and the church context can as well fit in it. By the way, I am tempted to believe that you no longer go to church judging from the way you criticize the church," I said.

"Yes, you have guessed rightly. I don't go there anymore. It is because of what the conventional churches are doing today that mushroom ones keep cropping up every day. Why should I be mingling with people who preach virtue and practice vice?" he asked.

"Well, I think you are making a mistake there. It seems you are going to church not for your own salvation but for those you criticize. If I were you, I would go there to get the preaching and use it to better my life than watching what they are doing," I said.

"Well, that is the way you see it but I don't see it that way. People are supposed, especially those who claim to be church leaders, to live by example. Besides, the church must not be that building where people go and gather. My church is in my heart," he said.

"Well, what else can I say? One thing is certain though and it is that only God knows who serves him truly," I said.

My friend shook my hand for saying that but went back to what young girls did in Yaoundé in the name of fighting for survival. He narrated a story of a particular case he knew.

"There is a young 23 years old lady living close to my house and she is in year two in that your university," he began. Her name is Nathalie and she was dating an official in the ministry of health. The guy is rich and he flashes her with a lot of cash. The hostel she lives in is one of the most expensive in the whole of our neighbourhood. She uses her body to compensate the man for his financial generosity. He uses her the way he likes both 'in front and back'. Her backside has been broken and the man does not want her anymore. She is now wondering what she is going to do as she was the one who took a group of friends out, lived in one of the most expensive hostels, worshipped around the neighbourhood and made a lot of noise among her friends. With the man pushing her aside, she is now unable to meet up with the high standard of life and has gone to the extent of visiting a witch doctor to get charm to get the man back. Unfortunately for her, the witch doctor informed her that she was not the only one the man was dating. Frustration has set in and shame cannot allow her think of taking the next step to the next stage. Instead of going and getting a room that befits her status, she is borrowing money from here and there to maintain the standards. That is the trap most of them come and get themselves into and end up frustrated. Be careful with those you mingle with. That is my only advice to you. The beautiful nature of the city could be very misleading. It is rotten right to the core."

We went to a bar not far from the hotel and emptied a few bottles before jumping into the car to begin the trip back. My friend kept his promise to show me something on our way back. We took the road that passed in front of the University of Yaoundé Teaching Hospital leading to Obili Round About. On both sides of the road were drinking spots almost every ten meters and in front of each drinking spot was a woman or young lady selling roasted fish. We stopped in front of one of them and my friend asked me to go out and observe one of the ladies roasting fish and ask the different prices she sold her fish. I got out of the car and a lady who must have been in her early 30s started beckoning at me saying that she was going to give me fish at a very good price. I could see six fishes already roasted in front of her and the prices she gave ranged from 400 francs to 1200 francs. But she added that there was a special one which cost 2000 francs and when she pronounced '2000 francs' she pointed at a key strapped on her left index finger. I told her that I was going to ask my friend in the car if he'd love to eat fish so that I could buy for both of us at once. With those words I returned to the car where my friend remained patiently waiting.

Once I entered the car and locked the door, my friend told me that I did not need to narrate anything to him because he had been watching everything.

"She pointed at a key and talked of a special fish whose price was more than those of all the fish in front of her. That special fish is eaten in the room and you can now understand what I told you about them selling not just fish but also themselves. That is Yaoundé and it's a hard reality," he said.

He drove me back to my neighbourhood after that demonstration. I wondered if all the big cities in the world were the same as Yaoundé as I lay on my bed. I also doubted if I was ever going to have anything to do with any woman especially one who was at the university as myself. Only time alone was going to tell.

147

My thoughts soon went back to my younger ones as well as the attitude of my heartless father towards them. They were growing up and my father was growing old. I wondered if he was going to abandon his old ways as he grew older. If that was the case, what attitude were my siblings going to adopt? Was any of them going to be hard hearted as a result of his actions? Some people sometimes made families and destroyed them with their own hands. I think that was the case of my father. Whether such destruction is carried out intentionally or not, is a different story.

I was soon interrupted in my thoughts by Lillian who came in and asked where I had been all day. I told her that I went out with Henry and also told her where we went and what we talked about. She was uncomfortable as I repeated my friend's ideas on the prostitution of young girls to get money from men old enough to be their fathers. She wanted us to change the topic and asked what I had eaten all day. I told her that I had drunk a few bottles of beer. She became furious that I went taking alcohol on an empty stomach.

"If you were still a child, I would have taken you out and given you some lashes," she said.

That sounded funny to me as I did not know how I would react if someone picked up a cane to use on me then. I had not been beaten in a pretty long time and the mention of giving me lashes brought back memories of my father's furious face. A flash of anger swept through me and I imagined what I would do with him if one day he dared try to use a cane on me again. I did not want the image of my father destroying my day and I digressed by asking Lillian how her day was. Her response was that she had a nice time with Mr Keith but had a story to tell.

"You missed something here today," she began. "There is this woman called Madam Stephanie who lives in the third room closed to mine. I'm sure you know that she is married. She had the surprise of her life today. Her husband left Bamenda and bought so many nice things which he loaded his car with to come and surprise her. He got here and heard music booming in his wife's room. He knocked on the door and the voice of his wife inside the room kept asking who it was and he was not saying anything. He wanted her to come out and get the wonderful surprises he had for her. With no response coming from outside, the knocking soon began to irritate her. She opened the door in anger perhaps armed with some insults to rain on whoever was outside her door. And behold, there was her husband in front of her and she had just a loin cloth tied slightly over her breast. There was a man lying on her bed with only his sleeping pant on. Gripped by panic and guilt, she shut the door again and would not open it. But her husband had already seen everything and the hand writing on the wall became very clear. The man of about 45 or so burst out crying like a child. You can imagine what followed."

"I cannot imagine anything. Just tell me what happened," I said.

"Students love scandals and they are always ready to unmask those involved. Those who live around there heard Madam Stephanie's husband crying and came to find out what the matter was. He only sat outside his wife's door and was crying. Some of them guessed what it was and rightly too and threatened to pull down the door if it was not opened. Knowing that things could be worse if the door was knocked down, it was the man inside who opened it and was gripped by the boys who were outside. They made him to lie on his stomach and the people who had assembled there jeered and called him all sorts of negative names. Her husband soon stopped crying and asked his wife if what he saw there today was part of the master's degree program she left him and the children to come and study. I felt really sorry for him and did not want to just imagine myself in his position," she said.

"What happened at the end of it all?" I asked.

"He just left and asked some of the students there to accompany him to his car. I think he went and gave them all what he had brought for his wife. He had every reason to break down and cry. He bought things and drove all the way from Bamenda only to come and see that his wife was getting more than just master's degree lessons," she said.

I asked her if she thought the man was going to forgive his wife.

"When it comes to forgiveness, especially in matters of infidelity, women easily do that and not men. Men always claim that women have more jealousy in them but the reverse is true. The chances of him forgiving his wife's infidelity would be between 5 and 8%. But, from the way I saw him leave, forgiving his wife would be impossible," she replied.

I recalled entirely what my friend, Henry, told me earlier that day. I anticipated that I was going to start experiencing what he said much later but I was shocked to start getting such stories just a few hours after he told me. That notwithstanding, most of the things Henry talked to me about came to pass. There were scandals of lecturers sleeping with female students and in exchange gave them marks, rumours of some female married lecturers dating their male colleagues as well as some much younger male students, incidents of some students organizing themselves into a gang and recruiting some men in uniform to assist them rob innocent citizens, rape, incest, prostitution with push factor being poverty or pride, the list was really long. But the most frequent stories were those of young female graduates being forced by employers to trade their bodies for job opportunities. Young male graduates were not also left out. They were forced to practice homosexuality and in exchange they would get job opportunities or obtain visas to travel abroad where working conditions and pay packages were believed to be much better. With all those stories, I began to wonder how my life would be like once I obtained the BA Degree.

16

I began to see Yaoundé differently from what I imagined it to be before I got there. Some lousy critics referred to some parts of the city especially the student residential area as Sodom and Gomorra, already too ripe for destruction. The comments of my friend Henry really had an impact on me. The sad incident with Rose, the horrible stories I heard about university girls as well as the open scandals I personally witnessed and the fear of being infected kept me far away from girls. I had just a few of them in the university and the learning ground was our only meeting place. If any of them insisted on coming to my room, I made sure that I invited Lillian or a neighbour or any other friend to come over. I feared staying alone with a lady as the risk of falling into temptation became greater. For the three years I spent in Yaoundé, that was the way I fashioned my life in order to stay out of trouble.

The only serious incident that happened and involved me directly was when Mr Keith came to the university campus to see Lillian and met us together. It was at the start of the second semester in year two. He called me to one corner and handed my pocket allowance for the next two months. I went in for the next lesson of the day which was common Wealth literature with it. We were more than 450 students in that particular class. Many students on campus referred to it as the Chinese parliament. It was too tight and pick-pickets took advantage of it to carry out robbery. I was a victim that particular day. I stood at the back with many other students and had to struggle to copy notes standing. Since everybody around me was seemingly struggling to listen to lectures and take down notes, I least suspected that pick pockets could be among. Those of us who were taking notes standing were happy when the lesson ended after two hours. We were the first to get out of the lecture hall and it was one of my female classmates, Juliana, who alerted me that my trouser was torn behind. I touched my back pocket and all the money Mr Keith gave me was gone. The pick pockets used something like a razor blade and tore off a patch and it was through the hole they created that the money was taken out. At first, I was mesmerized by the tact with which the pick pockets did it without me feeling anything. I imagined that they really merited a trophy for their professional act. But that soon gave way to worry. I did not want to call Mr Keith to inform him of what had happened. If I did, he would have informed his friend and I did not know how he would have reacted. If I did not want to tell Mr Keith, there was no need telling Lillian.

How I was going to cope for two months became a real headache. Lillian always wanted me to come to her room for breakfast, lunch and supper. I did not like that and she realized it. So, she either came and got me or sent food for me. But that was not supposed to take away my need for money. I occasionally did some cooking and invited Lillian and other friends to come and eat. Immediate neighbours did the same thing and when there was no sort of pay back for such good gestures, gossips took over and no student wanted to be confronted with such a situation. I managed for the first month without money and could not go through the second. For that reason, on the first weekend of the first week of the second month in the second semester, I opened up to Jackson, one of my male friends. He too was not doing well financially because he came from a poor home. He told me that he had his way of making money and if I was interested, he would introduce me to it. I told him that I needed money and was ready to do anything to have it.

"Do anything?" he asked.

I said yes and he said that he was going to take me to Black Star Hotel, situated on the Northern part of the city of Yaoundé. Anyone coming from Bamenda entered Yaoundé through that northern part. We had the conversation in the morning and agreed to move to the hotel at 14:00. I waited for that time to come with a lot of anxiety as I was eager to get out of my financial woe.

We did leave our student residential area at 13:20 and covered some distance on foot before boarding a taxi. We got to the hotel at 14:20. The hotel was a four star hotel and situated just some 500 meters from the major high way. We walked into the hotel premises and went close to the large swimming pool which was directly in front of the hotel building. We saw foreigners who were probably tourists or business men and women and a good number of rich nationals and their kids swimming in the pool. There were a good number of others who sat basking in the afternoon sun by the sides of the pool. There was a guard who made sure that people who were shabbily dressed did not get too close to the swimming pool. Jackson and I were neatly dressed and had no problem getting passed the guard. We stood a few meters from the pool after passing the guard. There were a good number of boys where we stood. I asked my friend what we were doing out there and he said that we had to wait for someone who would come out of the hotel and if we were lucky, he or she would pick one of us to go and do some work. I thought he was referring to work like mopping the floor, washing of plates in the hotel kitchen or washing of sheets used on hotel beds. I asked how much the employer would pay after the work was done.

"15.000 Francs and if he or she is pleased with your work, you could get 25.000 francs," my friend replied.

"And is the 15000 or 25000 payment for one day's work or a whole month?" I asked.

"The money will be for the short time you will work now if someone comes and hire you," he replied.

I could not believe it but soon became sceptical as even the 15.000 francs was too much for just a few minutes or hours of work. What even made me more sceptical was the kind of job I believed was offered. I considered that anyone paying that kind of amount for just cleaning around or washing dishes certainly had too much money to throw away. But the fact that tourists and rich people brought in a lot of money to the place made me accept it. But I still had to see before I could believe.

A woman soon emerged from the main door of the hotel and started heading to where my friend, myself and a group of other boys stood. She was fair in complexion with a broad round face. She also had big breasts and they covered her whole chest. To me, they were too much for her alone. She was really fat and a lot of flesh could be seen in the pink blouse she wore. It seemed my friend knew her personally as he started walking towards her as she approached. I followed my friend and greeted the lady after my friend did.

"Who is this charming young man that has accompanied you today?" she asked.

"It is my friend. His name is Smith….Martin Smith," my friend responded.

"Is he interested in having some pocket money?" the lady asked.

"Yes," my friend responded.

"In that case, I would like to go and give him some work to see how best he can do it," she said and made a U-turn.

My friend urged me to follow her and I eagerly did. I felt that perhaps she was the owner of the hotel and wanted to help young men and women like me. I followed her to the lift of the hotel and she pressed button number 5. We got to the 5th floor in a flash and she took me to her room. One curious thing she did was to key the door once I got in but she did not take out the key. She then moved to the bathroom while I remained in the room. I observed the room and did not see any work I could do as everything appeared to have been in their right places. I started getting worried and moved to the door where I unlocked it without it making any sound but remained in the room. I wanted to see the kind of work she was going to come and give me.

She soon got out of the toilet tying only a towel. I asked her where the dishes or clothes were that I was supposed to wash. She said that what I asked for was too much hard work and that what she wanted me to do was very simple. She did not allow me to ask another question but asked me to sit on the bed and to make myself comfortable. I told her that I was already comfortable where I stood. I asked her to give me the work she had for me so that I could do it fast and get back home. She was surprise and asked if my friend did not brief me on the kind of work I had to come and do. I told her that he did not and she smiled and told me that she was going to tell me.

"The work you have to do is on me," she said.

"What do you mean? That I'm going to massage you?" I asked.

"That is just one of it. You also have to caress, kiss and make me feel like a woman," she said.

Looking at her with all the hanging flesh all over her body with her laps as thick as those of an elephant, the blood in me ran cold. For a second or two I imagined Rose in front of me but the only difference was that the sizes were a complete mismatch. Without thinking I ran out of the room. I did not go to the lift but decided to use the stairs. I ran from the 5th floor to the second floor. Anybody who saw me at that moment would have imagined that a ghost was after me. I started descending to the first floor but all of a sudden decided to stop. I asked myself why I was running when the woman was not in a position to hurt me physically. I decided to go back. I did not know why I was going back but I was going all the same.

Once I got back to the door of her room, I hesitated before knocking. It was as though she knew I was going to come back and asked me to come in. She sat on the bed and tears were streaming down her cheeks. I got in but left the door only half closed and did not go more than a meter from it. She kept staring at the floor and did not raise her head to look at me.

"The fact that you have come back shows that you really have a heart," she said. "The way you reacted reminded me of the rejection I suffer day in day out ever since I started ballooning out of proportion. I was married and had few years of happiness before sadness set in with this size I now have. I am not proud of what I am doing. People come close to me only for money or to have a conversation. But when it comes to making me feel like a woman, they consider me too beefy and unattractive. I like to have a man of my own who would always be there for me and make me feel like a woman. I want to feel wanted. But since no body feels attracted to me because of my size, I am forced to pay for the attention I get."

"What happened to the man you got married to?" I asked.

"He is in Dubai presently to buy his business goods. He comes and goes. I started getting fat after the birth of our second child more especially I was not doing anything. There were people to do everything I wanted. So, with no activity, I started putting on weight and he warned me he was going to leave me if I don't watch my weight. I started doing everything to cut down but all my efforts went in vain. It seemed the size increased by the day and he did what he warned me he would do. That is where we are now," she said.

I felt really heart broken by the words that fell from her lips that for a moment I lacked words to tell her that could really ease her pain. Everybody needs someone and everybody needs attention. Could I really blame her for 'buying attention' as she put it? And why was she buying attention not from men older than herself but from young boys? Well, it was not my place to judge her or question how she went about her sexual life. What she needed was a way out of her predicament and not pity. With that thought running through my mind, I found words at last.

"If the man you got married to left you, where do you get the money to throw on young boys?" I asked.

"My ex-husband is not a heartless man. He is rich and he opened a bank account for me with a lot of money in it. He puts money in it every three months. Don't ask me how much is in the account. I have registered in a gym and have been going there for the past two years. Nothing has changed. I was told by the doctor that the gene was inherited but cutting down was not impossible. I had hoped that

156

the gym and drugs were going to help me but I was wrong. I have lost shape and everybody is running away from me. I am buying attention out of desperation. What would you do in my place?" she asked.

I did not want to imagine myself in her place and carefully avoided the question. I gave her a proposal instead.

"If you have money, why don't you travel to any of the European countries and let them take care of that fat? They have all the instruments or machines that could help you. On the other hand, if you do not want to go there, you could enquire and order them from here. I have seen some of the machines that are designed in the form of belts. With those ones you just need to buckle them just as you do with any normal belt on any part of your body and they would help to drain the fat in you," I said.

"What you've said has never crossed my mind, I must say. I will try to travel out and also buy the machine you have talked of," she said.

"I think that is the wisest thing to do. I think it is better to take care of yourself and the attention you need will come to you with no effort instead of thinking that you could buy it with money. For how long would you do it?" I asked.

"Thank you for taking the courage to come back. I now know I have been using the wrong methods to help myself. How can I thank you?" she asked.

I told her that 'a thank you' was enough. I wanted to leave but she stopped me and went to the right bedside cupboard and pulled out some bank notes. She extended them to me but I was hesitant and did not want to take them. She insisted and told me that money was not her problem and added that she was not wasting the 40.000 francs she was offering me. I took it and dashed out of her room. At least she was smiling as I was leaving her and not in tears as I ran out the first time. I gave her a vital proposal which was going to benefit her. Perhaps that was the reason why I went back.

Once I was out of the hotel building, I felt some anger building in me. I could not actually believe that my friend took me to that hotel to prostitute myself for money. I was bent on him having a piece of me. I spotted him by the swimming pool as I got out of the hotel building and went to confront him. He started smiling as soon as he saw me without knowing what I was about to do to him.

"You have taken too long in there my friend. I'm sure she was very pleased with your work though you had to enjoy yourself too," he said smiling.

I was not at all amused and landed a punch on his chest which sent him into the swimming pool. Some people who were around the pool started cheering while some tourists who had their children in the pool jumped in to take them out. My friend was very surprised by my act but I'm sure he understood why I punched him.

"I thought you said that you were prepared to do anything," he said from within the pool.

"Anything does not mean doing that kind of a job you piece of shit!!! I did not do the job and so you can go and do it in my place. You should be really ashamed of yourself. I don't know why I ever met you in my life. You are disgusting," I said and left.

I hated my friend for seeking the easiest way out of his financial difficulties. Sleeping with a woman old enough to be his mother was the most disheartening part of it. I stopped seeing him from that Saturday afternoon and never talked about the incident to anybody. We met and greeted casually like two total strangers. I found no need telling Lillian of it since I had money without trading myself. However, for the three years I spent in Yaoundé, that was the most disgusting incident in which I was directly involved. I tried to forget it and move on with my life as much as possible. I visited Henry and he visited me too. Lillian and Henry were my only friends. I limited myself to them to avoid getting into trouble and also to avoid humiliating incidents.

17

In the twinkle of an eye, three years were over. I graduated from the University of Yaoundé with a B. A degree but the biggest headache was how to find a job. Each academic year, over 60.000 students were sent out of the different universities in the country but jobs were not available. Most of them became commercial motor bike riders and those who were unable to afford a bike either became prostitutes, armed robbers or went back to the villages. The ones from rich homes got visas and travelled abroad. Henry was already a military nurse and was on his way to becoming a military doctor. Lillian was lucky to pick up a job at the American Embassy thanks to her relationship with Mr Keith. I was out with the degree I had been running after but what I was going to do with it became a real headache. Mr Finley kept his promise to sponsor me up to the university level. I could not blame him if he decided to leave me at that point. I was not sure that I would ever have gotten there had his curiosity not led him to me at the abandoned house in Pinyin village. I was really grateful.

I deposited documents in over 30 companies in the cities of Douala and Yaoundé as soon as I had the degree in my hands. I waited for over three months before a reply came. I received a phone call from SAO, a company in Yaoundé that produced toilet tissues. I got to the company premises as soon as I could with the hope that I would get a job. I was interviewed and at the end of it, I was told that I would have a job but not at the company. I was going to work at the residence of the general manager of the company as a night watchman. I was going to be paid 35.000 francs. That was what my education from primary, secondary, high school and university could fetch me for a start. I could not fold my arms and keep waiting for other people to keep giving me a helping hand. I accepted the job with the intention of putting in my very best. Maybe my boss was going to be pleased with my work and offer me something better. At least that was what I thought.

I started work and was bent on pleasing my boss. So I did not limit myself to night watching but I took upon myself to weed the grass in and around the whole residence. He was very pleased and gave me 1000 francs tips occasionally. I soon added sweeping of the whole yard to the weeding only to please my boss. I think that was where I burnt my own wings as it turned out to be a terrible mistake. My boss and his wife decided to take advantage of it. They soon fired their housemaid for incompetence and I was asked to do all what she was supposed to do still on the same pay package. I did not object and did the work well. I must confess that it was more of slavery than fighting for survival. I had always told Mr Finley every time he called that everything was wonderful and I had a well-paid job in order not to continue being a burden to him. But after three months of slavery in the house of the general manager of SAO, I opened up to Mr Finley and gave him a true picture of what I was going through. I also explained to him why I had to lie from the beginning. He understood me perfectly well and told me that all his labour was not going to end up in some night watchman-houseboy nonsense. He promised to make arrangements for me to come over and meet him in Italy. With that information, I worked again only for a week and told my boss that I was going to quit because I was working too much and having very little as pay. He proposed to add 10.000 francs to the 35.000 he was paying me already but I turned it down. He became really furious and asked if I knew what other graduates like me would sacrifice to have only half of the amount he was paying me. I told him bluntly that if I was a general manager like him, I would not take advantage of desperate situations as he was doing. I thought he was going to get really mad but he composed himself as a man though I could see the anger in him. He then further asked if I had a friend or someone who was as hard working as I was. I responded that even if I had someone, I would not allow him or her to come and work like a slave

160

for such a menial salary. That was another provocative statement but he was determined not to let loose the lion in him. He remained silent for a while and then asked me to go.

Deep within me, I knew he was hurting inside as the thought of my eminent departure took hold. I had no regret for leaving given the kind of extravagance I saw around there. There was a lot to eat and throw away. I saw brand new clothes burnt because the destined owners did not like them. That was an indication that the SAO toilet tissue which was sold all over the country and some neighbouring countries was yielding a lot of profit. I could not understand why a man with so much would not be happy to help but preferred to exploit. Some human actions were very difficult to comprehend and I did not seek to understand further.

Things went pretty faster than I had expected. I applied for a passport and it was available three weeks later and Mr Keith was the one who was charged with following up my visa at the Italian Embassy. I did go there for interview but it was more for formality because my invitation letter made everything clear already. It was much easier for the visa to be granted because it was Mr Keith who initiated it. If I was the one who took the invitation letter myself to the Italian Embassy, there would have been rendezvous upon rendezvous and maybe at the end of the day, they would have simply said that they were sorry for not granting me a visa. No one was ever certain of being granted a visa at any embassy in Yaoundé, even those who had travelled out before. The reality was that the economic situation in the country was so deplorable especially for young graduates. The only option left for a good number of them was to leave the country. They often found every excuse for wanting to travel to a particular country. But most of those who went for visas were turned down after spending huge amounts of money sometimes borrowed. Consequently, there were scenes of frustration in many neighbourhoods once a demand for visa was turned down. No reasons were ever advanced on why almost all western Embassies granted very few visas. Perhaps it was because they felt invaded by the huge number of demands or because nationals who promised to travel out and return after a certain time lap, never did so after the visas were granted. There was therefore an atmosphere of suspicion but that did not stop people from coming in their numbers in the hope of obtaining visas. Even those who had previously made a demand and were turned down hatched up another excuse and returned. I guess luck was on my side that there was someone to stand ahead of me.

My journey was scheduled for Thursday November 17th at 22:00. Yaoundé had an international airport but it was Douala, the economic capital that was the gate way into Cameroon. All commercial planes landed there first before making a stopover in different airports around the country. A stopover in another airport depended on the number of customers available and the Yaoundé airport, not being the number one airport made things a little bit uncertain for me. I had to travel to Douala to be sure of being on board a plane bound for Italy. *Even if the pilot decides to make a stopover in Yaoundé after take-off from Douala, that will not be at any extra cost to me,'* I thought to myself. The only trouble was that I was going to go to the airport alone. Mr Keith could not come with me since he had a lot of commitment in Yaoundé. Lillian too was busy with work and so too was my very good friend Henry. His was complicated because he belonged to the military and needed permission to go anywhere. Going to an airport which was not even within the city only to see off a friend was not enough reason to ask for permission. They in the military had their strict rules and I understood that.

I left Yaoundé at 15:15 on board a Toyota Coaster belonging to the Guarantee Travel Agency on that same Thursday. There were thirty passengers in the bus. The bus driver plaid music and did not tune to any radio station for us to listen to information from around the world. Even after some pressure from some passengers who were lovers of information, the driver did not give in. There were those who enjoyed the music and those that were disgruntled for not getting what they wanted. The disgruntled lot wished that we got to Douala soonest.

We finally got to Douala at 18:30. I had no problem locating the airport as it was just at the entrance of the city from Yaoundé. I had just a little box and there was no need allowing the driver to take me deep into the city which I did not know in the first place. So, I alerted him of my destination and he stopped. I alighted and walked to the airport premises. There was a gigantic building and many doors led in and out of it. I did not know which door to get into. There were many people there but everyone seemed to have been in a mad rush either to get in or out. I felt uncomfortable stopping anyone who was in a hurry to ask for assistance. I loitered outside the airport building observing people who flew in, got out of the gigantic building and fell into the waiting arms of loved ones. I also watched people who had to travel move into the airport premises. I saw particularly the kids of influential people traveling out for Christmas holiday. They were accompanied by their parents. Each one who came there to travel was accompanied. One curious thing was that policemen in uniform came there in their numbers to accompany people who had to travel. I did not understand why. I saw them enter the building through a particular door and guessed that the door led to where people got checked before they boarded a plane. I followed a lady who was accompanied by a police officer as they headed for the gigantic building. I entered the door they entered and it led to a group of men in police uniform. There were some counters and some pretty ladies sat behind them. They checked passports and if everything was ok, they asked the owner of the passport to proceed to a policeman who stood very close to a door that led to the back of the building. He looked at the passport again and then handed it back to the owner and opened the door himself to let him or her out. Nevertheless, there were some policemen who were charged with searching the luggage of those who came there to travel.

The lady in the company of a police officer I followed into the airport building went through the routine checks. It seemed the policeman who accompanied her knew most of the other men in uniform who worked at the airport as he greeted, laughed and embraced a good number of them. He occasionally pointed at the lady she came with and his colleagues or friends nodded their heads and smiled. Her luggage was checked and an 'Ok' ticket was pasted on it. Everything of hers was ok and one last police officer stood by a door which probably led to the back of the airport, opened it for her and wished her a safe journey. When it came to my turn, the police men in charge of luggage checked my little box and pasted an 'Ok ticket' on it. When that was done, one police officer took my passport and examined it carefully. I thought that he was going to hand it back to me but he did not and instead asked me to sit on a chair which was there. Another one came and stood in front of me and began questioning me.

"Where are you traveling to?" he asked.

"Italy," I replied.

"Whom are you going to see there?" he asked.

"I thought your job was to make sure that questionable luggage don't get loaded onto planes and signatures as well as stamps on passports are authentic," I said.

"You are right but given the threat of terrorist attacks, we have been given the right to decide who travels and who does not. So, you should answer my questions and make sure that what you say is the truth," he said.

Fear gripped me and I became scared that they might do everything to stop me if I did not tell them the truth. I decided to tell him all he wanted to know.

"I am going there on the invitation of a man who has given me every reason to hope in this life," I said.

"And that man does not have a name?" he asked.

"His name is Mr Finley Banks and he is an American peace corp. volunteer who was here and decided to move to Italy when his work was completed. He wants me to come over there to visit and maybe go to school," I said.

"With someone like that, it is certain that you are going to have a bright future. You will run away from this poverty that is here and in a few years you would return as a tycoon and we would be bowing down to you. We have chosen this job which is a kind of prison and we cannot go anywhere without permission. There is no tangible reason we can give for wanting to travel abroad like you. For that reason we have to bruit where we are tied," he said.

I wondered to myself if I was the one who forced him into the police job and could not understand why he was telling me of his predicament in the first place. But his last statement stroke fear in my heart though I could not make any meaning out of it. So, I asked him what it meant.

"What I mean is that this place where we work is the only place we can make up for our inability to go out and make better money like you. If that your American guardian wants to invite you over, it means that he has a lot of money and must have given you more than enough of it to travel with. I want you to give me 100.000 francs before I would allow you go through that door like the others," he said pointing to the door he was referring to.

It was true that I was given some money to carry on me. But it was just for any unforeseen that might crop up and it was not much as he believed. I had just 50.000 francs on me and did not believe that bribing my way was the intended unforeseen it was meant for. I told him the exact amount I had on me but he refused to believe me. He thought that I had hidden the money and was trying to tell him a cow and hen story. He made me know the content of his mind by telling that he was not going to use force on me to get it out. I saw a good number of people who came after me, accompanied and went through the door that led to the back of the airport. I became convinced that he was going to stop me from traveling if I did not comply. I told him that I was going to give him the 50.000 francs I had on me and would give him the rest of the money the day I returned. Of course that was just talk to safe a situation as I did not believe in what I was saying at that moment. He too doubted if he would still be alive or still working in the airport by the time I returned. He turned down my offer and said that it was either the 100.000 francs or I was going to miss my flight. Those words made me feel like strangling him as I did not want to imagine that he was actually going to stop me. Without much ado I sprang to my feet and tried to force my way to the ladies behind the counters to have my passport verified. He tried to withhold me and that drew the attention of his other colleagues. He told them that my passport was fake and I was trying to muscle my way through the door to the plane. Without even looking at it, three of them grabbed me like a common criminal and took me to a cell. Once the door of the cell was locked from outside, they said that they were going to carry out investigations and would return to release me. I sat there waiting.

At 22:10, they came and freed me but informed me that I could no longer travel because the plane I had to board was already on the runway and only magic or a miracle could stop it from taking off. I took my little box and went back out of the gigantic building and saw the plane I had to board take off in a distance. I watched it disappear in the horizon and with it, my dreams of a better future. I could not believe that my hopes and aspirations were disappearing before my very eyes and I could not do anything about it. There was just one thing to do and it was to cry. I went down and lay on my back and cried like a baby. I cried at the top of my voice. If someone had seen me then, he or she would have imagined that perhaps I just received some terrible bad news. There were some men but it would appear they belonged to a private security company who worked outside the airport building. They were charged with ensuring the security of cars that were parked outside the airport building. Within a short time, one of them was bent over me. He had a batten stick in his right hand and was tapping it in his left palm as he spoke to me.

"It will be better for you and me and for the tranquillity of this place that you behave. No noise is to be tolerated around here and if you do not want to be ejected like an unwanted alien, you better behave," he warned.

I did behave and felt some relief after that loud cry. The next trouble was where to spend the night. I knew no one in Douala and the only place I could spend the night in was at that airport premises. I thought of going to the airport lobby to sleep on one of the numerous chairs it contained. But they were not comfortable enough because they were too erect and could not be bent. I did not see how I could sleep comfortably on such chairs. So, I went out to search for the security guard who bent over me when I was crying a while earlier. It was not difficult to find him and he immediately recognized me.

"It is late and I know you need a place to lay your head," he said.

"There you are right. If you have a sleeping pill which can plunge me into a deep sleep, I would be grateful to have it. I want to sleep and forget what happened a while ago. My future has gone with that plane which took off without me," I said.

He felt really sorry for me and tried to sooth me by telling me of his experiences there at the airport.

"I know you were prevented from traveling because you did not pay the 100.000 francs they asked for. It was first of all 50.000 francs but they moved it to 100.000 francs some years ago when they saw that there were more civil servants traveling out of the country when it was not yet the month of July. You know that anyone employed by the state is allowed to travel out of the country only in the month of July. That said, there are a lot of extortion, exploitation and corruption going on here. That is why people who come here to travel like to be accompanied preferably by men in uniform. Those of them who accept to accompany people do not do so for free. They are paid as well but not as high as the ones here. When they get here, they give money for beer to their colleagues working here so that they would not disturb those they accompany here to travel. So, you can see that there is a 'eat and let me also eat' kind of business going on here. Sometimes, they are only interested in money that they allow people with fake visas to travel, only to be caught at the airport of their destination or transit airport and repatriated. That does not speak well of us outside the country," he said.

I looked at him with some suspicion as I wondered if he was going to be any different if he was in the position of those who carried out the dishonourable acts inside the airport. There were people who were good at criticizing others who misused their offices simply because they had no opportunity of occupying such offices. But once they were given such an office, they behaved even worse than those they criticized while they were still out. Perhaps the guard was one of those. But that was not my business at that moment. I wanted a place to sleep and he took me to a pickup truck which was parked not far from where we were. He told me that the owner travelled out of the country for a few days and handed him the key. He opened it and it served as my bedroom for the rest of the night till morning.

At 06:05 the next day, I called Mr Keith and told him of my ordeal. He called his friend, Mr Finley and informed him of the situation. Mr Finley in turn called me and told me that he was at the airport waiting for me when his friend rang him. I told him of how I had cried all the tears out of my body. He told me that Mr Keith was going to come over to Douala to reschedule my flight so that I could travel the next day. Hope came back when he said that and I looked up to the moment when Mr Keith would show up with a lot of optimism. That notwithstanding, I still could not forgive the men in uniform who stopped me from traveling simply because they wanted money which they had done nothing to earn it. I did not know what I would have done to them if I was given the opportunity to punish them. If there was no one to assist me like Mr Keith, that would have marked the end for me. I could remember getting stories of parents who had become tenants in homes they were once landlords because they needed money to send their children abroad to seek a better life and were stopped at the airport by greedy police officers. I was living almost the same situation and could not understand how some people could be so cruel and mean to others. My heart was full of bitterness and since they were in a position of strength and I could not do anything to them, I only prayed to God to render justice. He was the only one who could really protect the weak.

The preventing of some people from traveling for no good reason was not the only surprise I had to acquaint myself with at the airport. Almost 45 minutes after calling Mr Keith and informing him of my ordeal, it was the turn of the guard who assisted me to come up with a demand which I considered a bit unusual.

"You have to pay for your 'hotel room," he said. "You have to understand that Douala is a very difficult place and one must do everything to survive."

I began to imagine that all those who were selected to work in and around the airport were carefully chosen only from the devil's camp. I did not argue or ask how much I was supposed to pay. I just took out a 2000 francs note and handed it to him. He thanked me and said that it was going to enable his family have breakfast that morning. *'Indeed, nothing goes for nothing in this world,'* I thought to myself. I was not certain that the owner of the pickup truck handed the keys of his vehicle to the guard without giving him some kind of financial tip. Even if he did not, I wondered if the owner was going to be pleased with the guard for turning his truck into a hotel room if he came to learn of it. In the days of old, people were going to call that a bridge of confidence but in recent times people called it fighting for survival and would be quick to say 'So long as he or she is not caught, there is nothing wrong.' Whatever the case, it was none of my business and I had to be preoccupied with getting on board the next plane bound for Italy.

Mr Keith arrived from Yaoundé at 11:10 and met me outside the airport building. He told me how sorry he was to hear of what happened and went on to tell me that everything was going to be alright. With the word 'alright' coming from him, I had total confidence as though the word was spoken by God Himself. He came along with some bread and salad which he handed to me. I sat out where he met me and started eating. While I sat eating, he left me and went in the direction of the town and returned only 45 minutes later. He entered the airport building and came out after 20 minutes to announce to me that everything had been taken care of. A smile lit up my face and I had difficulties hiding my feelings. He understood what that meant to me and told me that no one was going to stop me again as he was not going to leave without making sure that I was on board the plane bound for Italy. His words were again reassuring. I did not see how I would have taken my siblings out of the uncertain future they faced as well as the cruel nature of my father if there was no one like Mr Keith and Mr Finley to act promptly. That was another sign that heaven was at work through the two men who were bent on seeing me succeed in life.

However, I was not to travel that same day but the next day at 14:00. With the long hours to wait ahead of me, I needed a place where I could have a good shower and sleep. Airport Motel was not far away and we went there and booked for one night. There I had enough time to sleep adequately and rest. I also had enough to eat and drink. However, I asked during my thoughtful moments why two total strangers would be the ones to help secure a bright future for me while my own brothers, who naturally would have been the ones to take the lead were instead the ones trying to push me into the arms of hopelessness. There was no answer I could think of but simply concluded that life was full of surprises and one had to be prepared psychologically to face them. Those thoughts brought nothing but disgust and pain and I decided at some point to shove them aside. That notwithstanding, Mr Keith rang my phone towards evening on that day of his arrival in the evening that he was going to see me only the next day at the airport.

Thy next day Saturday November 19th, I was at the airport at exactly 13:00 with Mr Keith by my side. We entered the airport building at 13:10 and some of the men who rejected my passport barely 48 hours earlier under the pretext that it was forged were present. One of them walked up to us and greeted Mr Keith in pure military style. Mr Keith greeted him warmly. He then extended his hand to me for us to have a handshake. I did not want to be rude and took it though I was very cold. I withdrew my hand from his grip before he thought of letting go as I felt that he was holding onto it longer than expected. We then moved to the ladies behind the counters who were charged with the verification of stamps and signatures on the passport. It was Mr Keith who held my passport and handed it to them. They verified it and said everything was authentic. I took it and moved to the man closed to the door that led to the back. He checked everything and handed them back to me and then opened the door for me to walk out. I turned and looked at Mr Keith and he smiled. I smiled back and told him that I would call him just by gesturing. He understood and the door closed. I had to go about some 50 meters through what looked like a corridor before getting out to the back. There was a huge plane in front of me as I got out of the building. I saw those who came before me and were checked, moving on some steps that led to the womb of the plane. I followed them and climbed the steps and entered the plane. Once in it, I looked for a seat and sat on. But restlessness could not allow me remain seated as I kept imagining that someone, probably one of those airport police officers could move into the plane to take me out. I soon left the seat and went to the toilet and remained there. I was lucky that no one came there to ease his or herself. I came out only when I could feel the plane moving. I rushed back to my seat and fastened my seat belt. The plane started slowly and very soon, it gathered speed. I could not believe I was finally leaving Cameroon. What was even more amazing was how a passport which was judged fake just two days earlier could become authentic when presented for verification by someone else. I was glad I was leaving all that behind and could visualize the bright future I had always dreamed of.

18

The plane I was on board finally touched down at the Bologna International Airport after close to seven hours of flight. I had to through yet another checking process. Cold waves ran from my head to my toes when my papers and little luggage were being checked. The fear I felt in my stomach made me feel that perhaps the shadow of repatriation was hanging over my head. When at last I was handed my papers and wished a nice stay in Italy, I thought that I had speeded towards the exit door before someone had the bad idea of calling me back. That was exactly what I did and once out of the airport building, Mr Finley was there with a car waiting for me. I ran and embraced him as soon as I set eyes on him. He was not alone though. He was in the company of Catalina, his Italian wife. he had once talked to me about her in one of our phone conversations. They took me from the airport and drove through the city which I found to be very magnificent. It was better than Yaoundé which I considered to be the best city in the world when I was there for university studies. There were very tall and beautiful buildings as well as wide and well-constructed roads with no potholes. Catalina spoke English and was able to tell me the names of the streets and the different neighbourhoods. The names were all in Italian and some sounded like complex sentences to me. Since I did not understand Italian, I had problems assimilating the names. I nodded each time the name of a neighbourhood was mentioned just to give the impression that I was recording them.

We headed to the northern suburb of the city where they lived. The house was a simple not too isolated duplex and Mr Finley told me that it was a gift to Catalina from her father on her wedding day. It was very spacious with a large sitting room and a dining room as well as four bedrooms. There was a swimming pool in front of the house as well as a garage. I had my room upstairs with a very large family size bed all to myself. There were three servants and they were the ones who did the entire house work. Catalina called all of them and introduced me to them. The only male among the three servants was introduced as Gholetti. The two ladies were Maria and Esperanza. She asked them to take care of my things just as they did with all the other things in the house. The two ladies smiled and said 'welcome' to me. Gholetti did not smile and I had the impression that he did not like me. He wore a very stern expression and I wondered if he was naturally that way. Only time was going to tell. They all understood the English language and I imagined that was one of the conditions they met before being hired. Mr Finley did not understand Italian much and it was therefore important for the servants to understand the English language. They all left as soon as the introduction was over to go and continue with their various tasks. Mr Finley left the sitting room and went to their bedroom leaving just Catalina and I.

While we sat there, she asked if I had any dirty clothes which needed some cleaning. I told her that I didn't and she went on to say that each time I had any, I should just pack them together and call Gholetti to collect them. Now, that was something new. I had always done my things by myself and asking or allowing someone to start doing things for me to the extent of washing my clothes made me a bit uncomfortable. With the kind of expression on the face of Gholetti at the time I was introduced to him, I wondered if he was ever going to do that for me. Besides, I wondered if he was going to be washing them with his bare hands as I did back in Cameroon. I could remember watching European movies back in Cameroon in which people put clothes in a machine, introduced a good amount of detergent in it, pressed a button and came back a short while later to take out the clothes already clean and dry. Some of my friends who watched such things on TV called it the Whiteman's witchcraft. I knew that kind of machine was definitely in that house and I planned on asking Gholetti to teach me how to use it than handing my clothes to him to take care of. She equally asked me to call the attention of Esperanza for anything that had to do with cleaning in the rooms, the sitting room and the kitchen. Maria on her part was charged with the cooking and serving of food. The only thing she told me was that if I needed water to drink, I should call her attention. She did not mention anything concerning food because there were specific times when food had to be served and everybody had to eat in the dining room. Food was served three times a day and not many times as was the case back in Cameroon. I just could not help comparing everything and what ever happened in the house with what obtained back in my country.

Mr Finley who went to the room when we entered the house soon re-emerged and he and Catalina went out leaving me in the sitting room alone. They asked me to feel free in the house and call the attention of the servants if I needed anything. I could not feel free as they instructed. I was different from anybody else in the house and even a half blind outsider who came in would have noticed that. I did not know how the servants would react towards me if I asked them to serve me with anything. As a result, I resolved to stay put in the sitting room watching TV and switching from one channel to the next. When I got tired, I went to my room and had a nap while waiting for the time Mr Finley and wife would return. I could only feel free if they were at home.

My hosts did return home at 17:00 on that day I arrived Italy. We watched TV for some time and at 19:00 we moved to the dining table. While we ate Catalina asked the kind of food I loved best back in Cameroon and I told her that I loved every meal except those that were slimy in nature. She smiled and Mr Finley did as well.

When we had all finished what we had in our different plates, we all moved to the sitting section where the TV set was. Mr Finley searched through the channels and stopped on CNN. He was very much interested in what was going on in his homeland. The threats of terrorist attacks were frequent in the news and Mr Finley sighed each time they were mentioned. "What could really push a human being in his right frame of mind to strap explosives round his waist and blow up himself in the midst of many innocent people with the sole intention of killing them? Why hijack a plane and go crash it only to kill people? What is wrong with the world?" he wondered aloud.

"If you start asking questions as those, you would end up with more of them in your hands without answers. The world is a stage on which we are mere characters. When your part is over, you have to leave it just as those that carryout such horrible acts. Leave it to the one who created all of us to take care of them," Catalina said.

Mr Finley sighed again and then turned and asked me to write as many job applications as possible and hand them to him. He cautioned me to leave spaces meant for the sender and receiver's addresses blank. He was going to fill the spaces himself and deposit them where he felt I could be employed. But he had his worries about the labour market in Italy.

"Do not carry your hopes too high," he said with a sigh. "Your African certificates do not have much importance here as in many western countries, though your standard of education back home is very high. That explains why African students perform extremely well in most western universities but the colours of their skin become hindrances to them finding jobs. That is very sad but people are the way they are and it is difficult to control the way they think. This country happens to have one of the highest unemployment rates in the western world and foreigners cannot be given jobs when nationals are jobless and starving. Somewhere, we cannot really blame them but rejecting someone because of his skin colour or origin is very disturbing. I am indirectly telling you that you are going to face difficulties dealing with people here. You might even face open physical xenophobic attacks from some unemployed as they would tend to see you as the one who is taking away the jobs that would have been meant for them."

I knew that integrating myself in a society which had people who looked physically different from me was not going to be easy but having to face physical attacks sent shock waves down my spine. At that point, I asked myself why life had to place difficult choices ahead of us most the time. I had the choice to ask my host either to send me back to my homeland or to stay there and face the hostilities he just made mention of. But returning back to my homeland meant that I had to face the ever grinding poverty with jobs that offered church rat salaries. Staying in Italy was not safe either but it offered chances of a better pay if one succeeded in picking up a job. Elsewhere in the world especially in Eastern Europe, people got killed because they were seen as those who stole opportunities or rare jobs. I resolved that there was risk involved in everything including life itself and I had to take it. However, Mr Finley could read the impact of his words in my silence and tried to dispel my frustration by telling me that I could always count on his support and that of his wife. That was soothing to hear.

It was 21:40 when I decided to go to bed. The thought of the difficulties I was going to face simply because I looked different kept troubling my mind. I asked myself why the heart of man was filled with so much wickedness. There was no end to my frustration and the torturing thoughts soon carried me off to sleep.

I soon found myself back in Cameroon in the town of Bamenda, precisely at Savannah Junction leading to Old Town. I was in the company of Johannes, a business man who owned a huge shop in the Bamenda Main Market. He was taking me to the home of his friend, Jacob, to hand a parcel to him. He indeed held a plastic bag in his left hand which contained the parcel though I did not know what it was exactly. However, after about some twenty minutes' walk into Old Town neighbourhood, we took a little narrow path which led to the home of his friend. It was some three hundred meters from the tarred road. Once we entered the house of his friend, I discovered that there were many other people there. I think they were holding some kind of meeting. But one curious thing that I noticed was that though there were so many people in the house, there was not even a single woman among them. The owner of the house walked up and welcomed us both while at the same time pointed to the dinning section for us to move there. That was the only place where there were still some unoccupied seats. All faces lit up with smiles as they watched us move to that dinning section.

I sat down only for a little while and had to move to the lavatory to ease myself since I had drunk a lot of water some time earlier. On my way back to the house after easing myself, I met an old lady who was passing in front of the house we came to, to go to a neighbouring house. She stopped and looked at me with a very sad expression on her face.

"What are you doing here? Do you like entering this type of a house?" she asked and continued on her way without waiting for me to provide answers.

I stood on the spot where she met me really perplexed and wondered why she had to ask me such questions. I had never seen her before and was not certain that she knew me or any of my relatives. After pondering over her questions for a while I decided to run after her to get some explanations. But there was no trace of her anywhere. I concluded that she was probably trying to tell me something or to warn me against something and went back to the house.

When I regained my seat, the owner of the house came up to me and lined a variety of foods and drinks. The drinks were only alcoholic ones and I did not drink alcohol. I was not hungry and refused to take anything there. Johannes' friend was not happy with my attitude and did nothing to disguise his frustration. He tried to cajole me into taking even a little bottle of beer but I was firm on my decision not to take alcohol.

"Why don't you want to eat or drink something?" Jacob asked. "A little amount of alcohol has never killed anybody. A Cameroonian who refuses to take even a little bottle of beer is really strange."

He sounded like a real hospitable and caring man and asked what I wanted to drink. I told him that I wanted to drink water and he insisted that there was no water. I told him that he could send somebody to buy it but he insisted that I had to drink only what was available there in the house at that moment. I told him that I was going to pay for the water if he did not have the money. He became furious and I could not understand why. He turned and faced his friend.

"What kind of an individual have you brought here today," he asked.

My friend turned to me and asked me to stop behaving like a little boy and behave as a man. The words of the old lady to me a few minutes earlier re-echoed in my mind. There was something unusual about that gathering. I could not understand why I would turn down an offer which was my absolute right and it would become a problem. Jacob left in anger and went back to the sit he occupied before we walked in. I remained observant on my seat and noticed that the mood in the house had changed drastically. My friend was not happy and there were no smiles on the other faces either. The people just went on eating and drinking in silence.

Jacob soon left his seat and went into the kitchen. He re-emerged with a mug of water and a glass. He did not hand the glass to me when he got to where I sat. Instead, he told me that if I wanted to pay for the water I was going to drink there, it was not going to be with money. I asked him how I was supposed to pay and he asked me to look into the mirror which hung on the wall in that dinning section. In it, I saw the images of my siblings and he said that I was going to use them in paying for anything I consumed there. I said it was alright and he poured a glass full and extended it to me. Since he stood an arms' length from me, I kicked the glass from his hand and it chattered the mirror on the wall. Immediately it was broken, I found myself back at savannah street junction. I could remember that we started off at that Junction but no longer had an idea of the direction my friend took me to. I started wondering aloud what was happening to me and jumped into the road without looking left or right. By the time I came back to my senses, I found myself in the middle of the road just about three meters away from an oncoming vehicle at top speed. A collision was inevitable and I began to cream. I jumped up and found Mr Finley and wife sitting on both sides of my bed. Catalina took me into her arms.

"It was a nightmare," she said.

It was then I realized that it had all been a dream. But I could not just discard it as a mere dream which had nothing to do with reality. Johannes was indeed my one time friend and behind the door into his shop hung some bank notes. I didn't know if they were real or fake. I once asked him why he hung the money behind the door and he just smiled and said nothing. I told Mr Joel about it when I was still selling in his shop and he told me that many of the business men in that market belonged to sacred cults. He further explained that the bank notes that hung behind the door were intended to attract customers and the money in question was given to them in their sacred cults after they had sacrificed people. I avoided Johannes after learning of it. That dream was probably telling me what would have happened to me if I had not broken up our friendship. Mr Finley and Catalina prayed with me before leaving for their room. The rest of the night was peaceful.

The next day, Mr Finley and Catalina left for their respective jobsites. I was left at home with the servants. I wrote the applications Mr Finley asked for and watched television all day. I did everything possible to avoid the servants as I did not know how they would behave towards me and I was not prepared to face any embarrassment. The best way to avoid it was to adopt 'a do it yourself policy'. My host came home after work that same day and I handed all the applications to him. He promised to do his best in finding a job for me. I thanked him immensely for all what he had been doing for me to see that I succeed in life.

For the rest of that first week in Italy, everything was a routine with Mr Finley and wife leaving for work every morning and returning in the evenings. I on my part stayed at home watching TV, sleeping and eating. I took care of my things myself and never asked or ordered any of the servants to do anything for me though I had been given the authority to do so. Life was really boring, I must say and it was going to last for three months after my arrival in Italy. To ward off some of the boredom, I decided to be very observant around the house. I noticed that Catalina never entered the kitchen and did not take care of her husband's clothes as well. She ordered the servants all the time to do them. That was in sharp contrast to the situation I knew back in Cameroon. Housewives could allow their maids to do everything but not take care of the food and clothes their husbands had to eat and wear. Housewives always had a suspicion for their female maids as a good number of them passed through food and the caring of clothes to snatch their husbands. They had every reason to be suspicious as there was a common adage that 'the best way to a man's heart is through his mouth'. The man could start by appreciating the food the servant prepared and the way she took care of his dresses and that would develop into a relationship. Wives became wise and restricted the activities of their female maids. They therefore had to proof their love for their husbands and sustain it by taking care of their foods and their outfits themselves. I therefore assumed that there were high levels of divorced rates in the western world because women neglected such duties. Whatever the case, I planned to advice Catalina on such duties when I was certain she was in her best of moods.

That notwithstanding, I used my idle moments to watch mostly news channels. Hardly did a week or month go by without reports of Africans landing on the Italian islands of Lampeduza and Cecily by

181

sea in a bid to escape the grinding poverty back in their home countries. What was appalling about the reports I got on TV was the inhuman conditions under which those who survived the dangerous crossing were subjected to in detention camps. I could not understand why countries of the north were fond of coming to give us lessons on democracy and the respect of human rights when they could not practice them on those that entered their territories, though illegally, begging just for crumbs. I guess the old sayings that 'do what I say and not what I do' fitted squarely in such a situation.

Nevertheless, December soon came and since majority of Italians were Christians, the feast of Nativity and St. Sylvester were taken very seriously. Those were the few days during which a good number of youths went to church. During normal times, mostly the elderly did so. Catalina and her husband as well as myself drove to church which was some two kilometres away as one family. We became the centre of attraction when entering the church and when mass was over. Some people made comments in very low tunes while others giggled especially the very young ones. Some came to where we were to greet but I could read curiosity on their faces. I could not tell what was on their minds. Many people blamed foreigners there for any wrong doings and I wondered if the people were seeing just another thief, armed robber or trouble maker in me. Whatever the case, that was the new society I found myself in and had to try as much as possible to change such a mentality by showing the good side of me.

On New Year's Day, we went to church and moved back home when mass was over, just as on the day of nativity. I had a slight headache and decided to lie on my bed after taking some drugs. I just felt like remaining in bed all day but was worried that I might have difficulties finding sleep when it was dark. I then left my room at 14:00 and went to the sitting room to watch some movies. The house servants had all been given that day off to go and celebrate with their loved ones. Catalina came into the sitting room and asked if I would like to go out with them and I said yes. I asked her where she intended taking me to and she said that it was going to be a surprise. I went to my room and put on my outing clothes. Mr Finley, Catalina and I left the house at 15:00.

19

We started heading to the southern part of the city and when we got to the city centre, we turned east. I had all the time to admire the splendour and beautiful architecture of the buildings. Catalina told me that some of them dated back centuries. The roads were wide and well-marked too. The level of development was really breath taking and I wondered when towns and cities in my home country would ever get to such a level.

At 15:50, we drove through a gate that led to a house which was identical to the one we lived in. I asked Catalina where we were and she said that I was going to meet her parents and the rest of her family. As we left the car and were about to enter the house, a strange sensation swept through me just as when someone set his eyes something really frightful. I did not know what to make of it but concluded that it might have been a premonition to something that was going to happen that day. I began to wonder how they were going to treat me and the kind of words that they might utter. But for that moment my fear was unjustified.

We entered the house and found a much older man and a woman as well as one young man and two young ladies. One of the ladies wore an oxblood blouse and a pair of jean trousers while the other wore a black gown. They all rose and shook hands with those of us who just walked in. Catalina introduced the much older man and woman as her parents. The young man, Giorgio, was her younger brother and Juliana in the black gown was his fiancée. The lady in jeans was Estephania, Catalina's younger sister.

Soon after the handshakes, we were asked to move to the dining table where varieties of food were served. There were seven plates on the table. Everybody sat where there was one and the seat I occupied had no plate in front of it. A maid was called and asked to bring one more plate which was meant for me. The plate which was brought was identical to the other ones on the table but it had a little crack on it. The crack was so little and one needed to examine it really closely before seeing it. A set of cutleries was brought as well. After saying grace before meals, it was time to eat and I became the centre of attraction again just as outside the church house. Those I was meeting for the first time were curious about seeing how I was going to eat and if I was able to use the cutleries like they did. Those I had looked really blunt and the effort I had to employ in using them made those who had their attention on me laugh. I got tired of trying to use them.

"Eating is not supposed to be done under stress," I said.

My comment provoked more laughter but I was not that type that loved to pretend. I requested for some water in a little bowl to use in washing my hands. It was brought and after washing my hands, I used my fingers to tear the chicken that was in my plate. The enjoyable manner in which I ate and the finger licking that accompanied the exercise made them want to try it. Juliana washed her hands and started eating with her fingers too.

"The food tastes different when eaten with finger," she said. Estephania and Giorgio did the same thing but the rest just smiled and refused to try it. Mr Finley was already used to it. He used to eat with his fingers when I was still living with him back in Cameroon. But there since he had already begun eating with the cutleries, it was better to just continue than soil his fingers.

We all moved to the sitting room once we were through with eating. There, we sat conversing while feeding our eyes on some news items on TV. Our conversation was mostly centred on life in Africa and the different kinds of problems people faced. I gave answers to all the questions they asked and they were satisfied with my responses. The relationship established during our interaction was warm and I felt happy that I was accepted. At least that was what I thought.

At 18:00, we had to leave for our own residence. Catalina's parents went out with us to see us off. But as we all boarded the car, I remembered that I forgot the key to my room on the dining table where we ate. I wanted to be taking care of my things myself and did not want the servants to do them for me. So, I developed the habit of locking up my room even when I had to go only to the sitting room to watch TV. That day was no exception. I left the car and dashed again into the house and made my way to the dining room. I found the key where I sat but equally saw something which was very disturbing. The plate I ate in and the cutleries I attempted using and gave up were lying in the waste basket. I was devastated and felt that the world was crumbling on my head. I really had difficulties establishing a link between the warm people I dined with just a few hours earlier and the act that lay bare in front of my eyes. I asked myself a good number of questions. I wondered if it was the servant who took the initiative to dump the plate I used or it was the master of the house who gave the instructions. There were no answers. I left the house and tried really hard to conceal my emotions and frustration. I entered the car without a smile or saying goodbye to the parents of Catalina. Mr Finley knew me as though he was the one who made me. Just taking a look at me, he immediately noticed that there was something wrong. He did not ask me what the matter was just then. He waited until we were on the move. In response, I told him that it was the headache which had not really subsided. I had to lie because I did not want to steer up trouble between Catalina and her parents or family members. She was that type that did not tolerate any nonsense and I knew she was definitely going to confront her parents then and there had I spoken the truth. We got home that evening and I went straight to my room and locked myself up.

The next morning, I remained in my room and fought hard not to let the incident of the previous day get to me . Somewhere, I was happy that it happened because that was one of the things I needed to build my spirit so as to better face the society which was hostile in its outlook. That was the reason why I rarely went out alone and preferred the boring routine at home. Taking care of my things helped a lot in warding off some of the boredom.

On 5th February, which was three months after I got to Italy, the phone rang in the morning and it was Mr Finley who answered the call. He told me that it was coming from a company and they wanted me to come over for some interview. I did not know where it was located and so Mr Finley had to alter his program for that day to take me there. I got ready as soon as possible, motivated by the excitement of finally finding work. I was grateful that one response came out of the over twenty applications I wrote. But there was an inner voice in me which kept telling me not to get my hopes up yet. Asking me to come for interview was no guarantee that I was going to get the job. One thing was certain and it was that if I did not get the job at the end, I would have still been contented that at least a response came.

We were at the company premises in 30 minutes. I could see the name of the company but it was in Italian. We walked in with Mr Finley moving in front and I behind him. Since Mr Finley was versed with the company, he led me straight to the office of the manager. He knocked on the door of the office and a voice within asked us to come in. We did and the man in the office got up from his seat and shook hands with us both. He then offered Mr Finley a seat, after which he turned and asked what he could do for me. I responded that I was supposed to have an interview there that morning.

"An interview here this morning?" he asked astonished.

"Yes," I responded.

"I'm not sure. I think there is a mix up somewhere," he said.

It was then Mr Finley stepped in.

I don't think there is any mix up," he said. "If you can remember, I brought a hand written application and curriculum vitae to you a few months back and you told me that you were going to study them and get back to me. The documents were his and you asked me to bring him along for interview this morning. Well, here he is."

The man took a deep breath and I understood that I was not going to have the job. Mr Finley too could read meaning in his reaction.

"I understand that you are not going to interview him and he is not going to have the job," he said.

"I'm sorry my friend," the man said. "You just have to understand. You know the kind of society we live in. I cannot….."

Mr Finley did not allow him to go ahead. "You do not have to elaborate. I understand," he said and we both left.

Mr Finley was very disappointed that he moved ahead of me to the car without uttering a word. He kicked the car and was on the move even before I had time to close the door. Scared that in anger he could lose control and even cause an accident, I asked him to stop and take a deep breathe three times. He did but did not continue immediately after the exercise. We remained at the spot for about ten minutes during which I tried to console him instead of the other way round.

"What is wrong with human beings? How can someone be competent on paper but would not be granted an interview or given a job simply because he looks different? How can someone be rendered incompetent by his skin colour?" he wondered aloud. "If I had known that guy was a coward, we wouldn't have wasted our time going there. But don't worry, we will find a job and a good one. For that, you can trust me."

"I don't think competence had anything to do with his decision not to interview or hire me. My physical appearance was the problem. He is a business man and might see me as an object that could slow down his business," I said.

"Whatever the reason, the fact is that you will not have the job," he said with a sigh.

We did not say anything to each other until we got home. I had to resume my routine back at home while waiting for the day when a job would be found for me. Mr Finley went into the house and went to his room to pick up something. I was in the sitting room when he came out to go to work. He stopped for a few seconds and looked at me and then asked what it would feel like if a job was found for me but outside the city. I told him that I had no problem with that and he told me that he would call another friend in the southern part of the province and then would get back to me. I thank him for the effort and sacrifice he was making for me. He left and I remained in the sitting room watching TV.

At 10:50. I got tired of watching TV and decided to go outside. I went and sat by the swimming pool. The day was bright and looked promising and I wished such brightness could take away the dark cloud of uncertainty which still hung over my future. The fact that Mr Finley was there and was doing everything possible to secure a job for me gave me hope which helped to take away part of my anxiety and psychological stress.

20

Two weeks after my host announced that he was going to contact a friend outside the city for any possible job prospects, he informed me that there was a job at a ranch in the southern part of the province. The job consisted of taking care of animals. I loved animals but had never had the chance of taking care of any. I did not ask what kind of animals I was going to take care of but was just excited that at last I had something to keep me busy. The amount of money I was going to be paid was not very important at that moment. All I was interested in was work. I knew that no matter how small the salary turned out to be, it was going to be better than what I earned back in Cameroon as a house boy- night watchman.

On February 21st, I packed all what I had as belongings and boarded Mr Finley's car and we started the long journey to the southern part of the province. He told me that the name of the place was Monzuno. He opted to take me there since it was a weekend and he had no major plans in mind. He asked Catalina to come with us but she refused saying that she was too tired to travel especially by road. I said goodbye to her promising to write often and to come over to visit whenever I could.

We arrived at the ranch in the afternoon. Mr Finley told me that the greatest part of Italy's animal farming took place there. It was very rural in outlook and there were vast areas of grazing land. He also informed me that a lot of milking was done there and big companies in the towns and cities came there to collect the milk to use in most dairy products. That gave me a clue to the nature of work I was going to be doing there. The curious thing was that it had nothing to do with my field of study at school. I guess when people go into a specific field of study and upon completion there are no jobs, they end up in fields they never initially thought of. That probably explains why most people in the world today are not happy with their jobs.

However, we soon drove through an open gigantic iron gate and went some two and a half kilometres before meeting a house. Once Mr Finley turned off the engine of the car, a man who must have been in his late 50s emerged from the house and embraced him. After he did that, he turned to me and extended his right hand. I took it and he asked Mr Finley if I was the young man who had to work for him. Mr Finley said yes and he called two of his employees to help take my things out of the car. He gave directives on the room they had to take them to while he took us to his sitting room. There, we met his wife and two daughters who greeted us very warmly. From their interaction, it was obvious that they knew him very well. I was still new and so, there was need for some introduction to be made. Mr Finley told them my name and they all said 'welcome' to me again calling me by name. He went further to introduce my new boss as Mr Salghetti. His wife's name was Mrs Salghetti Garcia and his two daughters were Celestina and Christina. Their warm smiles made me wonder if they were going to be different from Catalina's parents. I had become suspicious of any act of kindness towards me because Italy had become more or less a licking roof under which I found myself and could not appreciate the rhythm of the rain. As for whether they were going to be different, only time would tell.

Mrs Salghetti soon left us and went to the kitchen after her husband commented that their guests must have been starving after the long journey. She invited us to the dining table twenty minutes later. There was fruit salad, spaghetti and bread as well as a five litre container of red wine. There was quite a lot to eat. Since spaghetti was something I loved so much, I ate quite a lot. Mr Salghetti too urged me to eat as much I could. "Food in enough quantity and quality is good for the body," he said. Smiles lit up the faces round the table as he said that. There was conversation between Mr Finley and our host. He sought to know from Mr Finley if he planned on engaging on the long journey back that evening and he responded that he was going to leave the next day.

Mr Salghetti took us out to visit his vast estate after we had finished eating. He wanted all of us to go on horseback but I could not ride one myself. I got on the one Mr Finley was riding on and used the opportunity to see a good number of his employees. Some of them were of African origin like me and that was a good sign that I was going to really feel at home there in Monzuno. There were five of them and they smiled as I passed by with Mr Finley and my new boss. I was itchy to meet them individually to know them and their experiences.

We soon returned and the only thing left for me to do was to take a shower and then go to bed. I was taken to my room by Armah, who told me that he came from Ghana. I told him that I was from Cameroon and he called me his brother. I did not want to start bothering him with many questions as I knew that we would have enough time to know each other the next day which was Sunday. Sadly enough, it was that Sunday morning that Mr Finley had to head back north to the city of Bologna. I wondered how I was going to say goodbye. However, the next morning, I woke up at 05:30. The eminent separation that morning with Mr Finley started troubling me. I knew that I could travel up north at any time I wanted to see him. Added to that was the telephone. I knew he could opt to call me every day if that was going to make me happy but all that did not take away my anguish. I then wished for that moment to pass quickly so that I could concentrate on the activities of the coming days.

That moment came at 07:30 when I was already dressed for church. I left my room and met him in front of the house in the company of his friend.

"Are you ready to go to church?" Mr Finley asked.

"Yes," I responded.

"I am glad to see you carry that spirit everywhere you go. God is at the centre of our lives and we must never part with Him for one second," he said.

Mr Salghetti embraced his friend and wished him a safe trip back. It was my turn to fall in the arms of Mr Finley and the look on my face said everything.

"My friend here has promised to allow you come over at any time you want. So, I don't want you putting up that face," he said freeing himself from my grip.

He got into the car and started the engine. It was really painful watching him leave. I think Mr Salghetti could imagine how I felt and put his arm around me as we both watch Mr Finley disappear in a distance. He asked me to go to church adding that we would have a little chat when I returned.

From the house of my new boss, I did not need to ask for directives on where the church was located. It was situated by the side on a slope some 20 minutes' walk away. As I set on my way to church, the images of Mr Finley disappearing in a distance and his lasts words to me flashed in my mind. He had been more than a father to me. He found me in an abandoned home, hunger stricken and decided to take me out of it. He had seen me through secondary, high school and university education. To crown everything, he took me over to Italy because he wanted to help find a job for me. I felt at that moment that if angels did walk the surface of the earth, he was one of them. I also knew that my presence at that estate was a sounding bell to the fact that time had come for me to take my destiny into my own hands. Back in Cameroon, a father had to lead his son into adulthood and bringing me to that estate was Mr Finley's way of leading me into adulthood. I knew that the moment when people had to stop asking me who my father or mother was, had to begin there. I therefore had to either walk out of that place a real man or a total failure. Determination, dedication, devotion in all I had to do, as well as honesty were the ingredients I needed to successfully make it.

I got to church at 07:55 and walked straight into the church house. It was not very large as the one in the city. It was full to capacity that some people lacked seats. What I realized was that people of all ages were there unlike the city where mostly the very old and the very young went to church. I suppose surviving in the city was more demanding than in the countryside and that explained why people of all ages in the countryside could find time to go to church.

At 09:45 the mass ended and I went back to my new home. I was eager to know what Mr Salghetti wanted to tell me and moved to the main house as soon as I took of my clothes. He was there sipping coffee alone and watching TV. When I was seated, he asked Christina to bring a cup of coffee for me which she did.

"My friend told me a great deal about you," he said.

"I'm sure what he told you must have been nice things," I said.

"Sure, they were. He told me that you are a very hard working young man and know what you want as well as where you are going. Those are the qualities I expect all my workers to have and that is what motivated me to ask him to bring you," he went on.

"I promise not to disappoint you sir," I said.

"I am a man who takes a lot of pride in defending and protecting those I call my own. What I am trying to say is that we live in a very complex society and it is easy to blame someone else than oneself when things don't go right. If you want to go out of this place, make sure someone knows where you are going and make sure you actually go where you said you were going. If you say that you are going to Rome and instead go to Milan and something happens to you there, I would have no arguments to back you up. Let those around you know what you can do and can't do. This is a small place and most of my workers here are not from here. Once in a while, crimes are committed here and there and the easiest people to target are those that are strangers here. I cannot defend you in such a situation if you

195

keep putting up different character traits. Make yourself as predictable as possible and I would have the weapons to fight for you if you find yourself in trouble," he said.

I thanked him for his kind and wise words. Drawing up a time table for myself and following it religiously was on my agenda ever since I got to Italy. What I desired most was staying out of trouble by all means and if there was someone as Mr Salghetti who was prepared to defend me, there was no reason not to take his advice seriously. But he still had more things to tell me.

"I and my workers form one family. We take breakfast, lunch and supper together but they are free to cook in their rooms if they do not like what I have to serve here. I try as much as possible to make everyone comfortable. I cherish dialogue a lot and I believe that solutions to problems could be found through dialogue. If you have any problem with any of your colleagues or with the way you are treated here, let me know and we would find a solution through dialogue," he reiterated.

I told him that I'd heard all what he said and was going to do my utmost best not to disappoint him. I then asked him about the nature of my job.

"You would have to be taking some of the animals to the hills for grazing. At some point in time, you would leave them in their enclosure and go for the grass they would eat using the chariot. You would also have to milk the cows as customers from town would come here almost every day to buy the milk to use in their dairy products," he replied.

I wanted to ask him about my salary but was scared that might give him the wrong impression that I was more interested in money than the work I came there to do. I decided after a second thought to get the information some other way. Waiting for the end of the month was one way and finding out from Armah how much he earned was another. From his pay package, I could guess what I was going to be paid. He then added that I was not going to begin work the next day but would learn how to sit and ride a horse first. I was going to be taking the animals to the hills on horseback and it was essential for me to know how to ride it. I thanked him for schooling me and being honest to me. After saying that, I asked him to excuse me as I wanted to have a little chat with Armah. He asked me to go but said that I should remember to come in for lunch at 12:30. He smiled as he said it and I smiled back.

I met Armah outside his room and he was just returning from the bathroom where he went to have a bath. He had just finished feeding the animals in the enclosure he had to take care of that morning. He had to freshen up before lunch. I waited for him to go and dress up and come out before I started asking my questions. In my first question, I sought to know how he got to Italy. He had a chilling story to tell me.

"The world is really wicked my brother. Our enemies are only our own brothers," he began. "I come from a very poor family. When I say 'poor', I mean every sense of the word. There were times my parents, six younger ones and myself would beg on the streets just to survive. Life was not easy."

He paused for a while probably reliving the nightmare of the past again in his mind. I was anxious to hear the rest of his story.

"I could play football but needed to get into a sports academy to perfect my talent," he went on. "There was a man who always came to the dusty playground I always practiced on, to watch me and my friends play. He walked up to me one day and told me that I had great potentials and he was ready to link me up with a good sports academy here in Italy. I began to see football as the only means through which I could dethrone poverty from my family. I started dreaming of one day playing in a big club like Real Madrid, FC Barcelona, Manchester United, AC Milan and all the rest."

A smile lit up his face as he enumerated the different clubs. But it dried up as soon as he called the last one. *There is nothing worse than living in the shadows of a shattered dream,* I thought to myself. I tried to imagine his ordeal but thought that it was better to let him paint the picture himself.

"You needed to see me training after the man I just talked about made that promise," he went on. "I considered my body a machine and was prepared to work myself to death. I believed that success was to come only through the amount of time and energy I put into my training. One Saturday morning after training, Big Boss asked me to take him to my parents so that he could have a chat with them. Big Boss was the name the man was fondly called. I took him to where I lived and he told my parents that he was an agent and had links with big football clubs in Europe. He convinced them that I had great talents that were wasting. My parents asked him what they could do for him to link me up with one of the big clubs in Europe and he said that all they had to do was raise the sum of $7000.00. They complained that the money was too much and there was no way they could ever lay hands on that kind of money. He told them that I had potentials and my first contract in a big club was going to fetch millions and not thousands. With such comments, my dreams and those of my parents climbed higher and higher. The only home we had and the only piece of land we had back in the village were sold and the money was handed to Big Boss. He helped me make a passport, obtained a visa for me and bought a ticket as well. He brought me to Italy and we landed in the city of Bologna. He then took me to the poor neighbourhood on the western part of the city and we checked into an inn. He paid for two nights. He left me on the day we checked into the Inn telling me that he had to go and meet the managers of the big sports academy he wanted to hook me up with before returning. He did not come back that day and I hoped that he was going to do so the next day. I waited the whole day but Big Boss didn't show up. After spending the second night in that Inn, I was asked to move out if I did not have money to pay. I had to move out with no documents on me or money to face that big city. You will not imagine what I went through in that city. The streets became my home and I survived for four months by begging from passers-by. At the same time, I had to be running away from the police. I never saw Big Boss again."

He paused again for a short while and I could see tears streaming down his eyes. I understood then why he had to begin by saying that our enemies were our own brothers. My blood ran cold and I felt really terrible about what happened to him. I tried to console him by telling him that there was a God up there who was watching everything and Big Boss certainly had his reward waiting for him.

"Big Boss really taught me a lesson. Now I know that if someone comes to you claiming to be an agent of some sort, he should be the one putting money on you and not you giving him money," he said with a sigh.

I started feeling that asking him further questions would be torturing him but there was just one I wanted to ask to completely satisfy my curiosity. I wanted to know how he found work with Mr Salghetti.

"He went into a supermarket to buy a few items and had some difficulties transporting them to his car. I was outside the supermarket begging as usual and ran to assist him. I spoke and he realized that my English was fluent. He asked me a few questions and I gave him some answers. He did not take me on that first encounter. I knew that he was definitely going to come back there to buy things some other day. The fact that he talked to me and had the patience to listen to me made me have the conviction that he was a good man. And you know, good people always draw other people to themselves. I kept praying and hoping and the second time he came there, I still opted to carry what he bought though he would have carried them by himself. He asked me what I was still doing there and that was when I opened my chapter. It was my story that finally rescued me from that street life," he explained.

I glanced at my watch and it was 12:28. I told him that it was time to go for lunch and we both went to the sitting room where everybody was already seated.

21

After saying grace before meals, everyone dished what he or she could eat. We began and it was punctuated by conversations led by Mr Salghetti himself. He used the opportunity to introduce me to his other workers and equally told them where I came from. They might have had difficulties picturing Cameroon on the map but they knew that it was a great football nation. He introduced those I was seeing there for the first time. I learnt that I was the sixth African to join his group. There was Uche and Chukwudi from Nigeria, Armah from Ghana, Didier from Ivory Coast and Justin from Liberia. There were five Italians. Four of them were of the Roma tribe. They considered themselves Italians because they were born there. But the Italian state did not consider them its citizens. However, they told me that their great grandparents and grandparents came from Romania. They all came from outside Monzuno. The none Roma there was a native of the locality. The two daughters of Mr Salghetti worked in the estate too. They took care of the customers who came there to buy and also ran the accounts of the estate. I was curious if they had a salary at the end of the month as the rest of us. In a lighter mood Mr Salghetti voiced his wish to see his large family remain united and work together as it was good for the health of the estate and all the people living on it.

We left the dining room and retired to our various rooms to rest and prepare for the afternoon shift. The animals had to also eat and they were not to be taken to the hills. They had to remain in their enclosure and their food had to be brought to them there. It had to come from the hills and the workers had to go and get it. It was a tedious job and so the workers needed to have enough rest that afternoon.

I did not remain in my room for the rest of the day. I left it at 15:00 and decided to accompany Armah to the hills to cut the grass which the animals had to feed on. I seized the opportunity to ask him a few more questions. I asked him how much he earned as salary.

"I can boast of between 1100.00 to 1200.00 dollars per month. Only $1000.00 is already a lot of money back there in my native Ghana. I sent the salary I earned for the first two months back home and a house was built. My whole family is living in it now. I later on sent more money and pieces of land were bought around Accra and the village. I have been working here for four years and plan on leaving at the end of this year to go back home. Life is in stages and you must know when to leave from one stage to the next. Once you fail to leave a stage at a particular time, you would remain stocked for the rest of your life. I think that the time to graduate from a servant to a boss of my own is fast approaching. The end of this year is that right time. I am still wondering how I would say goodbye to this man who has been an angel to me. He represents hope for the hopeless and the marginalized," he said.

He paused a little and looked at my face to see perhaps if I had any reaction concerning the attribute he hung on Mr Salghetti. I did not say anything and could not tell whether he read something from my expression or not.

"I don't want you to think that I am showering him with too many praises," he went on. "That man is really an angel down from heaven. Look at the workers; most of them are foreigners from poor African countries. Look at those from Italy here from the Roma tribe. They have white skin as other Italians but let me tell you that they are marginalized as those of us who come from outside. They are placed on the same second class or third class scale with us. Some people here in this country do not see people like you and I as human beings. They call us black monkeys, criminals, trouble makers and anything that could be considered bad. People of the Roma tribe sometimes suffer the same fate. But lucky enough, a man like Mr Salghetti is there to give us hope. I don't just know how I would go about telling him that I intend to leave after all what he has already done for me. I don't just know."

He provided answers to the many questions I had in mind in his long explanations. I decided to digress a bit to the other workers of African origin. He told me that Uche and Chukwudi told him that they escaped grinding poverty through the Sahara desert with the aid of smugglers to Europe and they found their way to Italy illegally. But he added that they fought hard and obtained legal papers as they started working and earning money. As for Didier, he suffered the same fate as he Armah, at the hands of a dubious man posing as a football agent. He was abandoned in the city of Milan and finding nothing to do, he decided to head to the southern part of Italy. It was on the way south to nowhere that Mr Salghetti found him when he had walked for days and nights with no food and water and started begging from drivers in passing vehicles for a lift. I could feel the pain of the others because all those who had known poverty definitely knew suffering. We headed back home after loading the grass we went out for on a chariot pulled by a horse.

I started my training on horse riding the next day. It was not something which had to take long. I knew how to do it in barely a week. After learning how to do that, my life became a routine. I took animals to the hills and the water bodies around, milked cows, went to church, made one trip to the city of Bologna every month to see Mr Finley and Catalina, assisted the daughters of my boss on Sunday afternoons when there was not much work to be done in improving on their English. I always made sure someone knew where I was and what I was doing. Things were to be that way for four and a half years.

I tried to compare my first employer back in Cameroon with Mr Salghetti. They were complete opposites. My first employer in Cameroon was wealthy and I put in my best to please him by doing work which he did not initially hire me for, in the hope that he could give me a pay rise or give me some tips. Unfortunately for me, he took advantage of it and exploited me. I was doing some extra work too at the home of Mr Salghetti like teaching his daughters English. He did not take advantage of it. He gave me extra tips for that. All my trips to the city to visit Mr Finley were paid for by him. I expected him to deduct what he paid for my trips from my pay package at the end of each month but that never happened. He even gave me money for food on the way whenever I had to travel. There were moments I considered that my employer was too good to be human. He taught me a great lesson by his way of life. I learnt from his example and that of Mr Finley to judge people individually and not as a group. That was why most people we came across were generally hostile towards us mostly because we looked different or were foreigners or were potential job thieves, but I could not generalize that Italy was hostile to foreigners or was a racist society because I did not have the time to get to know each and every one. I guess those who were hostile toward us did so because they did not know who we were and were not willing to know. All the same, that was the world stage and it was not imperative that all the characters be only good ones.

However, two and a half years after I started working with Mr Salghetti, I went for my usual once in a month visit to the city of Bologna. It was on the second Saturday of the month of April. Something really unusual was waiting for me in the city that day. I climbed down from the bus at the spot I usually did and crossed the road. I had to walk for about 250 meters before getting to the point where I had to board a taxi to head to the northern part of the city where Mr Finley and Catalina lived. I had barely gone 100 meters when some two boys who must have been in their mid-20s approached me from the opposite direction. They all wore sky-blue pair of jeans but one had a red tea-shirt and dark hair while the other wore a green tea-shirt and had blond hair. The guy with dark hair seized my little bag which contained my few clothes. I tried to take it back but he threatened me with a little batten stick he held in his right hand. I stopped trying to have it back. Being on the alert not to receive an unexpected swing of the stick became more important. The one with blond hair said something in Italian but soon realized that I did not understand anything he said. He then said something else in Italian and they both laughed. Though I could not understand a word of what he said, I knew it was something derogatory. The guy with dark hair switched to English though his English was not perfect and asked if I understood what he said. I said yes.

"Whatz arre you dzoing here?" he asked.

"Do you mean here on this spot or in this city" I responded though it was yet another question.

"What are you doing in my country?" the guy with blond hair stepped in, moving from my face to behind me while his friend remained in front of me.

I did not say anything and thought that it was the best way to avoid a confrontation with them. But my silence seemed to have angered them instead.

"Did your father or grandfather leave anything here for you to come and take," the guy with blond hair asked again.

"I am not here to look for trouble and wouldn't want to hurt anybody," I said still on my guard.

It seemed my answer did not only anger them further but infuriated them as well. The guy with dark hair dropped my bag and swung the batten stick he had in his hand with the intention of hitting me on my left arm since he was in front of me. I went down and the batten caught his friend who was behind me on the left rib cage. It was really severe and I knew that it was going to take some time for the pain to subside. That was my opportunity to get away. The guy in front of me tried to use the batten again but did not have the time to really stabilize himself as I grabbed it with my left hand and landed a powerful punch on his nose with my right hand. It sent him crashing to the ground. At the same time, blood started oozing out of his nose. The pain he inflicted on his friend had not subsided and so I picked up my bag and started running to where I had to pick up a taxi while they laid there on the street nursing their wounds. I was running and looking behind and soon noticed that the two who tried to hurt me had more friends. In fact, it was a whole gang and they were after me. I prayed to God to safe me because I was scared of what they were going to do if they finally caught up with me.

Behold, it seemed I called for God's help just when He had His eyes focused on me. A young lady on a scooter came from the opposite direction and turned just in front of me.

"Come on," she shouted.

I jumped on the scooter and she whisked me away. She started off towards the direction I intended boarding a taxi to head home but soon negotiated a bend and headed west. We were to go some two and a half kilometres in that direction. There were a lot of garbage heaps and overflowing garbage bins on our escape route. Mostly simple houses of at most three bedrooms were in that direction. She rode into an open garage of one of the simple houses and locked the gate once we were in.

"None of those guys would come to look for you here," she told me. "You just have to stay here for a while and let the tension die down.

"Who are you and why did you decide to help me?" I asked.

She did not answer the first part of my question but gave an answer for the second part.

"I have seen many foreigners beaten and sometimes killed here for no good reason. I just happened to be at the right place, at the right time today to help you because I did not want those guys to hurt you," she said.

"Do you go around helping foreigners who run into trouble?" I asked.

The question went before I had time to think. I realized that the question was ill placed and stupid and tried to digress but she insisted on providing an answer.

"It is not my job to go wandering around town looking for foreigners in trouble to rescue. I could not be there and allow them hurt you without doing something. You would have done the same thing if I was in a similar situation, wouldn't you?" she asked.

"Of course I would have helped," I responded.

She left me and went through a door at the back of the garage that led into the main house. My curiosity on whether she lived there or not was taken care of. She returned just four minutes later with two sandwiches, one in each hand. The one in her right hand was bigger and she handed it to me. "I know you must be hungry after putting in some effort to defend yourself. You might still need more energy to run when you get out of here," she said laughing.

I laughed too but went on to ask how she knew that I could speak English which was the language she used before whisking me off.

"Many people who come here and cannot speak Italian, speak English. I did not need someone to tell me that you are a foreigner. I knew it just by looking at you. Anybody can see that because you look different. But I am not like those who hate people for just looking different. That is senseless and mean," she said.

"Thank you for seeing things that way. I think you are an angel," I told her. She smiled and thanked me for such kind words. I was marvelled by her behaviour and started having the feeling that we could really get along. She put herself in danger to safe me whom she did not even know. That was something really wonderful though I felt that it was too risky taking a total stranger to the home she lived in with the rest of her family. Back in Cameroon I had known people who had wanted to help some strangers by taking them into their homes and the 'guests' ended up killing their host and raping their wives and daughters before making away with valuable items. Maybe she did not see things that way and did not consider the act a risk. Whatever the case, I was grateful that she was there to safe me from an angry group of young men.

We remained silent for a little while in that garage before she spoke again.

"Where were you going to when I found you?" she asked.

Without saying a word, I unzipped my little bag and took the address of the house which Catalina wrote and gave me. I showed her just as I did to any taxi driver I met for him to know my destination. My rescuer knew where that was but it was not her place to take me there. I took out my cell phone from my little bag and called the house. It was Catalina who picked up the receiver. She asked where I was and I told her that I had no idea. Startled she asked me to explain further and I told her that I was attacked by some young men and had to run to an unknown place. She asked me to describe what I could see around me so that she could come and pick me up. I handed the phone to the young lady who rescued me and she spoke with Catalina in Italian. She handed the phone back to me when she had given Catalina the description and Catalina told me that she was going to be with me between 20 and 25 minutes. She hung up after she said that.

While we waited for Catalina to come and get me, I asked her what her name was. That was the second time I was doing it.

"My name is Gloria. I have two brothers and a sister," she said. "As you can see, this is not a rich neighbourhood and if we are living here, it means that we are not rich. But since we never go to bed hungry and hardly fall sick, I can say that we are rich somehow. I ...," She halted abruptly and I guessed that she was probably asking herself why she was telling such confidential information to a total stranger. She was probably trying to sustain a conversation with the intention of making me comfortable but in the course of doing so, she was exposing her family to me. I could not blame her for stopping abruptly because the world had become a very unsafe place and that made it difficult trusting people. There was therefore need to be careful.

A brief but tense moment of silence ensued but the hooting of a car outside the garage gate was very timely. It was Catalina and Gloria was careful as she opened the doors of the garage. She did not want that anyone should notice that there was a stranger there. Catalina came in and the doors were shut again. I narrated the whole incident to her and how Gloria rescued me. She thanked Gloria for saving her son and invited her to come for supper the next day which was Sunday. She took me home and we decided that whenever I had to come over, I had to call when I was some 30 minutes away from the city so that she or Mr Finley could pick me up at the bus stop. Either of them equally had to go and see me off at the end of each visit.

Gloria came at 12:30 the next day for lunch. After eating, Mr Finley and Catalina went out and sat by the swimming pool. Gloria and I moved to the sitting room where we sat watching TV. I used the opportunity to thank her again because were it not for her timely intervention, I would have been either in hospital or a morgue. I equally got to know her better. I asked her questions on what she did for a living and her likes and dislikes. She gave me answers which from my judgment were very honest. I wished I had more time to be there but I really had to head back to Monzuno.

Catalina was the one who took me to the bus stop. We could not take Gloria along because she came with her scooter. We all left at the same time after exchanging phone numbers. I also gave her a description of where I worked and she promised to surprise me there some day. While in the bus, I thought of our encounter and smiled. I could not tell but something was happening which I had no power to stop.

22

I got to my destination and that incident with the gang of idle youths spiced my conversation with everyone at the estate. Everyone felt terrible about what happened. The solidarity was total and they all thanked God that by his grace, nothing happened to me. I also told them of Gloria who saved me and the promise she made about coming to visit me at the estate. My boss expressed his enthusiasm at meeting the young lady who saved me. He really looked forward to seeing her. But my African brothers sounded rather indifferent. It seemed they were already too used it and saw what happened to me more as part of the fate that awaited those that lived in a foreign land. Uche told me that I was really lucky to have gotten away unharmed.

Since I was back at the estate, I had to put the incident behind me and concentrate on the new chapter that was about to open in my life. Catalina certainly believed that Gloria only saved me and our encounter ended with that supper of appreciation we had together. What she did not know was that Gloria and I communicated almost on a daily basis after that incident. She came to Monzuno as she promised. I visited her each time I went to the city to visit my parents but I did not go to her home. We met at a little football field in her neighbourhood. When the relationship became really serious, my colleagues warned me. They told me that there were some Italians who were radical and could see our relationship as insulting. "You cannot be stealing their jobs and at the same time taking their women," Uche warned. I was aware of all that and knew that I could be killed. But that was not enough to stop me. I loved her and she loved me too. Just for that fact, I was prepared to take the risk. However, I took some precautions not to expose myself to unnecessary danger. I boarded a taxi even if it meant going for just five hundred meters. There was no need fighting for love if I was going to end up dead.

That notwithstanding, all was well until one year before I had to leave Italy. I went to visit Mr Finley and Catalina as usual. I made a stopover at the little football pitch where Gloria and I always had our rendezvous. We met and she decided that we make our relationship known to her parents. She told me that she was tired of meeting me in hiding and wished for it to end. Her family was not rich and I knew that if there was one social class where love, tolerance and solidarity thrived most, it was among the poor people. Race did not matter much so long as everyone was poor. I knew what poverty was and was certain that I was not going to encounter any resistance since we belonged to the same social class. I agreed to Gloria's proposal and we arranged that I come over to her house the next day in the afternoon which was a Sunday.

With the rendezvous already taken, I left for the main road which led to the northern part of the city full of excitement. It was when I got there that I decided to call to inform my parents that I had arrived. It was Catalina who picked up the receiver that day and told me that she was on her way. I knew that I would have to answer some questions when she arrived to pick me up. I did not call when I was 30 minutes away from the city as had always been the case. Telling her that I forgot was not going to be a realistic answer. "*What would I tell her if she asks?*" I asked myself. That was one hell of a problem and only a woman could put a man into it. Indeed, Gloria was the reason why I break laid down rules and had to ignore the risk of being attacked by the gang that once attacked me before. To solve the problem, I resolved to tell her the whole truth if she asked. After all, I was already a full grown up man and there was nothing wrong with having a girlfriend.

Catalina got to where I was and I jumped into the car. The first question she asked was why I did not call as usual before getting into town. It was then I made my true confession including the planned rendezvous we had the next day.

"Gloria must be a very lucky girl. I wish you both the best of luck," she said. . She was particularly happy because she knew me so well and saw my relationship as a mark of responsibility. She was right in seeing things that way because I was working and earning money. There was no better place to invest that money than in a family of my own.

When we got home, nothing was really interesting in and around the house because I had my mind focused on the rendezvous of the next day. If there was a means to make the time go faster, I would have done it. I spent the rest of the day imagining, singing to myself and feeling really happy. At some point I asked myself what was happening to me and wondered if other people who fell in love tended to behave and feel that way. I began imagining myself taking Gloria to that point where the mountain touches the sky. I believed the place was completely problems free. But all that was only wishful thinking. Whatever the case, I knew that a new stage in my life was to begin with that introduction the next day.

Sunday came and I went to church with Mr Finley and Catalina. When we returned home after church, it was Mr Finley who asked when I intended to go for my rendezvous. That question was unmistakable. Catalina had told him everything when they were in their room in the night. I told him the time and he congratulated me. He offered me a new black pair of trousers and a pink shirt to put on and advised me not to be late. They had no plans to go out and so Catalina offered to give me a lift to my place of rendezvous. We left the house at 11:55.

We arrived the neighbourhood at 12:20 and Catalina made a U-turn after dropping me off. But before leaving, she asked me to call her when I was through. I went into the family home of Gloria and she was there to welcome me. She held my hand and took me to the table where her father and mother were already seated. Her sister and two brothers were still awaited and they came in from their rooms shortly after. Gloria had to go and get her younger sister from the room. Everyone was wondering what she was doing that she had to keep people waiting. In some other homes, others would have started eating without the person who was absent but that was not the case with Gloria's family. Everyone had to be present because they did not want to give room to anyone to start feeling that he or she was not important.

When everyone was present, prayers were said and everyone started eating. Gloria decided to make the announcement just at that moment.

"You all know that Martin Smith here is my friend and I rescued him once from one of those gangs of delinquents in this city. I told you that we were just mere friends but for some time now, we have been more than just mere friends," she said with a smile on her face.

Her mother and her kid sister smiled but not the three males in the house. Her father and two brothers stopped eating. It seemed the information cut their appetite and the food which was very appetizing at the start became sour, tasteless and disgusting. Her two brothers left the table and went back to their rooms after giving me a very stern look. Her father did not leave but rose from his seat before speaking.

"All my life, I had worked hard to get my family out of poverty," he began. "I have fought really hard to provide for your needs. Just when I was about to achieve that dream of getting us out of poverty, recession set in and I lost my job. The only thing I can call my achievement is this house. I am still fighting hard even at this moment to provide this food which you are opening your large mouth to put in, by polishing the shoes of rich men in rich neighbourhoods in this city. There are times I receive insults from them when they feel that I had not done my job well. I swallow my pride and take the insults because of you and that is why I've continued doing that humiliating job. Where did I go wrong in all that? What have I done that you have decided to repay me like this? Instead of looking for someone who can help you when you are in trouble, you've settled for 'something' which is not up to a human being."

I lost my appetite and the reaction of the head of the house made Gloria's mother and kid sister to also loss appetite as well. I bent my head on the table after pushing the plate of food a little further away from me, wondering what on earth was happening to me. Gloria who had listened to her father without interrupting him decided to do so when he started calling me disparaging names.

"What has he done wrong to you and what is wrong with us loving each other?" she asked.

"That question is not supposed to come up," he blasted. "Have you taken just a little time off to think of me and what my friends and people around here would say about me? They would say that my daughter has fallen in love with some monkey from I don't know which part of Africa, and all negative things. You want to repay me for all what I've done for you by making me a laughing stock in this community."

"So this is all what this drama is all about...your pride," Gloria said.

I considered that I had heard enough and had equally over stayed my welcome. I left the house and went in front of the house where I called Catalina to come and pick me up barely 30 minutes after she came and dropped me. She could sense from my voice as I spoke that there was something wrong but when she tried to ask what the matter was, I just told her with a lot of insistence to come and take me home. Tears had built up and it took only the manhood in me to prevent them from spilling out through my eyes. Back in the house, there was still some heated exchange between Gloria and her father. I could hear them from outside as I waited for Catalina. She arrived and picked me up.

I poured out my frustration to Catalina on our way home. She felt really terrible and lacked words to console me with. There was dead silence until we got home.

I went straight to my room and fell on my bed. I buried myself in thoughts and asked myself what was in me that made some people like Gloria's father hate me so much. Was I really ugly that I could not be considered a human being and be compared only to a monkey? I just could not comprehend it. My self-examination led to self-pity but I was not supposed to let it get me down. I consoled myself that he was just one out of millions of Italians who had ever said such a thing to me. *"If he does not consider me a human being and sees me as a monkey, it is his right. But he never created me and my destiny does not lie in his hands,'* I told myself.

I soon heard a knock on my door. It was Catalina who already opened the door half way and was wondering if I would let her come in. I asked her to come in. She did and sat on one end of my bed. She looked at me for a while in silence.

"I'm sorry about what happened to you today," she said. "There is one question I would like to ask you."

"Please go ahead," I urged.

"Would you turn your friend away if she comes here because of what her father said to you?" she asked.

I was direct and frank in my response.

"Gloria is an individual and her father is another individual. If there is someone whose actions I should hate, they should be those of her father. I have no problem with Gloria. On the contrary, I love her. There is no reason why she should suffer as a result of the actions of her father," I said.

"I know what your friend's father said to you was very hard. If you saw him in a helpless situation like in a ditch, would you help him out?

216

I began to wonder why she was asking me such questions. She could read from my looks that other questions were running through my mind. But I provided an answer all the same.

"Gloria's father is just a human being like me and I don't see why I had to allow his words hurt me in the first place. If he was my God, I would have had every reason to be worried. Now that he is not, I will just consider him as many other people who act out of ignorance. I will help him if I find him in trouble. What I hate are his actions and not him. I am hopeful that he shall one day come to realize that there is more that unite us humans than separate us. The differences between us lie only in what the eyes can see," I said.

"That was the response I was expecting to hear. Never let anger take hold of your heart. The destructive force of anger could be compared only to that of a hurricane. If there is one thing I admire you for, it is the way you reason. I am proud to call you my son. Well, there is someone down in the sitting room who really wants to talk to you. I will go to my room and allow you talk freely. You will have quite much to tell each other, I'm sure," she said and left.

I went down to the sitting room and found Gloria there. She rose to her feet as soon as she saw me.

I moved to where she was and put my arms around her.

"I'm so sorry about what happened today," she said with tears streaming from her eyes.

I just held her and did not say anything. I was certain of one thing and it was my love for her. That was one thing that was really worth fighting for. She was scared that the reactions of her father and brothers were going to push me to abandon her out of fear. That did not cross my mind even for a second. I was not prepared to let her be taken away from me without a fight. However, I had one worry and it was how we were going to continue seeing each other. It was already crystal clear that I was no longer going to loiter around her neighbourhood. If I were going to be caught around there by one of her brothers, it was obvious that I was going to beaten mercilessly. It was imperative that we sought a way out of the situation we found ourselves in more especially as we already knew those who did not want to see us together.

Gloria was the first to attempt a proposal which she thought was going to be a magic wand that would solve our problems.

"People always say 'Time heals all wounds.' I think it can apply in our situation. If they are not prepared to accept or realize that you are the one I love, it means that they are not interested in my happiness. I will leave them and follow you wherever you go and I'm sure that when they discover that we actually love each other, they would accept it," she said.

That was too radical and I did not want her to start making a choice between me and her family. There was love for sure between us but we hadn't had a real situation to put it to test. I was not certain about the future as far as taking care of her needs were concerned. Besides, if she turned her back on her family with my blessing, what would she become if something happened to me? How would she return to her family that she had earlier rejected? The act of leaving her family and coming with me for them to later on realize that we were meant for each other was not bad in itself but it was too risky given the degree of uncertainty that still hung over the future. I made it clear to her that for that moment I was just a stranger and was not supposed to be more important to her than her family. I proposed to her that the first step to take was to begin by convincing her mother and sister who were already sympathetic to her situation to remain on her side. As for her two brothers, they were jobless and probably wanted their sister to hook up with someone of substance who could provide solutions to their job problems. I was sure that they were going to move over to her side if they came to realize that I could also do something. They were obviously not going to be much of a problem. But her father was definitely going to be a very hard nut to crack. His problem was not whether I was man enough or not but that I looked different and that was going to be an ulcer in his pride.

218

But even if her whole family were against her, it had to remain the ultimate refuge when all is lost. It was therefore important to take measures that would not side-line them but would keep them close by.

I was happy that I dissuaded her from taking a hard stand against her family. I could not afford to look at the situation simply from the side of her family. I was not sure that if we had met in Cameroon where my own family was, they would have welcomed her open handed. I was certain that there would have been resistance from my paternal family as they would have seen her as 'that foreigner'. The risks were obvious already on her side and highly possible on my own side and that was the reason why I urged her not to side-line her family out of anger. Moreover, we concluded that we would continue communicating on the phone as we had always done and she would come to Monzuno from time to time. I was also going to see her each time I got to the city but we were either going to meet at the home of my parents or in any other public place in the city far from her neighbourhood. We separated after arriving at that consensus on a lighter mood. I made her to understand that it was important that she spent more time at home so as not to give her family the impression that she was meeting me in secret.

23

After she left, I knew things were going to be different and hard for her from that day on. Her family was going to keep a close eye on her and probably follow her sometimes whenever she went out. I just could not understand why two grown up people could not decide to fall in love without having to face some resistance from some quarters. I had no quarrel with Gloria's family members worrying about her wellbeing but her wellbeing was not the issue in that particular case. The clash of interest was the real issue. Whatever the case, there shall always be interests to protect or defend and that shall remain part of human nature that must be tolerated.

However, Mr Finley who was not at home when Gloria arrived excitedly asked how the introduction went. I narrated the story to him and just like Catalina, he felt really terrible. He understood how badly I must have been feeling and decided to call his friend, Mr Salghetti, to tell him that his son wasn't going to be returning that Sunday afternoon because he had a depression. I had to travel back to Monzuno only on Monday afternoon. He decided to help take away some of my pain by taking me out to the cinema with Catalina. We left the cinema and went instead to a restaurant to have dinner that day. It was all fun and I enjoyed it. I spent the morning period on Monday watching TV and left for the bus stop at 13:30 from where I started my journey down south to Monzuno.

I got to the estate in the evening and went straight to the sitting room where Mr Salghetti was watching TV.

"Welcome back son," he said with a smile.

"Thank you boss," I responded and smiled back.

"I trust you had a nice trip," he said.

"Indeed sir, I had. Thank you," I replied.

My boss was a very caring man and I knew he was going to ask what happened before I sunk into a depression as his friend called and informed him. He asked me to have a seat and the question did not delay in coming. I narrated what transpired and he shook his head in disapproval.

"Only an uncivilized person would look at the back of a book and claim to know all what is written in it. If they do not want you, it means that they do not love you. It would be better for you to go to where people would accept you the way you are and appreciate the qualities in you and not simply throw a glance at you and assume that they already know everything about you. I'm only happy that the times are changing and legislations have been passed making it possible for people of African origin to become nationals here. It is already a step towards progress but those who become nationals here would still have to fight for acceptance and recognition. The road ahead is long and difficult but with determination, they would certainly make it," he said with an uneasy smile.

A little moment of silence ensued during which he fixed his eyes on me. I'm sure he was probably feeling sorry for me and those who were in the same situation like me.

"I have never really understood why some people would take upon themselves to make this life which happens to be very short a living hell for others. The sad thing about it all is that mostly youths between the ages of 18 and 35 engage in such devilish acts. Perhaps that is the reason why they die too young leaving their parents behind. Don't worry, there is a God who is alive and I know He will always stand by those who are persecuted simply for looking different," he said.

I thanked him for his usual wise words and asked him to excuse me because I wanted to go to my room to have a shower. He urged me not to take long as supper was already ready.

I returned twenty minutes later as I did not want to keep them waiting. I was not really hungry so after eating alittle I went to bed.

I was not feeling sleepy and my mind would not settle down either. I remembered the words of Mr Salghetti after I narrated my ordeal to him. I tried to make some meaning out of what he meant by 'leaving people who did not want me and going to those who would accept and appreciate the qualities in me.' Could it be that he was indirectly inviting me to be part of his family? His two daughters were not married and as a man who loved people and children, I imagined that was certainly a problem to him. But going out with one of his daughters was definitely out of the question. I loved them just like sisters and considered them as such. *"Oh well, maybe I'm just allowing my imagination go too wild and Mr Salghetti had no such intention in mind when he made his statements to me. All that is just total nonsense,"* I said to myself and decided to shove the thoughts aside.

The next morning, I went back to my routine which was to last for the next three months without any major incident. I rang Gloria regularly and she called me too. She visited me twice within the three months after the incident I had at her home with her father and two brothers. I also visited her all the times I went to the city within the three months. Everything was perfect and I considered that it was almost time to move our relationship to the next level. It was my turn to get tired of meeting the woman I loved only in hiding. But what to do with her brothers and father became more preoccupying. There was no way I could impose myself on them. What could I do to make them love me? If I knew where I could find the three wise men from the East back then, I'd have gone to them for inspiration.

However, at the start of the fourth month after the humiliating introduction, I called Gloria. I could sense a lot of uneasiness in her voice as she spoke. So I got worried and asked her what the matter was.

"A man of about 28 years old called Totti has been coming to our home for some time now. He drives a big car and comes from a wealthy family. He has told me and my parents that he loves me and would want to marry me. He is bringing gifts for my father and brothers and in return they are piling a lot of pressure on me to marry him. Smith I love you so much and want you to come and take me out of this dilemma," she said in tears.

"A man can force a horse to the stream but he can't force it to drink water. The solution to that problem is in your hands," I told her and hung up.

I was in my room when I made that call and crashed on my bed as soon as I hung up. I was in a foreign land and had to fight with a rich and powerful adversary who was not my match, over the love of one woman. With his money and power, he was capable of crushing me with ease. He could decide to pay some tugs to eliminate me and get away with it. Many have suffered that fate and nothing happened after that. I was not different from the victims. I was really powerless and could feel my manhood shaken from its very foundation. I dreaded finding myself in situations I could not handle. But all hope was not lost simply because Totti was interested in her. There was still a little string on which I could hang and it was the fact that Gloria was the one to decide whether to give in or not.

Within that fourth month, I was really hurting inside though I pretended to do things normally. I was determined not to let anyone know of what I was going through. I considered that it was my problem which I had to handle it alone. I called Gloria two days after that hurting announcement and it was her elder brother, Giorgio who picked up the receiver of her phone. I asked him where Gloria was that he was the one taking her calls.

"Smith or whatever you call yourself, stay away from my sister if you know what is good for you. Someone who is a real man has come to marry her and if things go as planned, she would be getting married in two months. Go for a woman who is as inferior as yourself and stay away from us. That is a warning and I will not sound it again. If you will not behave, then you will do so in the grave," he warned.

I tried to ask him why they were so unkind to me but he insisted that he had warned me and I had to stay away if I knew what was good for me. I could feel the world crumbling on my head and I found it hard to believe what Giorgio told me about Gloria getting married. I became bent on finding out if indeed she was going to get married from her in person. I called with a lot of insistence but never had any response for the three weeks that I kept trying. I concluded from the non-response that perhaps she had fallen in love with Totti and was going to be happy marrying him after all. Since I could not find any other reason for her long silence, I gave up and prayed that she find happiness in her marriage.

I did not go to the city to visit my parents during that nerve wrecking month. I called and told them that there was too much work and I was only going to visit them the next month. They asked me to take care and to extend their greetings to Gloria. Little did they know that my world was falling apart and Gloria was at the centre of it all. I kept thinking and wondering why love could sometimes be so cruel. I tried to brave it as a man but it took its toll on me. I started losing weight and isolated myself from the other workers most of the time. Even when I was among them, I was always silent. I wanted to keep my problem to myself and was lucky that no one questioned my attitude.

I went to the city on the third weekend of the next month and Mr Finley came and picked me up at the bus stop. While we were on our way home, my phone started ringing. It was a strange number. I answered and it was Gloria on the other end. It was a bit loud and Mr Finley could hear her as she identified herself. She inquired if she could meet me at home and I told her that I was going to wait for her. Mr Finley looked at me and smiled after she hung up.

"I can see that the two of you are really going to go far," he said.

I smiled uneasily which gave him the impression that my love life was perfect. "I am not growing any younger and should be thinking of building a family of my own," I told him. My heart bled with pain as I said that. Frustration started enveloping me and I became afraid that it could spill out through my voice and Mr Finley would immediately know that there was something wrong. So I decided to remain silent until we got home.

When we arrived home, I went to my room and stayed there. Mr Finley remained in the sitting room switching from one TV channel to the next. Catalina was not at home and had to return only in the evening. I waited in my room for the time Gloria would arrive. There were so many questions I wanted to ask her.

I heard the doorbell ring 45 minutes after we entered the house and I left my room to go and see if it was Gloria. Indeed she was the one and Mr Finley ushered her in and offered her a seat. He went back to the seat he occupied before she came and continued watching TV. I sat down for a while with them there.

"I can see that the two of you would make a wonderful couple," Mr Finley said to Gloria. "I know you women could be gentle like flowers when you are happy but could sting like serpents when you are angry. Please Gloria, when that time to sting comes, don't be too severe on my son, Ok?

Gloria laughed and promised to do everything not to sting at all. His comments also made me laugh. But I was itchy to take her outside and fire her with the tons of questions I had in mind. I asked Mr Finley to excuse us as I had something really important to discuss with Gloria.

I took her out of the house and we went and sat by the swimming pool. There was some gap between us and I did not look at her in the face. She looked nervous. She tried to narrow the gap between us by coming closer and taking my hand but I shifted away.

"What is it? Have I become so cold to you simply because I told you that Totti is running after me?" she asked.

I did not answer the question and went straight to what I wanted to ask her.

"For some time now, you've not been taking my calls. I've called several times and have either had no response or your elder brother who informed me that you were getting married in a few days from now. He also warned me to stay away from you and your family if I know what is good for me. What am I supposed to make of all that?" I asked.

She drew again closer and I did not shift. She took hold of my left hand and I could see tears running down her eyes. She opened her mouth to speak but it seemed the words got stocked in her throat. The silent weeping intensified and I had to take her into my arms. I was heartbroken seeing her like that. I calmed her down and then she started narrating what she had been through.

"You would not imagine what the past months have been for me. My cell phone was confiscated by my brother with the blessing of my father. Some of your calls could not be answered because your number was registered in my phone. My movements were restricted. I managed to visit you down at the estate because I had to deceive them that I had to go to the hospital for some medical check-up or the salon for a hair do. My life has been a living hell since that day I introduced you to my family. I am under intense pressure to marry Totti," she said.

"I'm really sorry to hear that. I know what it is to be under pressure. But tell me something; are you going to marry Totti?" I asked.

"Smith, I don't love Totti. The only one I can feel love for is you. I love you so much," she replied.

"Does that mean that you are not going to marry him?" I asked again.

She did not say anything but kept staring at me. I could not read anything in her silence or looks and urged her to say something.

"I have to marry him for your sake. If I turn him down, my brothers could come after you and if they do not come, they could hire someone to kill you. I will never know peace if something

227

happened to you because of me. Do you know what it is to live with guilt on your conscience?" she asked.

"You have just said that you don't love Totti. In that case don't marry him. Are you going to sacrifice yourself to satisfy the greed of some of your family members to the detriment of your own happiness?" I asked.

"If it was just for the sake of my family, I would not do it. I'm sacrificing myself for you because I want you to stay alive. If you can still remember, I suggested running away with you but You objected to that proposal and from what you said, I really got to realize the importance of a family. I am ready to abandon mine to come with you but I would need your own family to shield me. Can you guarantee that if I leave here and we get back to your country, your family will welcome me with open arms?" she asked in tears.

I did not have an answer to that question. Instead I went on to plead.

"If really you love me, don't marry him I beg of you," I said almost in tears.

"Please Smith, don't make this more difficult for me than it is already. I have made my decision and will carry on with it," she said and left in tears.

I remained seated there by the swimming pool with my world which had come to a standstill. I did not know what else to do. If it was possible for me to disrupt the wedding on the day it had to take place, I would have done it. But taking such a risk meant that I had to carry my casket along. I just had to accept defeat and get into my head once and for all that Gloria was not meant for me. Life made it that there were to be winners and losers. I had lost at that moment and had to accept it.

I left the place I was seated by the swimming pool two hours after Gloria left. I went back into the house and found Mr Finley who had dosed off after watching TV for long. I passed with the intention of not waking him up. Just when I was about to take the stairs, he asked me if my friend had gone. I said yes and he was surprise that she left without even saying goodbye. That was a bit unusual and he had the right to be surprise.

"I hope you did not have a fight," he said.

"There was no fight. She came and found you asleep and did not want to disturb. But she asked me to inform you when you woke up that she had left," I lied. I went to my room without another word and crashed on my bed.

I slept all afternoon and when it was time for supper in the evening, I did not leave my room. Catalina who had returned was probably wondering what I was doing in my room that I did not come out to greet her. It was obvious that she was going to come to see what was wrong. I heard a knock on my door and immediately knew she was the one. I asked her to come in and the first thing she did was to place her palm on my forehead. Realizing that there was nothing wrong, she still asked if she could call in a doctor. I objected to the idea insisting that I was alright. I was conscious of the kind of illness I had and no medical doctor could help me. I told Catalina that I just wanted to stay in bed and rest because there was a lot of tiring work at the estate of Mr Salghetti. That was convincing enough and she smiled and left my room, closing the door behind her.

When I was certain that she was down stairs, the full weight of my hopelessness and powerlessness came back in full force. I seized that moment alone in my room to cry a little. That helped me to see and understand better the turbulent nature of the world adults lived in.

24

The next morning, I did not go to church and pleaded with Mr Finley to take me to the bus stop. He did not ask any questions. I knew that he must have sensed that I was in some kind of crisis but did not want to ask. I had no intention of telling him about my love troubles in the first place. However, I boarded the bus destined for Monzuno at 07:50. He said goodbye to me and got back into his car and left. At 08:00, the bus was on the move. In the course of the journey, I planned on burying myself in work once I got to the estate. Any moment of idleness was going to push me into thinking of Gloria and thinking of her was going to bring nothing but pain. That was what I did until the eve of her wedding day which was a Friday.

On the said Friday, I still had a deep feeling within me that a miracle could happen and the wedding would not take place the next day. I wanted to ring her phone but refrained after a second thought. I did my morning chores and completed it at 11:20. I had to begin the afternoon shift at 14:30. That time lap between the morning and afternoon shifts was too much and if I did not find something to keep me busy, wishful thinking was going to kill me. I got on one of the horses and decided to visit all the hills my eyes could spot around Monzuno. I informed my boss and some of my colleagues of where I was going. I explored the hills and admired the beautiful sceneries of the environs. Though they were a source of distraction, they reminded of what I had lost because I wished I was there with Gloria. It became obvious that Gloria was going to occupy my thoughts for some time to come. By the time I thought of going back to begin work, it was already 14:00 and I was quite far off. So, I hurried as I could though I got to the estate 25 minutes late.

I did my work for that day and in the evening, I joined the rest for supper. I went to my room after that and since there was no work to be done, my mind went back to Gloria. There was nothing I could do to avoid it. I did not sleep all night and kept wishing and wishing. But I knew that my aspirations at that moment were going to remain just wishes.

On that Saturday morning of her wedding, I had a terrible headache and could not get out of bed. Uche whom I had to work with that morning came to my room to fetch me perhaps after getting tired of waiting. He knocked on my door, walked and called. But from my reaction, he knew there was something wrong. He went and informed Mr Salghetti who wasted no time in calling in a doctor. I was prescribed some drugs and two days bed rest. I took the drugs but my mind was greatly troubled. I believe they could not work effectively as they would have because I did not have a peaceful mind. My treatment was only going to be effective when the reality was bare in front of me to see. Mr Finley was informed but asked not to worry because I was in good hands.

At 15:20 that same Saturday, I went out of my room and moved to a slop which was close to the house. There was a gentle breeze blowing and I enjoyed its coolness on my flesh. I assumed at that moment that the man of God must have pronounced Gloria and Totti as husband and wife. It was psychologically soothing as I became convinced beyond every reasonable doubt that there was no possibility left for Gloria and I to ever be together again. My psychological and emotional pains subsided and that was the best moment for the drugs I took that day to start working effectively. I watched the sun set as I sat on the slop. Though the weak rays of the setting sun fell on the surrounding hills and added to their beauty, my love not only for Gloria but women as a whole set with it. I did not have interest in women or looked at another woman until I left Italy.

I did not have two days bed rest as prescribed by the doctor. I was feeling much better the next day which was Sunday and went to church. The homily that day was centred on letting go things that could prevent us from moving forward in life. That was a very timely message from the man of God and I capitalized on it. Gloria's love belonged to Totti and hanging onto it was like hanging onto a broken dream. It was therefore important for me to let go that love which had already left me. So, I convinced myself that losing the love of Gloria was not the end of the world and it became imperative that I pieced the pieces of my life together and move on. With that galvanizing thought, I started work soon after church.

From that day onward, I did all I could not to think of Gloria as a lost treasure. I respected her as a married woman. I never saw her again face to face but that does not mean that I stopped communication with her. I did not call her but she always called me. She kept speaking to me as though we were still lovers and cried out her nightmare of living in a loveless marriage most of the times. She compared me to Totti a good number of times. I sometimes felt sorry for her and thought that our continuous communication was perhaps making things difficult for her. Maybe cutting links with her completely was going to help but she told me she was going to die if that were to happen. I sometimes ran out of words to use in consoling her. Out of frustration, I asked her to take the love for Smith and give it to Totti whom she decided to marry. That was the only way she could find happiness. On the whole, I don't think I had the right to blame her for anything. It was not as if she did not know what going into a loveless marriage would entail but I think she deliberately sacrificed herself to suffer for the wellbeing of her family. I was a good listener and a wall on which she could lean. That was what kept her in touch with me.

Six months after her wedding to Totti, I considered that it was time to turn over to a new page. I decided like Armah some years earlier to become a boss. I told Mr Salghetti that time had come for me to go back to my country and carry out some investment which would help take my family out of poverty. He was already more than a father to me and the announcement of my eminent departure created a lot of anxiety just as the other previous ones. It was not easy parting with someone who rescued me from unemployment and poverty. There was nothing in the world I could offer my boss to compensate him for all what he did for me. Besides, that was not the only nerve wrecking separation I had to deal with. I never saw what could bring Mr Finley to Cameroon. He told me that he intended moving to Nashville his home city in the United States in some years to come though he did not precise when. The two men were not only friends but fathers as well. But as a son, I had to leave them some day and forge my own path in life. That was the way destiny made it.

That notwithstanding, a very emotional send-off party was organized. Mr Finley and Catalina came in from the city. They all told me that I made the decision to be a man of my own at the right time. Though I was a son to them and they loved me very much, they had to let me go even though it was painful. They urged me never to stop going to church because everyone's destiny laid in the hands of God. I promised never to abandon the church and to be like their ambassador everywhere I went as I was determined to remain the good person they knew me to be.

I left Monzuno with some regrets because I was going to miss its people and the animals I was used to taking care of. Feeding the animals helped me cope with the shock of losing the one I loved so dearly in this world to another man. I was really going to miss that place. Nonetheless, I was on my way back to the city in the company of my parents. They were still not aware of what happened between me and Gloria because I didn't want them to know. Mr Finley asked what I was going to do about her at that moment that I was leaving Italy. It was a very disturbing question and I thought of making up a story and telling him. After a second thought I resolved that there was no need keeping the secret from them.

"Gloria is now a married woman," I broke the news at last.

It was as if I just dropped a bomb. Mr Finley who was on the steering wheel, pulled over and asked what I just said. I repeated it and he remained speechless. Catalina asked what happened and I told her honestly that I did not know. That was when Mr Finley started making sense out of my actions when I visited them not looking too well.

"Why did you not tell us," Mr Finley asked. "We are your parents here and your problem is our problem.

"Now I know what you have been through," said Catalina.

Shortly after she said that, my phone started ringing. It was Gloria calling. My parents were watching me to see if I was going to take the call. I did and she asked me how I was doing. I told her that I was doing fine and also informed her of my return to Cameroon. She asked when I intended to do that and I told her that I was on my way from Monzuno and intended making a stopover at home before heading to the airport. She pleaded if she could come over to see me at least before I left. I had nothing against her and saw no reason why I had to say no. I estimated the time we still had ahead of us before arriving home and asked her to meet us there.

As we got home and the car halted in front of the house, Gloria was already there. She held a little traveller's bag in her hand. We got out of the car and met her and all of us went into the house. We all sat down in the sitting room and it was Catalina who spoke first.

"My son just told us that you are a married woman now. You two formed a very wonderful couple and if someone came to tell me that you shall one day be apart, I would not believe it. What happened between you two?" she asked.

"It's a long story. Sometimes we want to do something knowing fully well the consequences but we go on to do it all the same. That is what happened between us and I now regret my action each day that goes by," she said with a sigh.

"Well, I don't know what else to say. We are soon going to see him off at the airport and I'm sure he has already informed you that he is returning back to Africa," he said.

"Indeed he has. I'm going to really miss him," she said.

"I think they would have one or two things to say to each other. Let's go and put our son's remaining belongings together," Catalina said to her husband and they left for my room.

Gloria and I were alone in the sitting room and she came and sat close to me. She took my left hand and held it before talking.

"I'm sorry about what I did. I should have thought of my own happiness first and not sacrifice myself to satisfy the whims and caprices of my family members. Now I know what it is to be engaged in a loveless marriage. Totti does everything to make me love him. He offers me everything I want, even those that I don't ask for. But I can't feel anything for him. My heart is with you. It has always been and will always be. I am now caught in a web and do not know how to get out. The only thing that makes me happy is that Carvalio, my kid brother has had a job in the company owned by Totti's family. He uses what he earns to keep the family. I also work there too. But I do not love the man I'm married to. That is the truth," she said.

"Don't you think you are sounding a bit weird? You are married to a man and professing your love to another," I said.

"Please Smith, I didn't come here for you to mock me. I am just pouring out my heart to you," she said.

I apologized for what I said as I realized that she was hurt. That apology swept her pain aside for a short while and a smile lit up her face. She went on to offer me the traveller's bag she came along with.

"What is in it?" I asked.

"Open it and see for yourself," she replied.

It was a three piece suit and from the material, it was obvious that it cost a fortune. I asked her if she took money from her husband to buy a suit for me. She felt offended and told me that she took money from what she earned. I apologized again and hug her for giving me such a wonderful gift. Her frustration vanished. I had another question to ask but started by pleading with her not to feel offended.

"Have you ever offered something like this to your husband?

She did not respond and I knew what it meant. I ask her to do so even if she did not love him because he was her husband. She promised she would try to get something for him. I insisted that it was not a matter of trying but actually doing it whole heartedly.

I soon considered that she had stayed too long and that was probably going to create some problems for her. I urged her to go back home. She insisted on having my physical address, phone number and e-mail address. I gave her my e-mail address and promised to send the others, once I got back to Cameroon. She gave me her e-mail address as well. She rose and made for the door. When she opened it, she turned and looked at me before stepping out. I thought that was the last time I was going to set eyes on her but she dashed back into the house all of a sudden and ran to where I was and fell on me. She hugged and held me so tight with her lips pressed on mine. I was powerless and did not have the strength to push her off because what we were doing was not correct. I just could not understand what was happening there. Don't ask me if I enjoyed it.

She finally left just when my parents re-emerged from my room and were making their way into the sitting room. It seemed they saw what she did before leaving.

"If she did love you that much, why did she marry someone else?" Catalina asked.

That was a question any normal person would have asked. But there was not going to be an answer. What was done was done and I was on my way out for good. I was accompanied to the Bologna International Airport on the evening of 4th November at 19:45. We got there and spent a lot of time in the lobby of the airport waiting for 22:00 when the plane had to take off.

At 20:45 the checking in began as well as the agony of separation. After everything of mine was checked, I had to go through the exit door which led to the plane but the looks in the faces of my parents prevented me from doing so. I turned and ran back to them and hugged them hoping that their warmth was going to give me the courage to go through the exit door. It did not and I had to repeat the running back process over three times. I'm sure the people at that airport were overwhelmed by the drama I was performing with my parents. What must have been very intriguing to them to see those I called mother and father looking so different from me. Anyway, whatever they thought or imagined didn't matter. My parents finally decided to leave first because that was the only option left. Seeing them was definitely going to prevent me from going through the door that led to the plane It worked and at 21:30 I was in the womb of the mighty bird that had to take me back to Cameroon. The plane touched down at the Douala International Airport in the morning of 5th November.

25

t 05:25, I was back in Cameroon. I had gone through the routine checks at the airport and was waiting for my luggage. It had to come after two hours and that was one of the problems with our airports. Luggage always took too long to be taken out of the plane and there were reports of some going missing. Before I left for Italy, there had been meetings on security of goods and persons in and around the airport but the realities on the ground remained largely unchanged. The meetings remained expensive talk shows where only lofty ideas were hatched but never saw the light of day in reality. There had been reports of items missing between the plane and the luggage room of the airport. If it happened to any of my luggage then, it would not have been a surprise to me because it was almost a normal thing. But thank God, I got everything I travelled with.

At 08:50 I left the airport premises on board a taxi to Guarantee Express a Travel Agency which was just 15 minutes away from the airport. I got there in no time and booked a bus bound for Bamenda, my home town. Six hours still separated me from there and I was anxious to get there.

I kept thinking a lot in the course of the journey. I wondered what my younger ones had become and if my father was still as cruel as he used to be. I wondered how they were going to react when they saw me again. There were just so many questions and I couldn't help asking then. I was anxious to see them and hug them again after so many years.

Santa Village laid on the way to Bamenda but I did not stop there because it was already too late in the evening. I decided to call my one time Boss, Mr Joel just when we arrived Santa and pleaded with him to kindly pick me up at the Agency. I gave the name of the Travel Agency and he told me that he was going to be there.

We finally arrived Bamenda from Douala at 19:30 because of the numerous stops we had to make on the way either to drop or pick up passengers or stop at police checkpoints. Mr Joel was there with his wife and their daughter, Rose, to pick me up. I asked him why he had to come with a whole delegation and he told me that he intended coming alone but after informing his wife and daughter that he had to come and pick me up, they insisted on coming too. I was glad to see them and we all loaded my things onto the pickup truck they brought and left for their family home.

They asked me a lot of questions about Italy on our way home. I told them that Italy was a nice country but people who looked like us had to fight really hard there. I talked to them about my wonderful employer and all what he did for me. I equally talked of Mr Finley and his wife, Catalina who were real parents to me. They asked me why I had to leave such wonderful people and come back to Cameroon. My response was that home remained home no matter what and I had to return because I felt that it was time to take my destiny into my own hands. That response pleased Mr Joel and he said that he always knew just by looking at me that I was going to make it in life. I just smiled and he went on to ask what I intended to do then that I was back in the country. I told him that I planned on investing my money in some business though I did not have any particular one in mind. A brief moment of silence followed after that.

I broke the short silence by telling Mr Joel that I was going to need his expert advice on which business to invest in. "I will always be ready to assist," he said with a smile. I thank him and then turned to Rose to find out whether she was still living with her parents. She said yes and I jokingly asked her mother why she still had to continue tolerating the presence of a full grown woman in her house. She replied that her daughter was never too old to be her child and for that reason she had to wait for that special man who truly loved her to come and take her away. That was the African way. With high rates of unemployment, children tend to stay much longer with their parents. Some ended up never leaving and ended up having children of their own. I wondered if that would have been my fate had I not run away from home and Mr Finley hadn't found me. Life was very tough and every day that went by, people had to develop thick skins to be able to face it.

At 20:10 we arrived at the home I was already used to. I asked if my room was still there at the boys' quarters and they said that everything was intact. I was really exhausted and the only thing I badly needed was sleep. I allowed them take out my things from the vehicle while I went in, had a shower, a bite and went off to bed.

The next morning, I woke up at 08:00 and went straight to the bath room to clean up. I went into the main house and had breakfast. I left the house after that to cash the money I sent via Western Union from Italy. I opened an account with the money in First Trust Bank. From there, my next destination was Santa village where my family was. I boarded a taxi at 09:50 and arrived Santa at 10:25.

The taxi driver wanted to end at Santa Motor Park and reload for Bamenda. I convinced him to change his mind by proposing something extra for him to take right below the house I once called home. Since he had to drive only along the major highway and not get into the muddy neighbourhoods, he accepted. However, as we drove across the village, I noticed that not much had changed after so many years. Only a few new houses were dotted here and there. The only place where real changes could be visible was around the Motor Park and its immediate environs.

At 10:45, the taxi halted some 45 meters below the house I was born in. I moved up the little slop that led to the yard but stopped some 15 meters from the main house. There were coffee plants and lots of plantain and banana suckers that obstructed the view of anyone on the yard who wanted to have a view of the highway below. From that distance and thanks to the obstruction of the plants, no one could see me. So, I stood there for a while to observe what was going on around the house. I could see my father sitting in front of

241

the main door. He was not alone. There were some three kids playing not some meters from where he sat whom I did not know. None of my younger ones were there. He was giving orders but no one was listening to him. The kids went on playing and when he tried to rise from his seat, they all ran in different directions. I could not believe that the man I was seeing was my father who used to rumble like thunder and no one would dare disobey him. He was just a shadow of his former self. The difference was too over whelming. Age indeed was a very cruel punisher.

I walked into the yard and all the playing stopped at once. The children ran to my father looking curiously at the stranger who just walked in. My father observed me for a while and I could sense that he had problems recognizing me.

"Who are you looking for or what can I do for you?" he asked.

I could not blame him for not making me out. I had changed from the skinny hopeless boy he was used to, to a huge bulky man over the years. Besides, the passage of time might have had their effects on his physical appearance and not his voice. It was still loud sounding and reminded me of the days he used to inflict pains on me with a cane.

"You mean to say that you cannot recognize me?" I asked.

"If I could recognize you, I wouldn't have asked who you are," he said.

I shook my head still to come to terms with the changes I could see before me. "Where is Jane, Benjamin and Joshua?" I asked.

That was when he recognized me but did not leap for joy as any parent would after separating with his child for a long time. It was not strange to me as I already had a fixed opinion about him in my mind. He went on to tell me that my younger ones had gone to the farm with their step mother.

"Who are these children?" I asked.

"They are your step brothers and sister," he replied.

"You have not been able to make anything out of those you already had before I left and have gone ahead to produce others? I can't believe this," I said.

"You are just coming back after so many years from I don't know where. You have not even sat down and you are already reproaching me. What is wrong with having more children?" he asked.

"I did not say that there was something wrong with having more children. My problem is having more children when you are unable to provide for them. Well, since you see no problem with having more children, I'm sure you are having no problems getting money out of your pockets to take care of their needs," I said.

"Are you by implication saying that I should have remained single after the death of your mother?" he asked.

"What would have been wrong with remaining single after the death of my mother? That would have been evidence that you truly loved her. I did not expect you to stay like that. When she was alive, you never loved her and that was why you kept a lot of concubines outside. But if you had to remarry, why didn't you go in for a woman who no longer wanted children?" I asked.

There was no response and I was already getting irritated with what I was seeing there. I asked him to tell me precisely where my kid brothers and sister went to and he did. They were in a farm some four kilometres away from home. I left again without entering the house and got to the highway where I hired a commercial motor bike to take me there and bring me back. With the 5000 francs I proposed, it was difficult for the bike rider to turn down because there was no way he would have made that amount even after working for the whole day.

I got to my destination just when my junior ones had just left the farm and were on their way back home with their different loads. They carried them on their heads and had to cover the four kilometres journey on foot. They dropped everything they carried as soon as they saw me. They looked really dirty as they did some tilling much earlier. With all that dirt on them, they all jumped on me and my clothes became soiled in a matter of seconds. The happiness of hugging them again made me to care less about the dirt on my clothes. I then went on to ask them a good number of questions about schooling and wellbeing. From their responses I gathered that Jane abandoned school in primary seven and preferred to learn a trade. Joshua and Benjamin also abandoned school and were not doing anything apart from assisting in the farm when they felt like. Concerning their wellbeing, they told me that they fed well through the use of force because their step mother always tried to feed her own children before giving them the left over. So most of the time, they seized the pot from her and took out the amount they needed before she could share the rest. When asked if my father still beat them so much, they told me that the cane did not mean anything to them because they were already too used to it. But Joshua was quick to point out that the old man was already tired and no longer had the strength to be manhandling them the way he would have loved to.

That was information which was enough to make me have sleepless nights. If my junior ones dropped out of school, it was because they did not see the importance of education. I could not determine whether they dropped out because of lack of finances or just sheer stubbornness. I think stubbornness was the probable reason. If there was something that I had to do, it was to reverse the situation as soon as possible by getting them back into school. At that moment I was talking to them, the academic year was already more than a month old. Time was therefore not on my side.

Nevertheless, the woman my father referred to as my step mother was not with them. I asked them where she was and they told me that she was still in the farm. I asked Jane to take me to her which she did. I introduced myself as the elder brother of Jane and she said that my father had told her a great deal about me. When I sought to know what kind of things they talked about, she did not say anything. That left me thinking that my father must have told her only nasty things about me. I had every reason to think that way because we did not separate on good terms.

I left her in the farm and was heading back to the road with Jane before remembering that I did not even ask her name. Jane told me that her name was Francisca. We took just ten minutes to get back to the road. I collected their loads and had them tied on the motor bike. I then asked them to hurry home while I went ahead on the bike. We were not going to use the same roads. They were going to use short cuts while I was going to use a much longer road since I was on a bike. But I was going to get home before them.

I got home and made known what I intended to do about my younger ones to my father. I told him that I wanted to take all of them to the City of Bamenda where I'd send them to school. I was just informing him. His opinion did not really matter because I considered that it was a failure on his part if they dropped out of school. But there were some problems I had to take care of before bundling them to town. I had to secure an apartment to ensure that they had a place to lay down their heads. I called Mr Joel as soon as that thought came to mind and asked him to call all the people he knew to keep their eyes and ears open to any news about a house to let. He told me that he knew an apartment whose occupant packed out less than a week before. I pleaded with him to rush there and see the owner if he had some time to spare. He told me he was on his way there. I did not see how I was going to carry my siblings to the one room I spent the night in at his boys' quarters.

I did not have quite much to discuss with my father and rose to leave. But he asked me to hold on a little. I did not disobey.

"You have said that you are going to take all your younger ones with you to the city to send them to school. What about these ones that you are seeing for the very first time?" he asked.

"I was taken aback by the question. I looked at him in utter surprise and started wondering if my old man was quite normal. That question was supposed to make me revisit the past but I decided not to. It was tough and had to remain a constant battle I had to fight with myself. I was not to remain with the anger I felt towards him for ever and delving into the past was going to make any possible reconciliation between us difficult. But there was nothing I could possibly discuss with him without it having a bearing on the past at least in my mind. I remained thoughtful for a while before responding to his question. I wanted to choose my words carefully.

"You cannot plant mangoes and expect to harvest guavas. You never invested in me and should not be expecting to reap anything from me. You never sought my opinion before manufacturing those children. I don't see how what happens to them should be any of my concern. You are their father and not me. They are your responsibility and not mine. I have decided to make my younger ones my burden. You have failed in life and so, should take care of those children to at least catch up or make up for the mess you made of my younger ones," I said.

He remained silent after I said that and I was convinced that he got the message clean and clear. I left when my kid sister and brothers were still to arrive home. I did not have time to wait for them because the house issue in town was very pressing. Even if I secured it, I had to equip it with at least three beds and chairs. I had to do all that before the next day.

I got back to town late that afternoon and went to Mr Joel's shop and he immediately took me to the house he informed me of. It was a simple house with three bedrooms and a large sitting room. The landlord who was there present and said that I had to pay eight months in advance and after that would be paying monthly. I accepted because I had the money. Houses were rare and I guess that condition of paying eight months first, was the reason why the house had to remain empty for more than a week after the last tenant packed out.

After paying and taking my receipts, I went to City Chemist Roundabout where so many bed-makers exhibited their furniture. I paid for three beds and they were dismantled and loaded onto Mr Joel's pickup truck. I then ordered a set of dinning set chairs to be made in three weeks. At least I wanted something on which my siblings could sit and study after school. Making a set for the sitting room was not so pressing and I planned on buy them later on. With everything set in the house, I went back to Santa village and took them to the city with me. I also handed some money to my father to take care of some of the problems he had.

I went and pleaded with the authorities of City College of Commerce to admit Jane and Joshua into the first year. The principal of the school was very understanding but had one worry. He wanted to know what I intended doing for them to catch up with the rest of their classmates. I told him that I was going to hire private teachers to assist them at home. That was a reasonable thing to do. That was not all; I also went to the office of the school counsellor and asked her to keep a special eye on Jane and Joshua. I was concerned that they were not going to focus fully on their studies if they did not first of all understand the importance of education to them and their future. As for Benjamin, he was supposed to be in primary six but given that it was an examination class and he was very ill prepared to face the official exams in less than nine months, he was admitted in primary five. My first objective was to get all of them into school and I achieved it on that first day of their arrival in the city.

In the afternoon after school on that first day of school, Jane came home and told me that she was not going to continue schooling in her new school. That forced some cold sweat out of my pores. The words were powerful enough to give me heart attack. I had to take things very calmly and find out why she opted not go to that school. So I asked her the question.

"There are so many little children in that class and I feel that I could be their mother," she said.

She was right. There were some of the children who got to secondary school at the age of nine Jane was probably worried about what her mates and teachers would think of her if those she called children were to challenge her academically in class. That in itself was to be an obstacle to her performance. I asked her what she wanted me to do at that stage. She told me that she wanted to go to an evening school. I found no problem with it given that she was going to sit for the official General Certificate of Education Exams in just three years and not five. It was all to her advantage. Age was one of the reasons why I could not have them registered in a government secondary school. There, the authorities were very strict on age limits. They could afford to do that because the tuition was very moderate and affordable and most parents preferred them. As a result, they were always solicited.

I did hire teachers to assist my siblings at home. I prepared special weekends for them to go and visit the school counsellor. It was important that they always bore in mind where they were coming from and where they were going to. However, with the school issue taken care of, it was imperative that I invested what I had left as money in some business before it was swallowed up by family problems from every angle. Mr Joel advised me to invest in food stuff. He did not precise any and asked me to decide. I thought of beans since it was farmed and harvested twice per year. In the far off villages, a twenty litre bucket of beans cost 3000 francs and in the grand metropolis like Douala and Yaoundé, the same bucket cost between 12000 and 15000 francs. I kept my price at 11500 francs and it made me a supplier. There were women who always called to command the number of bags they needed and all I had to do was supply. It was worth investing in beans and I made a lot of money from it.

Moreover, there were some travel agencies in town who often went around looking for 4x4 pickup trucks to hire in order to take tourists to the hinterlands through very rough and rugged terrains. I also thought that I could buy some second handed pickup trucks to lease them out to the travel agencies for that purpose. So, I called Mr

Finley who coincidentally was in Belgium and asked him to look for some second handed 4x4 Toyota Hilux trucks. He bought four at giveaway prices and shipped them to Cameroon. I also bought two more during an auction sale at the Douala Sea Port. In all, I had six of them. They were hired by the Travel Agencies as well as some road construction companies. The travel agencies hired one for $60.00 per day while the road construction companies hired one for $1000.00 per month. It was good business but it had its own disadvantages. The road construction companies often brought back the vehicles in very bad shape. For that reason, I had to spend a lot of money repairing the vehicles.

My success in business did not come without setbacks. I did not put in much time in seeing what my younger ones did at school and was out of the house most of the time. Lucky enough, I bought everything they could eat and kept. Jane was a big girl and became the mother of the house. She knew how to cook well and took care of her brothers. They also did well in school and I think the guidance of the school counsellor had a great role to play in it. I had to work for the money they needed to go through with their education but that had to keep me away most of the time from home. I guess in everything there are sacrifices to be made, right?

I kept in touch with my parents back in Italy as well as Mr Salghetti. They gave me advice on how to go about my businesses. As for Gloria, we communicated only via e-mail. When she wrote, I replied and when she didn't, I never wrote back. She was a married woman and I felt that too much attachment to her might jeopardize her marriage. Since my return from Italy, I had not been interested in women. I just buried myself in work and the hunt for money. Business became not only a profession but a hobby. I thought of it all the times and even in my sleep, I kept thinking new ways of making more money.

As my business expanded, I decided to explore other business avenues. I thought of the transport sector and bought some two

Toyota Hiace buses. They were to ply the Bamenda - Douala and Bamenda - Yaoundé highways. I could not fully trust the drivers who handled the vehicles because they were family heads and had needs. I was very frank with them and told them I knew that they were going to take part of the money they made for themselves but urged them not to overdo it as it was going to kill me and indirectly kill them as well. To ensure that they did not take too much, I gave each of the bus drivers an amount they had to pay into my bank account every week. It was inferior to what I knew they could be making a week and that helped to build trust between us. I just thought that trying to control them too much was going to provoke them into wanting to outsmart me. It was therefore better to give them a free hand to handle things the way that pleased them.

26

I went to the internet three years after I returned to Cameroon and saw a mail from Gloria in my mailbox as usual. The day was Thursday 26th May which happened to have been my birthday. The mail was unlike the others I'd received from her before. It read thus;

"My Dear Smith,

I have been in a loveless marriage for over three years now. Totti truly loved me but he had been unable to make me love him despite his hard efforts. We decided last week to behave like two educated and civilized people. Our marriage was not working and that was a fact we could no longer ignore. We filed for divorce and it is going to be pronounced soon. I am not claiming anything from him and would not accept any offer. I just want us to put an end to our sorrows and move on with our separate lives. I no longer live with him. I live with my parents and the rest of my family. My brother has not been fired from his job as a result of my break up with Totti. I have not been fired either. I still work in Totti's family company and earn a salary. Forgive me for breaking this kind of news to you on your birthday. I just thought that it was right to let you know. Happy Birthday my love.

G."

I did not know what to make of that information. I read it over four times and even printed out a copy. That day, some unexplained happiness filled my heart and I smiled all the way back home. I realized that the love in me that I felt was dead with the marriage of Gloria to my rival was actually just dormant. My hopes surged and my dreams of building a family with her were rekindled. I whistled on my way home and communication between us became more frequent than before. I felt I was alive again.

I went to Santa very regularly in the hope of dealing with the hatred I had for my father. He spent a good amount of the money I gave him for his upkeep on calls. I was the one he called most of the time. In some of such calls, he would ask me to come over even when he had nothing to tell me. He drew up his time tables and included me in them even without my consent. The time tables included visits to his friends and whenever he was with them, he would present me as his son who had just returned from abroad. His friends would greet me with a lot of respect and that I realized made him beam with pride. Those moments meant everything to him and seemed to be his only moments of happiness. I just felt sometimes like reminding him that he never did anything to me as a father and therefore had no moral grounds to be doing such things. That would have taken away the happiness and pride he had when in the company of his friends. I did not want to see him unhappy and allowed him do it within the first four months of my return.

I did try to curb the amount of time he wanted to take me out on such visits. He felt happy and proud whenever he introduced me to his friends but it never dawn on him that he might have been exposing me to danger. There had been stories of people like him who carried their well to do children and went round introducing to friends and such children ended up in caskets shortly after. I was afraid that one of his friends could become envious and would decide to harm me. In order not to offend him, I resorted to telling him that I was busy and whenever I went and saw him, I found one excuse or the other to leave. That was the only thing I thought of doing to stay out of harm's way.

Nine months after Gloria informed me of her divorce, she called and informed me that her father was very sick and her family did not have enough money to foot his hospital bills. I did not asked how much she needed but just told her that I was going to do something. I went to my bank and had $3000.00 sent to her. I did not call her to give the transfer details but sent them by email. I got a phone call from her the next day after she received the money, thanking me for it. That was just what I expected in return but wondered if she was going to inform her other relatives about it. It did not really matter if she did or did not but since my new found hope in us being together again, I thought it was important for our families to come together. She informed me of how positive her father was responding to treatment. I prayed for his speedy recovery and longed for the day he was going to accept and respect me as a human being.

A month after I sent the money, my phone rang and I was shocked when I picked up the receiver and heard the person on the line introduce himself as Gloria's elder brother. I expected something really nasty to spill out of his mouth but that did not happen. It was as though he saw the amazement on my face and told me not to be surprise because only fools were incapable of changing. I knew he was no fool but would never have believed that I was ever going to hear from him again after the humiliating treatment he meted out on me after learning that I had something to do with his sister. I asked him how he was doing. He ignored the question and went on to thank me for what I did for his father. I asked him how he knew of what I did and he replied that his sister told him everything. He then went further to apologize for what he said to me and the way he treated me in the past. I asked him if apologizing meant that he was going to allow his sister go out with me if she wanted to. He remained silent to the extent that I thought he had hung up. He was still there and said after a while that he was not going to stand in the way of her sister's choice if she made one. That was something I wanted to hear. The gesture I made moved him and he started seeing things differently. I sought to know if his father was informed of the origin of the money and he said no. I knew the man was hard hearted and only time and effort was going to make him change. I did not give up hope on him yet.

However, I did not have enough time to digest the positive shock of Gloria's elder brother calling me when another one came in just three days later. I got out of bed at 08:20 when my kid sister and brothers had all gone to school. I got my tooth brush and went to the toilet to clean up. I then moved to the dining table to have my breakfast. I barely began savouring the taste of the fruit salad with some bread when my phone started ringing. The number was a local one but not found in my repertoire since there was no name accompanying it. I guessed that he or she who must have been calling certainly got my number from someone I knew. I picked up the receiver and the voice on the line was that of Gloria. It was unmistakable. I wanted to know where she was calling from and she responded that she was in front of Dream Land Restaurant building. It was just a stone throw from Vatican Travel Agency in the City of Bamenda. That was the surprise of the year but there was no time to waste as I had to go and pick her up. I asked her not to move an inch from where she was and jumped out of the house without eating up all my breakfast.

I got to where she was in no time in one of my pickup trucks. I packed just a few meters from where she stood and jumped out. I ran and fell on her without realizing we had entered the road thereby obstructing traffic for about two minutes. The first driver who halted smiled and I imagined that he must have been in such a situation himself. He did not hoot but the long cue that was behind him kept hooting. Those who did most of the hooting were taxi drivers and that was because time to them was money.

With the deafening noises, I could not be indifferent and had to move her by the side of the road still fully in her grip. One of the taxi drivers who was not pleased with the short delay we caused was not going to find peace if he did not voice out what he had in mind. He actually halted where we could see him clearly before saying it.

"Go and fuck in your house or a hotel room and stop disturbing people's businesses," he said.

I took Gloria to the vehicle and loaded her things onto the open back. We drove home and she had a shower while I prepared breakfast for her. After eating, we had just a few minutes to chat as she badly needed some sleep. She made me understand that she left Italy the previous day in the morning and got to Cameroon in the evening. As she arrived at the Douala International Airport, she did not want to spend a night there in a hotel and so asked the taxi driver who was transported her to take her to a travel agency that could take her to Bamenda. She was taken to Vatican Travel Agency and after booking for her journey was informed that the bus was going to take off at 22:00. That was the reason why she got to Bamenda in the early hours of that day. Since she badly needed some sleep, she went to bed at 09:20.

27

The arrival of Gloria meant that I had to alter my program for that day. I had to prepare my siblings for what they were going to encounter that day after school. I remained at home watching TV until 15:00 when they all came home. I waited for them to eat and settle down before calling their attention. I went to my room and brought out one of Gloria's pictures which I had. I showed it to them and Joshua asked me who the beautiful lady was. Jane and Benjamin probably had the same question in mind.

"She is someone I met when I was in Italy," I told them and went on to recount how I once was about to be badly beaten and she was the one who rescued me. Joshua and Benjamin immediately expressed their admiration for her. I'm sure Jane too admired her but being a big and smart girl, saw things deeper than her younger brothers.

"You are definitely showing us this picture because there is something cooking, right? Is she going to become part of our family?" she asked.

I said yes and told them that she was sleeping in the house. They were very excited and Joshua asked me to go and call her. I told him that she was too tired after the very long journey and was asleep. I asked them to be patient and pleaded with them not to make noise. Since they were just back from school, I asked Joshua and Benjamin to go into their room and have a rest. As for Jane, she remained in the sitting room with me. I looked at her and saw that she was a bit worried. I asked her what the matter was.

"Brother, if you love the girl in the picture, I will love her too. But I have a worry. She looks different and getting daddy and his obstinate brothers and sisters to accept her would not be easy. I can already begin to sense the trauma she is going to go through," she said.

"I already know of that and have things already worked out. Anybody who rejects her automatically rejects me. They have never done anything for me in their lives and I don't think they should be in any position to dictate whom I marry. Don't worry, I would put everyone in his or her place," I said.

"You can always count on my support," she said.

"I know. Thank you very much for understanding," I said.

"I have no choice than to understand. I am a woman and sooner or later I would have to try to find my way into someone's family. I cannot stand on the way of another woman coming into mine because I don't know what would happen to me in the future," she said.

"I like the way you reason. Very few women would reason that way. Many would try to bar the road for women coming in to marry their male children or male relatives but they often forget that life is a continuous cycle. Thank you for understanding," I said.

Even though I was talking tough with my sister, I knew I was not supposed to be too harsh as I sounded. I had to be diplomatic first and if that did not work, I could then employ harsh measures. I planned on going to visit my maternal relatives the next day to introduce her to them. It was important that I did that as soon as possible to avoid rumours flying left and right. My two brothers and sister were already on my side and that was already an achievement. I had the conviction that I was not going to face any opposition from my maternal relatives. They were those that were extremely poor but they sacrificed all they had when it came to serious situations. My biggest headache was going to come from my paternal relatives. Whatever the case, I had to be ready for anything.

Gloria emerged from the room at 17:45 and moved to the sitting room where I and my two brothers and sister were seated. She stopped just a few meters from where we sat and all eyes were turned towards her. I rose and moved to where she stood and put my left arm round her neck. I then presented her to my sister first and then to my younger brothers. There were smiles on every face and Benjamin in particular wanted her to sit near him. She did and we watched TV for a while before I dismissed them to go and revise what they did at school. At 19:25, we had our supper and I went back to watching TV with Gloria while they all went back to their books.

With just two of us remaining in the sitting room, I thought it was time to ask her some burning questions I had in mind. My first question was to know if her family was aware that she was coming to Africa. She responded that only one person did not know about it and it was her father. My next worry was on the legality of keeping her without taking permission from her family. She told me that she was more than 18 years old and had the right to hook up with whoever she wanted with or without the consent of her family. "That is the way it is in Europe," she reiterated. That was a convincing response and getting the official permission from her family to live with her for ever was my next target. The soonest that happened, the better for both of us. On her part she found no reason why getting the permission of her parents had to be too much of a priority to me. All left to her, we would have had our children before going to get the permission of her parents. I did not dispute her line of thought and told her that we were going to proceed as time went on. However, she told me that she was going to join me in whatever activity I was involved in the very next morning. I tried to talk her out of the idea by telling her that she needed a lot of rest after such a long and tiring journey. But she was adamant. I really did not want her to engage in any work just then and to shift her away from it, I proposed that we go and see my maternal relatives in Bafut, which was situated some 20 km from Bamenda City. She had no problem with that and we planned to leave for Bafut at about 08:30 the next day. Since it was a weekend, a good number of them were going to take advantage of it to rest from farm work. I called Aunty Regina to inform her that I was coming with a guest the next day which was a

Saturday. I knew she was going to inform my other aunts, uncles, cousins and nephews who were around her.

We got out of bed on that Saturday morning at 07:30. Though it was weekend and my siblings did not have to go to school, they still got up early to take care of house chores. Each one of them did something in the house before going to school or going out. By 07:50, they were through with work and Jane invited us to the table after preparing breakfast. At 08:30, I bundled them into one of my pickup trucks and we all headed for Bafut.

At 08:52, we arrived at our family compound in Bafut. It was streaming with family members who had come to see us especially my siblings after a very long time. I introduced Gloria to them but did not tell them that we had anything in common. I wanted to assess the environment first before breaking the news. It would have been imprudent for me to just assume that each and every one of them there was going to accept Gloria with open arms.

After so much hugging and kisses, we were ushered into the main house. Two chickens had been slaughtered that morning for us. Varieties of traditional meals were also prepared. I wondered if Gloria was going to like any of them. As we started eating, Aunty Regina asked me to the hearing of everyone when she shall see her daughter-in-law. There was a loud roar in support of that question all-round the house. A brief moment of silence ensued during which all ears were waiting for an answer. I asked what type of woman they wanted me to marry. Aunty Regina who seemed to have been the self-appointed spokesperson said that they were prepared to accept any woman I brought so long as she was going to give them children. I asked what they would do if the woman was a foreigner. They all responded that her origin did not matter to them. That response paved the way for me to make a special announcement with a lot of confidence.

"Life has not been easy for me and my younger ones since the death of our mother. You all know the kind of person my father is. If

I did not run away from home, maybe I would have been a thief or criminal or prisoner locked up somewhere. I think God was always with me directing my steps. I went to the country of that woman I came with and things there were not easy especially for one who was a foreigner. She had to rescue me once from some guys who wanted to harm me simply because I looked different. If she did not come along that fateful day, I think I would have been beaten to death. We had been friends ever since she risked her life to save me. There could be no love greater than that. So, I have come here today to present her to you. The daughter-in-law you all long for is here today and you can all see her," I said.

Aunty Regina tuned a traditional song and it was sung by all those present. All my aunts and uncles there took each a slice of chicken from their plates and put in Gloria's. That was an indication that she had been accepted into the family. It was an intense emotional moment for me. I revisited the long and rough path I had been through especially the humiliation her family subjected me to. That acceptance was enough to take all the pains of my past years away. I guess there is always sunshine after a stormy weather, right? Well, having Gloria at last was probably my reward for persevering. But there was one person I wished was present in that compound at that moment and it was my mother.

The little celebration was not going to go on all day. At 14:20 we were on our way back to the city. I called my father to inform him that I was going to see him that very afternoon. He too told me that he had something really important to discuss with me. I ended by telling him that I was going to be there in an hour or so.

When we got to town, I allowed everybody at home and got Gloria's picture and headed for Santa Village alone. I got there at 15:50 and met my father in the sitting room. He was drinking Spanish red wine. He asked me to get a glass and join him. I declined the offer telling him that alcohol was not too good for me. I had no intention of spending too long there and asked him what he wanted to discuss with me.

"My son," he began. "There comes a time in a man's life when he must think of building a family of his own. Since you returned from abroad, I have not seen you or heard that you are with any woman. As your father, I am getting worried and want to ask you what you are thinking."

"Thank you for worrying about me. It is true that since I returned, I've been running only after money and have not had time to be looking at women. I have not also had time to discuss with you about the kind of life I lived abroad and some of the difficulties I faced there," I said.

He asked me to tell him everything. I told him precisely where I lived in Italy and the difficulties faced by foreigners who looked different there. I told him of the incident I had with the gang of boys and the timely rescue of Gloria. After narrating everything to him, I took out Gloria's picture and showed it to him. My father was a seasoned crook and had a lot of experience as far as man and woman relationship was concerned. He smiled as he looked at the picture and asked why I had to show him the picture of the girl who saved my life. I just smiled and sat looking at him.

"Don't tell me she is the one your heart has settled on," he said with an uneasy smile.

"What if she is the one?" I asked.

"Then there will be a problem. I will give you my reasons…..she is a foreigner…..she is a white…..she does not know anything about our culture…..she does not know our mother tongue….it is not certain that if you die someday, she would remain here….there are just too many problems," he said.

I was really downcast with his comments that for a moment I ran out of ideas. I began to ask myself why I had to go there to even inform him in the first place. That was a man who would have destroyed me had I not ran away from home and he was there trying to make a decision that was going to affect my life for ever. I did not see why I had to let him do it and told him that I had made my choice and anyone who had a problem with it had to go to hell, including him.

"It is not because that ghost saved your life that you feel you have an obligation towards her," he said.

I sighed and left in anger. I was so furious that I got back to Bamenda in no time. When I entered the house, I tried hard to disguise my frustration. I told Gloria that I had some headache, went to the bedroom to lie down. I just couldn't come to terms with my father's comments . I began to see him as a man with no sentiments. Even if he did not like the lady, he would have at least pretended to love her for my sake. Accepting the woman that made my happiness was the least he would have done to make up for failing to be a good father. What a man!

I did not get out of the room even when it was time for supper. I did not feel like eating. Gloria joined me soon after supper and we had a serious chat. She wanted me to tell her all about my business and activities. I told her everything and she proposed that we go in for a bank loan and use the money in buying more buses. I hated loans with all my soul and saw them as closely related cousins to poverty. I had seen people who were well to do go in for loans but were unable to pay back in time and everything was taken away from them. Their lives turned upside down in a matter of seconds. I was also aware of the fact that life itself was a risk and if nothing was risked, nothing was gained. Based on that fact, I did not reject her proposal but insisted that we go in for a little loan and see what came out of it before going in for another. She agreed and we both went to First Trust Bank and applied for a loan 48 hours later. I had an account in the bank and that facilitated the granting of the loan.

As concerns my father, I decided not to go to Santa or call him after our disagreement. He tried to call me a few times and I rejected the calls. I changed my mind only the next Saturday which was exactly a week after he annoyed me and decided to call him. When he answered, he asked me to come over so that we could talk things out as father and son. I told him that there was nothing to talk about while at the same time hammered on the fact that he had no choice than to accept the person I had chosen as a wife. He was really sober and pleaded with me to come over so that we could settle our differences. I told him I was going to be there at 14:00.

Before I had to leave for Santa village, Gloria wanted to know when I intended taking her to see my father. I replied that it was not proper to just surprise him with a woman without prior preparation. Besides, I did not want the occasion to be identical to mine when she wanted to introduce me to her family. She agreed with me and I informed her of my little trip to Santa village. I wondered how she would have felt if she knew that I was going there to see how I could impose her on my paternal relatives. The experience of rejection was too traumatizing and I did not want her to go through it.

I got to Santa village at 14:00 as I promised my father. I got there with the conviction that he must have realized that he could not come between me and Gloria given the manner in which I left the last time. I was wrong. Instead, there was a surprise waiting for me when I entered the house. There I found all my aunts and uncles as well as a good number of my paternal cousins. It seemed they had a discussion and were just waiting for me to announce their decision. It was my father's eldest sister, Aunty Juana who addressed me.

"You children of today think that you know everything and we your parents have become too old fashioned, having only outdated ideas to contribute. Your father has assembled us here so that we can join and help stop the madness you are about to engage in. He informed us that you want to marry a foreign white woman. Have you looked at all the women in this country and none has caught your heart? If you could not find one by yourself or had a problem of choice, you would have asked us your family to assist you get one. Has the father of that girl accepted you as a son-in-law? How are you going to pay her bride price? Are you going to go there and do it or you would import her and her father for it to be done here? Please my son, you are wise and we know that you are capable of making a wise decision. It is not yet late. You can change your mind and we would find a girl that would make you happy for the rest of your life," she said.

"Aunty, I wouldn't want to sound rude but permit me express my disgust with this gathering. What are you afraid of? Is it of the fact that the woman I love is a white? Or is it because you have foreseen that there would be problems to pay her bride price? Which is which?" I asked.

There was no answer to my question but there was a lot of mumbling in the house. They considered my remarks as insulting and their spokesperson took the floor again.

"We are not afraid of anything. We don't just like that strange woman. She could be a threat to our culture. We have already taken our decision and it is that we will not be part of any possible union between you and any stranger. You will have to choose between us your family and that woman," she said.

I resolved that there was no need arguing with them as they had already taken their decision because asking further question was only going to prolong matters. I decided to cut the annoying meeting short by releasing a bomb shell.

"Well, I have heard what you've said and will want you to listen carefully to what I have to say. I will accept any woman you will bring for me to marry on the condition that you also bring along a receipt of any franc you have ever spent on me," I said.

There were smiles and a good number of those in the house nodded when I talked of accepting any woman presented to me. The nodding and smiles were a sign of victory to them but they soon disappeared when I talked of receipts. They all knew that they had never done anything for me and could not produce them. The atmosphere in the house changed from a very heated to an icy one. I could read guilt and frustration on every face. That was victory for me and it galvanized me to go on since no one could dare take the floor, not even my father.

"On the day I was born, a good number of you in here appeared and disappeared shortly after. Some did not even come. You only reappeared again on the day my mother died and disappeared once more when the mourning period was over. How do you think we, the children she left behind were surviving during all those years you were gone? Is it enough to give birth to a child and claim the child to be your own? Giving birth is the easiest part and anybody can do that. Where were you when it was time to take care of the child? You were nowhere to be found and you never cared. I have fought very hard going through a lot of difficulties which you have not even bothered to know about. I have made it and that is why you have all responded to my father's invitation. Had it been I became a failure, would you have bothered to come here? You are here today, bold enough to tell me that you have taken a decision and I have the option to choose between you and the woman I love. If you wanted to take decisions that affect my life, you would have taken care of me and see me through all the stages of education. None of you did and so have no right to tell me who I have to marry and who I'm not supposed to marry. As for you my father, I don't want you going around introducing me to your friends as my father. You know that you've never been a father to me. You did the easiest part which was giving birth to me and then embarked on a mission to destroy me and my siblings. Today you have the guts to summon your family to take a decision about me. Well, you asked me to make a choice. I have made it and it is to marry that white woman. She is living with me in the city. Each and everyone here will have to make a choice....either you are for me or you are against me. If you know that you will not accept my woman, never set foot in my home or even call me. If you want to get to me, you must go through my woman. Her name is Gloria," I said and left.

266

With the dead silence that enveloped the house even when I was leaving, I was certain that some of them were probably regretting why they came there in the first place. I reflected again on everything I said and some guilt crept in me. I felt that I was a bit too severe but somewhere deep within me I felt some peace after speaking out my mind to my paternal relatives. Whatever the case, I planned on making amends if later on it turned out that I went too far. Though they were very hostile to my choice of woman, I still needed them by my side as a family.

28

I got back to the city at 16:30 and made a stopover at a shop where mostly mobile phones were sold and bought one plus a new SIM card. I took out my own SIM card and inserted it in the new phone and inserted the new SIM into my own phone. Gloria was going to have my old number while I had a new one. My intention was to get my paternal relatives to accept her. I considered the rejection of the woman I loved as a serious issue and I had to employ every means at my disposal. Moreover, a change of number meant that I had to inform by business partners of it. If I didn't do that, my business was definitely going to suffer. So, I wrote a text message and sent to all of them that day before getting home.

Later that Saturday evening, I called Gloria to the room and told her everything that transpired that day. I felt that it was important for her to know what was going on. She felt really bad to hear that my paternal relatives hated and rejected her without even knowing her. It was normal for her feel that way and I could not blame her. There was therefore need for her to know who was on her side and who wasn't. We agreed that she was not going to visit my paternal relatives until things were sorted out with them. But with my old number in her hands and being the one my paternal relatives had, trouble was not going to delay in coming. But in the meantime, we were not there just yet.

Within the third week after we applied for a loan, a call came from First Trust Bank informing us that it had been granted. I asked that the funds be deposited into my account. I had to travel to Douala to deliver bags of beans to some women there within that same week. With the possibility of withdrawing money in any First Trust Bank branches in other part of the country, I planned to withdraw the money in Douala to use in buying the buses for which it was intended. I travelled there with Gloria and after making my deliveries, we went to CAMI TOYOTA, a company specialized in the importation of Japanese vehicles into Cameroon. After negotiating for three Toyota Coaster Buses, the company's bank account number was handed to us. We went to First Trust Douala and transferred the money into it. After the transfer was made, we carried the bank receipt back to the company and all necessary papers were handed to us. One problem cropped up and it was how to get the vehicles to Bamenda. We forgot to make arrangements with drivers who were supposed to help us drive them to Bamenda. Lucky for us, I had the phone numbers of a good number of my maternal and paternal cousins who had driving licenses but were unemployed. I called one paternal cousin and two maternal cousins. They had to travel from Bamenda to Douala, which was a journey of not less than six hours on that same Friday. They took off at 14:00 while we had to remain there in Douala waiting for them.

While waiting for my cousins, Gloria and I decided to make a tour round the economic capital of Cameroon. We went first to Bonanjo, the seat of all financial institutions in the city. From there, we went to Akwa. It was considered the heart of business because most businesses were established there. Along many major roads one could see parks of second handed vehicles. A nice looking Toyota Hiace bus caught the attention of Gloria in one of such parks and she wanted us to go and take a look. I did not hesitate and looked for an ideal spot along the road where I packed the pickup truck we had been driving in. We went and examined the bus and saw that it was in good shape and could be used for at least a year before some repair works could be done on it. We asked how much it cost from the car dealer.

"Five million francs," he said.

That amount was exorbitant and I asked him to take us to his office where we could negotiate better. He did and after so much bargaining, we settled at three million. The money was paid and the necessary paper work taken care of. When that was done the key of the bus was handed to me. I handed it to Gloria who had then to drive it to CAMI TOYOTA premises where the other three buses were still packed while I drove our pickup truck. When we got there I suggested to Gloria that it was imperative for us to go and book for an inn given that it was not proper for my cousins to arrive and then we take off again almost immediately without them having adequate rest. She bought my idea and we immediately went to Airline Inn which was very close to the airport. There we booked for three rooms. Gloria and I were going to occupy the first room, my paternal cousin occupy the second, while my two maternal cousins occupy the third room since they were from the same home. With all those arrangements already made, we waited for the moment when they were to all arrive.

At 20:15 they arrived and called me to pick them up. I did and took them to the inn Gloria and booked earlier. They did not want to spend a night in Douala. They told me that they came with the intention of starting off soon after arrival. I could not understand the hurry more especially as they were jobless. Curious, isn't it? I insisted that they either spent the night or booked a bus bound for Bamenda. I had to do that because many accidents which were too frequent on our highways were borne of fatigue. I did not want to see that happening to a family member or anybody else. Besides, if that were to happen, their parents would not want to listen to any explanations from me. They would accuse me of sacrificing their children in some money making ritual. Horrible, isn't it? That was the world under the African sky I had to deal with. Asking them to make a choice was the only way of forcing them to spend the night in Douala.

The next morning, we woke up at 06:30 and ordered some breakfast. I did not want my drivers to complain of hunger when we eventually hit the road. After eating, we arranged an order in which we had to move. I was to be ahead and Gloria was to be right behind me. The rest of the three buses had to follow in any order. I made it very clear that no one had to try to overtake me on the road. I just wanted to avoid any form of reckless driving. I used it as a test to determine which of them was going to be a driver in the agency. Lucky enough for all of us, they behaved by following the pace which I dictated in front. We used the normal six hours as other road users did. They were given some money to take back home to their families upon arrival to Bamenda while waiting for the moment they would be called up for work.

Gloria was a woman but acted more than a man. When she had her mind focused on doing something, there was nothing to stop her. She did not like unnecessary delays as well. I thought she was going to spend the next day after we drove from Douala to Bamenda with the buses in bed resting. But that was not going to be the case. She woke very early the next morning and went to the branch office of the ministry of transport and the Bamenda City Council office for the necessary authorization papers. She was given three days to come for them. That was pretty fast. Any other person who went there for the same purpose had to run after those charged with granting the authorization papers for weeks and sometimes months. For those that wanted quick services, brown envelops had to exchange hands under the table. I did not know what portion Gloria used on them.

Maybe it was because she looked different. It was no news that those in power were more welcoming and nice to foreigners who came from western countries or looked different than to their fellow Africans that looked like them. Weird, isn't it?

Things went pretty fast when Gloria had the authorization papers she was asked to come for in three days. She organized a meeting with the bus drivers who happened to all have been my family members. There were three from my maternal family, one from my paternal family and two others I had no blood relation with. She told them that she was going to treat them like employees and not her in-laws. That meant that she was going to fire any of them that was not doing his job well or violated the rules she laid down. I knew what she could do and knew that she was going to manage the agency well.

That was the reason why I decided to stay completely off the management of the agency and concentrated more on my food distribution business. As for those that had to manage the branches that had to be opened in different towns in the country, flight tickets were sent to Gloria's elder brother and younger sister and they flew in. With just six buses, only two branch offices had to be opened in other towns. One was to be opened in Yaoundé and placed under the charge of Gloria's elder brother while another had to be opened in Douala and placed under the care of Gloria's younger sister. Gloria planned on slashing a few francs off the fares paid in other travel agencies. That way, she was going to attract customers and keep them. With everything set, Gloria & Smith Express took off just one week after the buses were driven in from Douala to Bamenda.

Two weeks after our travel agency took off, Uncle Julius, my father's elder brother, rang my old number. It was Gloria who took the call since the number belonged to her then. It seemed he spoke to her rudely. I could read the sad expression on her face and asked her what he said to her. She did not tell me the hurting thing he said but only told me that my uncle wanted to talk to me and handed me her phone. As soon as I made him know that I was on the line, I told him that I was not interested in anything he wanted to say since he found it so difficult to be polite to the woman that made my happiness. I hung up after that though he was the one who called. I would like to think that he understood the message I communicated to him by my action because he was at the meeting my father organized for them to take a decision about me. I think by being rude to Gloria, he was probably trying to see if I was indeed going to prefer my woman over them who were my family. He realized that day that I was not joking.

He called 24 hours after that incident to apologize to Gloria. Soon after she accepted his apologies, he told her to tell his son, that's me, to send him some money to enable him go to the hospital. There, I did not know what to make of his actions because I could not determine if his apologies to Gloria were genuine and sincere or if he just did that because he needed help. Whatever the case, I intended to exploit the situation to my advantage and that of Gloria to change the Stone Age mentalities of my paternal family members. I asked Gloria to call him and invite him over to the city to come and receive better medical attention. She did and when he arrived, she was the one that took him to the hospital and took care of his bills. When that was done, she took him to the market and bought some items for him to take back to his family. I did not offer him anything and when he asked me why I could not take some of my jobless cousins and put them in the travel agency, I told him that I was not the manager but Gloria. He told me that I was the man and was not supposed to leave everything in the hands of Gloria who was just a woman. I told him that there was a risk in everything and entrusting the agency in the hands of Gloria was a risk worth taking. Though my comments left him mouth wide open, there was nothing he could do. He was happy with what Gloria bought for him and the money she gave him when he was leaving.

I knew that one act of kindness, that put a smile on the face of Uncle Julius was going to mark a turning point in the attitude of my paternal relatives towards Gloria. I knew he was going to speak of the warm treatment he got from her to his brothers and sisters and that was going to prompt them into thinking that they were losing a lot by hating her. Indeed, he became Gloria's ambassador in my paternal family. A good number of his brothers and sisters as well as cousins changed their attitudes towards Gloria. Since all of them were farmers, they always sent raw farm produce to us in the city. The women sometimes came with cooked food right to the city but I could not trust them totally. I was not completely certain that they did not have any intention of hurting Gloria and so I never allowed her eat any cooked food that was brought without first tasting it myself. Before doing that, I first chewed some leaves which I was told were anti-poison. But there was someone who was so determined not to change his attitude towards Gloria and it was my own father. I guess there is one in every family, right? It did not matter much. He depended heavily on me and I knew how I was going to bend him.

On the 7th month after Gloria's arrival to Cameroon, I started noticing some changes on her. She started growing fat and slept a lot. She also threw up many times she ate something and complained of tiredness. I carried her to the hospital and after some tests were carried out it was confirmed that she was pregnant. That was good news for both of us as I was already wondering if she was ever going to bear a child. For the more than three years with her former husband, she was never pregnant and I never understood why. Maybe living in a loveless marriage kept her in frustrated thoughts all the time and that was why she could not take in. Well, it no longer mattered as her pregnancy confirmed that she could have children and I was not impotent. I kept wondering how she was going to react if it turned that I was impotent? It was a torturing thought and I did not like thinking about it. Her pregnancy was indeed relieving to me. What would have been the need amassing wealth when there wasn't going to be a child? I really felt the anguish of childless parents who really wanted to have kids of their own but couldn't when I kept waiting for Gloria to tell me that she was pregnant.

29

That good news of Gloria's pregnancy was not going to be without hitches. We were not yet married and the problems of legality and legitimacy started staring me in the face. I had to do something and the first thing to do was to legalize our union. I needed permission to take her as my wife and the most important person to give me the permission was her father. I was certain that wasn't going to happen just then but securing those of her brothers, sister and mother was not going to be a problem. Gloria called her mother and she gave her blessings but told us to call her husband when the marriage was signed. We agreed and scheduled our court wedding for the moment when her pregnancy would be exactly three months old. That was to be in three weeks after we learnt of her pregnancy.

On the day of the ceremony which was a Saturday, we sent one of our drivers with a bus to Santa village to go and get those of my paternal relatives who wanted to be part of the occasion. He went and brought them in at 08:30 to the house but my father was not among them. I called him and told him that I was no longer going to take care of his needs if that occasion went by without him showing up. As for my maternal family members, a good number of them were already in the city on the morning of that Saturday to take care of cooking and decorating the house. At 09:30 we all moved to the council premises where we were first of all schooled on what we were getting into. After the lectures, papers were signed and we went back home.

It was after we had already returned home that my father called to say that he was at the Commercial Avenue in the city in front of Press Bookshop. I sent Jane to go and get him. There was a lot of eating and drinking. I thanked all those present for coming and also used the opportunity to announce that my wife was going to be a mother in six months. My father drank as much as he wanted and conversed with his brothers and sisters. Everybody looked happy. When it was almost time for them to go, I rose and told them that their moral support and harmony in the family was all I wanted. To my father, I told him that I did not want him coming to any occasion that concerned me only after threats. I equally told him that it was hypocritical for him to be accepting money which I gave him and at the same time hated the woman who helped me make it. Whether that meant anything to him or not was difficult to tell. Gloria and I squeezed some bank notes into the palms of our guests as they left our house.

The constant tiredness and dizziness ended after our court wedding and Gloria went about her managerial occupation. With all the money that came in and with three of our pickup trucks rented out to two road construction companies for two years, we paid the loan that we owed the bank. Some was used to pay our workers. What I made from food distribution was swallowed up by our household needs. Family members that came for one kind of assistance or the other had their problems partially taken care of or fully taken care of depending on what we had at hand. All in all, the biggest problem we had was paying the loan and after it was settled we could then start realizing something for ourselves.

When Gloria was seven months pregnant I decided to take her to Santa village, not to visit any of my family member but to show her the places that helped to shape my life. It was a Sunday and we arrived Santa at 10:20. On driving across the village we saw my father very close to the Santa motor park. He noticed our car and I halted after realizing that he had seen us. He came closer to the car and greeted Gloria first. He then asked if we were coming to the house to see him and I said no. He again sought to know if we were there to see other family members and my response was still negative. He was surprise and asked yet again what we came to the village to do. I told him that we were there to see the people who helped me when I ran

278

away from home as a result of his cruelty. That comment dried up the next words he intended voicing and left him totally speechless. Gloria looked at me with unblinking eyes. She had every right to because I had never told her anything about my difficult life in Cameroon before I got over to Italy. However, with my father remaining speechless, I couldn't remain there burning fuel as I did not turn off the engine. I started moving again and it was then that Gloria decided to speak.

"You once ran away from home?" she asked.

"My love, I took you out today because I wanted to show you some things and people who influenced my life in one way or the other. Running away from home was just one episode in my difficult life and there were other episodes before that one. If I delve straight into the runaway part, I would be starting the story in the middle. Just wait until we get to the primary school I attended and I would begin the story," I told her.

Catholic primary school Santa was just three kilometres away from Santa Motor Park. We got there in no time and I took her around the buildings which showed signs of old age and badly needed repairs. Some of the classrooms had no doors and I imagined that the benches were still there only thanks to the honesty of the villagers. Some of the walls had been coated with white-wash but the floors were largely dusty and uncemented. We entered one of the classrooms and I cleaned a desk on which she sat. There I told my story from the moment my mother died till when I ran away from home. She was eager to know where I ran to when I left home but I asked her to be patient as we were going to move there shortly after. We then moved back to the car and were on the move again.

Our next stop was at Pinyin village and it was quite some distance from the primary school. We soon got to the abandoned house which I took refuge in, after running away from home. There was still a lot of grass in front of the house to show that it was uninhabited. The only difference was that a third grave was added to the two I knew when I was there. The front main door was locked but the back door was open. I went in with Gloria walking steadily behind me. I showed her the room I slept in and told her what I used as my bed. I also told her of the kind of food I ate and where I got it from. As we were leaving the house, I pointed to the stream I used as a source of drinking water until Mr Finley's curiosity led him to me.

We left that house and went just a kilometre further and I showed her the house Mr Finley lived in. I told her of the length of time I lived with him in it before he left for Italy. We did not need the car to go to my former landlord's house. It was very close to the one Mr Finley lived in. We just took a short walk there and we found him seated in front of his house. He became attentive and was ready to attend to us once we got close to him. He did not recognize me until I introduced myself. He was happy to see me and asked whom my companion was. I introduced Gloria to him and told him that she was my wife. She congratulated me and added that I was a good example of what parents expected of their children. That was a different man speaking to me then. I only hoped that he had changed from his old ways. I asked of the whereabouts of his wife and he responded that she was in a nearby farm looking for something they had to eat later that Sunday. He left us there in front of his house and went to call for her. They both returned and she fell on me. She was so happy and asked us to enter the house. I told her that I intended to show my room to my wife before coming.

I took Gloria to my former landlord's abandoned house. There I opened the door of my former room and we both walked in. Nothing had changed in it but for the fact that grass could be seen growing from the un-cemented floor. The papers I used to block some of the holes on the perforated walls were still there. I told Gloria everything including the nightmares I had to go through preparing for my exams. She was overwhelmed with my story that she broke into tears. Then and there, she promised never to be a headache to me and to be a very loving and understanding wife.

Those words were so touching and I took her into my arms. I guess she understood then that there could be different levels of poverty. She could see clearly that poverty in Cameroon was different from poverty in her own country. She probably might have imagined that she had lived the worst form of poverty back there but my experiences taught her a new lesson. I guess that was the reason why she cried after feeling and seeing what I had to endure growing up.

We soon left my former room and went into the house of my former landlord. There, we were offered seats and the only bottle of wine I could spot through the glass of their cupboard was brought out alongside two wine glasses. We each sipped one glass full and I decided to end there given that I was not used to drinking. With the high alcoholic content in it, I was scared of getting tipsy and that would not have been good for driving. Gloria equally decided not to drink further given that she was pregnant. We spent time entertaining our hosts with stories of our encounter and life back in Italy. They were so moved by the story that they in turn decided to tell us how they met and the different places they lived in before returning to settle in the village. I asked them where their children were and they told us that they were in different parts of the country fending for themselves. Our visit lasted for two and quarter hours.

When it was time to go, my former landlord and his wife accompanied us right to the car. My landlord was moving ahead with Gloria while I was behind with his wife. She thanked me for remembering to come and see her after so many years. I told her that I was one person who never forgot those I met on my way. She told me that she knew I was going to go places from the effort I made when I was living around her. I took out some bank notes and squeezed them in her palms without her husband's knowledge. I gave it to her because I knew she was going to spend it for the home for everyone to benefit from. When we got to where the car was parked, I opened the back door of the car and asked them to offload it. There was a bag of rice, a carton of soap, two packets of magi cube, and five litres of cooking oil. They did and started carrying them home while I drove my wife back to the city. She went about her business and I took care of mine

Two months later, I rushed Gloria to St. Mary hospital because she started having some contractions. It was 10:50 when we got there and she was immediately taken to the labour room. It did not take long for her to put to birth. A midwife came out 30 minutes after she was taken in to congratulate and announce to me that I was the father of a bouncing baby girl. I called my father first and informed him before calling other family members. Aunty Regina was the first to arrive the hospital and immediately went and made up a bed in one of the private wards of the hospital. She came and we both waited for Gloria to emerge from the labour room with the baby.

She emerged 45 minutes after the announcement of the midwife looking very exhausted. She was supported by one female nurse while another carried the baby. She was handed to my aunt and we all moved to the prepared private ward. Family members and friends started streaming in with gifts for the baby. Most of them were detergents and soaps. Mr Joel and his wife came with five litre tins of powdered milk and Ovaltine as well as a packet of sugar. One person I was not expecting showed up and it was my father. He called me outside the hospital gate and I went out to take him to where my wife was. At the gate, he asked me where his granddaughter was. I was not pleased with that first question because I had expected him to ask first how my wife was doing before going to the baby. I decided to put some knowledge in his head then and there.

"Someone said that if you want to eat a fruit, you must visit the tree. Even if you buy the fruit in the market, someone else had gone to the tree in your place. You cannot reject a tree and then claim to be interested in the fruit it produces. That is hypocritical and I will want you to make a U-turn if you know that you are going to make my wife uncomfortable in any way," I said.

"Please, the birth of a child calls for celebration and reconciliation. I am not here to provoke a war but to take part in this happy event," he said.

I had learnt to be suspicious of him all my life but still believed in his ability to change. I took him to where my wife was and he handed the three one kilogram packets of detergent he brought to her.

"My daughter, will you ever be able to forgive me for the treatment I subjected you to ever since I knew that my son was going to marry you? I have not been a good father-in-law to you and have realized that by hurting you, I am equally hurting myself. I will like us to begin a fresh start with the birth of this angel. Is it possible?" he asked holding her hands and looking straight into her eyes as she sat up on her bed.

"I have never had anything against you. In fact I have been longing for this to come soonest and by the grace of God, it has finally come," Gloria replied.

"Thank you very much for having that kind heart. Thank you even more for making me a grandfather to this beautiful baby," he said taking her out of the cot.

To me, it all looked like a dream. I was expecting to see him concentrate only on the baby and completely neglect my wife but things happened differently. I only hoped that the forgiveness he asked for was truly from his heart and not out of excitement of being a grandfather. That reconciliation at that moment was so beautiful to see and I longed for the day my father-in-law shall also accept me as a son-in-law.

I sat and watched my father hug his granddaughter with a lot of admiration. He asked if we had already thought of a name for her and Gloria said that she intended to give the name of her husband's late mother to her. My father smiled and referred to the baby as 'the reincarnation of his wife'.

Unfortunately, he had to leave us shortly after to go and take care of the second family he decided to create after the death of my mother. His new wife spent most of her time in the farms working and working. She often left in the mornings and returned almost late in the night. A good number of my family members who came on that day the baby was born had to return to their various homes to take care of their families. The only person who remained with me and Gloria was Aunty Regina. If my mother were still alive, she would have been the one to stay with Gloria after the birth of the baby to take care of them. But since she was gone, her sister had to take up that responsibility. Gloria and I were indeed fortunate because Aunty Regina's last child was already 17 and could take care of himself. So, there was no need for her to want to rush back to Bafut. She was very excited because the name of the baby; Lum Emilia reminded her of her late sister and she called her 'my sister'.

30

We spent three days at the hospital not because the baby had some problems but because the medical practitioners wanted to keep her under observation and to also administer her first vaccines. Aunty Regina was always there. She left Bafut on the first day I called and announced to her I was taking Gloria to the hospital with her clothes. She left for Bafut only on the day we had to leave the hospital to go and see how her home was faring. But shortly after we got home, she joined us there. She had to be with us for three months and her job was to take care of the baby and her mother. Gloria had to start doing things again for herself only three months after giving birth. That period was to enable her regain her strength. Even her work at the Agency had to be suspended and I was charged with managing it until she returned. I did not have to go and be at her office all day since there were assistants there. I went there only to verify, balance the accounts and take the money to the bank. As for my food distribution activity, I continued going to the interior villages to buy the food stuffs but did no longer travelled to deliver them in person. I took them to the travel agency and dispatched them to their various destinations through the drivers. I called my customers and directed them to where the food items could be collected.

When the three months were over, I went to the market and bought some items for my aunt to thank her for all the sleepless nights she spent up to take care of the baby when she was crying and her time and energy she spent for our sake. She was sad to go but had her home to run. I was compelled to employ a baby sitter to assist Gloria in and out of home. I did not find one immediately Aunty Regina left but two months later. During those two months, Gloria had to stay home most of the time while I continued doing her work. When she was able to assume her duties fully, the first thing she did was get pictures of our court wedding as well as some of our born baby and put in an envelope. She addressed it to her father and handed to me to take to the post office. I did and wondered how her father was going to react when he received them and saw my face on some of the pictures. I did not expect him to call even his daughter. But just as in the case of my father, I was optimistic that he too was capable of changing.

For the next three years after the birth of our first child, business was good for both of us. We accumulated a lot of money and bought more new buses. That meant that new jobless people found jobs with us. Some of my paternal relatives who felt that it was their relative's company and were as a result untouchable, decided to break some of the company rules. They were not allowed to pick passengers on the way as it led to unnecessary waste of time. That made a lot of customers to complain a lot with some threatening not to travel with the company in the future. After some warnings from my wife, they openly told her that it was their brother's company and she was just a care taker. I was definitely not going to allow any of my relatives disrespect my wife and decided to take the drastic measure of firing them. That was not going to go without consequences. Their sackings created some friction between Gloria and I on the one hand and the parents of those we fired. They blamed mostly my wife for being behind the sacking of their children. But I always believed in the power of dialogue in solving problems. I went to them and explained that I could not continue to keep people who were going to kill my business because that was exactly what their children were doing. I pleaded with them to keep my wife out of the problem as the decision to do away with bad elements within our company was entirely mine.

We did not sack my paternal relatives without any compensation. We gave them something to start up a business with and told them that if they so pleased, they could come and occupy some of the empty stores which were built within the company premises.

However, letting the parents of my paternal cousins know that the decision to sack their children was entirely mine freed Gloria. It was easier to blame and hate her because she could easily be brandished a stranger. I was always keen on doing away with that kind of image in the minds of my paternal relatives. For that reason I sent her to take care of their needs instead of going there myself. It greatly improved her relationship with them as they soon realized that the difference between her and them was only in the skin colour. What made my paternal family members get even closer to Gloria was her ability to speak a few words in my mother tongue. They were always very excited when they heard her trying to speak it. Where necessary, they made some corrections when she pronounced some words wrongly. I could only be happy knowing that my family at last got to accept my wife after long periods of hostilities towards her. In the long run, I did not really blame my relatives for behaving towards my wife badly. She looked different and all through history, people had always been scared of people or things that looked different. But when they got to know her, that fear was gone. That notwithstanding, the growth witnessed by our business obliged us to open more branches in Bafoussam, Buea and Victoria.

Moreover, exactly three years after the birth of Emilia, Gloria was pregnant for our second baby. Things became different between us. There were some times she became unnecessarily hostile towards me and did not just want to set her eyes on me. During such moments I either spent the nights in the living room on the couch or in the guest room. At other times she did not want me to leave her side for a moment. She wanted just me and no one else to do things for her. Anything that I did poorly was rewarded with insults. There were moments I just could not take it anymore that I had to remind her of the promise she made to me on the day we went to Pinyin village to visit my former landlord. She would apologize but would start tormenting me again not long after. Her actions pushed me to regret why I had to go in for a second child. I went to the extent of inviting

Aunty Regina to come and spend sometime in the house in the hope that her presence was going to help the situation. But Gloria only wanted me to do things for her. Aunty Regina told me that the pregnancy was responsible for such behaviour and that I only had to be understanding. All the food she wanted to eat had to be prepared by me and sometimes when she requested a particular meal and I prepared it, she would say that she wanted something else. I became furious each time she did that but I was careful not to let her notice that I was hurt. I prayed for the ninth month to come. I vowed never to go in for another baby after that second pregnancy.

She became less hostile when the pregnancy was six months old. She ate a lot that I became scared that the baby was going to become too fat and she might have difficulties giving birth when it was time. But I could not dare stop her for fear she could become hostile. Besides, her stomach became bigger than when she was pregnant for our first baby that I began to think that it was not only one foetus in her womb but two. During the 8th month of her pregnancy, I accompanied her to the hospital for her normal clinical check-up and had a little discussion with the doctor. I told her to examine my wife carefully and tell me if the large size of her stomach was just normal. When the doctor saw me after examining her, she told me that I was going to be a father of twins. That explained everything. I focused my mind on the twins I was going to have and bore every annoying thing she did after that news with all the tolerance I could.

She finally gave birth on December 12th to twins as the doctor told me. One was a boy and the other was a girl. I intended having two children and heaven sent three. That ended my chapter on having children. Family members came in just as they did after the birth of our first child. They brought all sorts of gifts. With the birth of twins in our family, we had to adopt some titles. I had to bear 'Tanyi' meaning 'father of twins'. Gloria on her part had to bear 'Manyi' meaning 'mother of twins'. Aunty Regina was still there to take care of the babies. I had to occupy the office of my wife until

288

when she was able to run things again. I really felt like a fulfilled man after having my complete family. Business was moving perfectly well. My younger ones were doing excellently well in their studies. Jane decided to enrol in the school of medicine after her high school . Joshua planned on doing the same as his elder sister. As for Benjamin, he told me that he was going to be a doctor in future. I guess it was just the dream of an adolescent. But I needed time to see clearly into it given that he was more inclined towards the arts than the sciences.

Going back to Gloria and myself, I would have really loved our marriage to be problems free. But it was not the case. We sometimes had our differences especially when we went out to occasions and girls kept looking in our direction. I guess they kept looking at us because she looked different and anything different always attracted attention. But Gloria did not want to think that her being white was the only reason why eyes were often thrown in our direction. She saw the young ladies who kept looking at us as potential rivals and accused me of making things easier for them by flirting with them. Besides, she had it in her mind that no matter what women did for their men, the men always went out. I always tried hard to convince her that I was different. I used my number she inherited as evidence to find out from her if any other woman had ever called her and given her the impression that she had anything to do with me. Her response was of course negative. I gave her all the numbers of my female customers just for that suspicion to go away. But it never did. I guess there is nothing as a perfect relationship or a perfect marriage given that such differences are sometimes necessary. The good thing was that we always talked our problems out to each other.

Though all in all my life was blissful, there was still one problem that remained unresolved and it was my wife's father. He never bothered to call us. Even when Gloria sent back money home in his name, it was her mother that always called to confirm that they did receive it. She called and told us that they saw the wedding pictures and the pictures of our first baby. We did not send pictures of the twins but Gloria informed them of the good news on the phone. Only her mother called me to congratulate me but her father never did. I began to wonder if one day he was ever going to accept me. Gloria proposed to me once the twins were five months old that all of us travel to Italy to visit their grandparents. That was an excellent idea but I had my fears. I did not know how her father was going to treat me and the fact that he never bothered to call me even after getting news of the births of his grandchildren made me imagine the worse. But I planned on going when the scheduled time finally arrived.

That time came when our babies, Daniel and Britney were both twelve months old. They were already able to play and move around. Taking care of them then was not going to be too problematic for Gloria and I. That said, we did not want to arrive Italy in the night with the kids and so decided to travel on a Sunday morning. At 07:50, we were already at the Douala International Airport. While there, I took the opportunity to call my parents, Mr Finley and Catalina, to inform them of our eminent arrival. We started checking in at 08:20 and at 09:30, the plane was on the runway and took off for Italy.

The plane we were on board touched down at the Bologna International Airport later in the afternoon that same Sunday. The journey was long and tiring though it was not my first time to undertake it. My parents were there to pick us up and immediately took us home to the northern part of city. There, we decided to spend the night and planned on seeing Gloria's parents only the next day which was Monday.

In the course of the night I pondered a lot over what awaited me the next day. I did not want to assume that the coming of grandchildren was going to automatically make Gloria's father change his attitude towards me as was the case with my father towards Gloria. I hatched a plan that night with Gloria. According to the plan, she had to carry a microphone as she was going to enter her parents' house with the children. I was going to remain outside in front of the house in the car which I already asked permission from Catalina to use, listening to what was going on inside the house. If things were rough, I planned on driving a few meters away from the house to wait for my family. I did not want to leave anything to chance.

The next morning, I woke up early and had a little chat with Mr Finley on what my wife and I planned to do later that day. I asked him where I could find a listening device. He rushed to town and returned a few minutes later with one. He helped me with the connection and did the testing too. When everything was set, he wished me good luck and went to take care of his own business.

At 10:20, I was behind the steering of Catalina's car with my wife and three children. We headed to the western part of the city where her parents lived. As we got closer to the neighbourhood, my heart pounded faster and fear gripped me. I told Gloria about it and she told me that it was normal. At 11:10, I halted not directly in front of her parents' house but a few meters before the house. That way, even if her parents heard the sound of the stopping car, they would have imagined that the owner was probably going to the home of a neighbour. We verified the mic she wore on her ear to make sure that it was functioning properly. It was and they all went out of the car and moved towards the house. When she knocked on the door, she showed me her fingers which were crossed. I did the same and prayed that heaven intervened.

The door was soon opened and it was her mother who emerged and fell on her. I could hear her hugging and kissing the children as well as saying how beautiful they all were. A short while later I started getting the voice of her father from inside the house. It was obvious that he was in the sitting room.

"Gloria my child," he said with a lot of emotion in his voice probably falling on her too. "These must be my beautiful grandchildren."

"Yes papa," Gloria replied as they were already inside the house.

I could hear him kissing the children. It was soon over and I heard him he ask the children to come and sit down by him.

When I could no longer hear moving footsteps, I knew they were all seated.

"Gloria my child, I can see that you look really healthy and happy. Will you ever forgive me for the terrible things I did to you in the past?" he asked almost in tears.

"I love you papa and there cannot be love without forgiveness," she said.

"I allowed myself to be consumed by empty pride. It was that pride that pushed me into hurting you by forcing you marry someone I knew you didn't love. I am so sorry. I now know that I have to allow my children choose the paths they want to take in life. You have chosen yours and I have seen that it is the right one. Your brother and sister are there in Africa with you and I know that they too would make it. I almost destroyed my own family with my own hands," he said really sobbing.

"Papa, all that is in the past now. We have to move forward after learning from our past mistakes," Gloria said.

"You are right my child. But there is one person I must make peace with before I can be able to move forward. Where is the father of these children? He did not come with you?" he asked.

"He came with us but since you have never written or called him, he did not know how you were going to react," Gloria replied.

"If he is here in Italy, please call him to come to the house. This is his home," he said.

"He is not far away. He is outside waiting in the car," Gloria said.

While she was saying that, I drove from where I previously parked to another spot directly in front of the house. Immediately I turned off the engine of the car, the door of the house opened and my father-in-law came out. He was moving slowly and cautiously as if he was on his guards. He did not take his eyes off the car and I remained seated in it waiting. I guess he too did not know how I was going to react.

As I watched him get closer to the car, I left the steering wheel and went round to meet him. He held me on both shoulders and started going down on his knees. I stopped him just before his left knee touched the ground. I just could not let him do it. I told him that whatever happened in the past was supposed to remain in the past. His action there outside his house was enough to tell anyone that he was truly sorry for whatever crime he might have committed. I thought that there was no need going back to details. He insisted on telling me what he had in mind because it was really a burden in his chest. I did not object but insisted that he had to do it only inside the house.

Once we were inside, he started apologizing for the kinds of things he said to me on the day Gloria brought me for introduction. Gloria's mother considered that there was no need for the children to be in the sitting room listening to adult problems they knew nothing about and might never understand. Though they could not make anything out of what was being said, certain actions were bound to push them to start asking questions. For that reason the children were immediately taken to the room. We were thus left in the sitting room just the two of us.

"I tried to separate what God had destined to be together," he went on. "You might have been wondering why I had never bothered to call you even when the news of my grandchildren reached me. The truth is that the full weight of the kind of words I said to you weighed down on me. Since the words already left my mouth and you consumed them already, there was no way I could withdraw them. Guilt took away all courage from me which prevented me from apologizing and making amends. Even when I summon some courage, I was afraid of taking the wrong approach. You don't know what life had been for me ever since I saw your wedding pictures. I allowed my pride to blind me to the fact that it was one God that created all of us," he said in tears.

"As I said a while ago, what happened in the past must remain in the past. The most important thing is that we have all realized ourselves. Besides, we came here to make merry by presenting your grandchildren to you and not to be grieving over issues long passed. It is now over. Let us begin all over, shall we?" I asked.

"Thank you for forgiving me. I now feel that a heavy burden has been taken off my chest. Thank you for coming here today because if you had stayed back, I would have remained with my burden," he said.

I did not say anything again after that because such conversations made me nervous I wanted it to end so that we moved to something else. The children were brought from the room and he still hugged them. He ordered for wine to be brought from the cupboard and we sipped from the same glass and that marked the start of a new beginning.

We had planned to spend just a week in Italy and I knew that we were going to spend most of it at the home of my parents. But that had to change with that reconciliation between me and my father-in-law. The first night we spent there ended up being the only one. We went there during the days but never spent beyond three hours. I squeezed some time to travel down to Monzuno to visit my former employer. I took only some pictures of my family to Mr Salghetti and his family. He told me that if he were to die that moment I visited him, he would die in peace because I was part of his achievements. I smiled and thanked him for everything he did for me and as well as all the underprivileged people who also worked for him. Unfortunately, time was not my best ally and I had to leave after spending just two and a half hours with him.

Back at my father-in-law's house, things were really wonderful. He was proud to have me as part of his family and was ready to defend me even with his blood. We took some short walks in the evenings around the neighbourhood and he introduced me to some neighbours and friends. I could feel nothing else but happiness. But one thing was against us and it was time.

We left Italy again on the following Sunday with me very contented that I did not travel there for nothing. I considered that the reconciliation between me and Gloria's father as the greatest achievement not only for me but for Gloria as well because we succeeded to make our one time hostile families accept one another. There was more joy in unity especially one gotten after hard struggle. I felt really happy that I wished there was a possibility to extend our stay in Italy. But our businesses back home badly needed our attention. We had to return. My parents, Mr Finley and Catalina as well as the parents of Gloria accompanied us to the airport. We took pictures and hugged before parting, even though it was painful. Well, that was life and we had to accept the encounters and separations. With our backs turned on Italy, we set a new target that was to work hard to give our children a better future.

The End